The BOX in the WOODS

ALSO BY MAUREEN JOHNSON

Truly Devious
The Vanishing Stair
The Hand on the Wall

13 Little Blue Envelopes
The Last Little Blue Envelope
The Key to the Golden Firebird
On the Count of Three
Girl at Sea
Devilish
Let It Snow

The Shades of London series
The Suite Scarlett series

The BOX in the WOODS

MAUREEN JOHNSON

 KATHERINE TEGEN BOOKS
An Imprint of HarperCollins Publishers

Katherine Tegen Books is an imprint of HarperCollins Publishers.

The Box in the Woods
Copyright © 2021 by HarperCollins Publishers
Map art by Charlotte Tegen
All rights reserved. Printed in the United States of America.
No part of this book may be used or reproduced in any manner whatsoever
without written permission except in the case of brief quotations embodied in
critical articles and reviews. For information address HarperCollins Children's
Books, a division of HarperCollins Publishers, 195 Broadway, New York, NY
10007.
www.epicreads.com

Library of Congress Control Number: 2021934356
ISBN 978-0-06-303260-6 — ISBN 978-0-06-308213-7 (intl ed)

Typography by Carla Weise
21 22 23 24 25 PC/LSCH 10 9 8 7 6 5 4 3 2 1
❖
First Edition

For Billy Jensen, real-life crime solver

The investigator must bear in mind that he has a twofold responsibility—to clear the innocent as well as to expose the guilty. He is seeking only the facts—the Truth in a Nutshell.
— Frances Glessner Lee

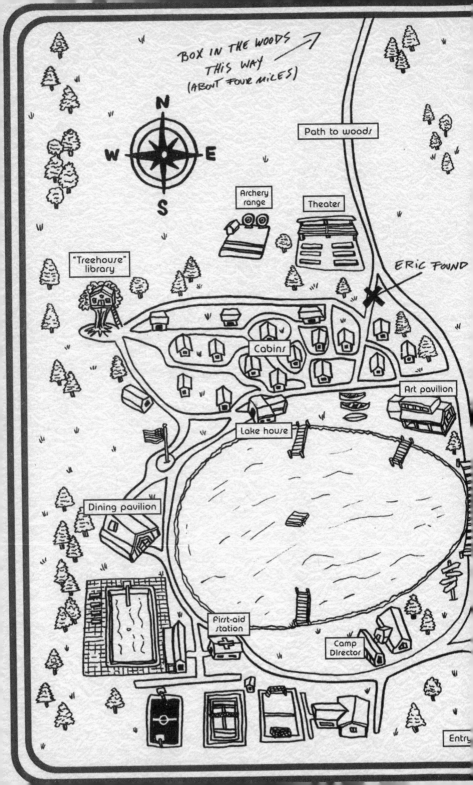

Camp Wonder Falls

POINT 23

ARROWHEAD POINT

Public campground

July 6, 1978
11:45 p.m.

Sabrina Abbott was doing something *illegal*.

Impossible.

Sabrina had never done anything illegal. She was Barlow Corners' paragon of virtue. The valedictorian. The library volunteer who read to children. The person who hyperventilated for ten minutes when she accidentally skipped a class because she was too deep in her research at the school library. The one who every parent of a younger student pointed to and said, "Be like Sabrina when you get to high school."

What would they say now if they saw her in Todd Cooper's notorious brown Jeep as it bounced down the dirt road through the woods, juddering as the tires made contact with the many pits and bumps along the way? The green fuzzy dice hanging from the rearview mirror banged together from the impact, almost in time with the Led Zeppelin pulsing from the stereo. The headlights were the only thing that cut through the dark between the trees and the sky with its sliver of a moon. Sabrina didn't particularly like or trust Todd, who was the captain of the football team and the son of the mayor. Todd was an asshole. But he came with the package tonight. He had the car.

Here she was, breaking camp curfew and going into the

woods—both prohibited activities. But those infractions were nothing compared to what they were going to do once they reached their destination.

She pressed herself into her companion's side. Eric Wilde was her new— Was he her boyfriend? They hadn't gotten that far yet in the discussions. She had no doubt that he wanted that title, and she had just freed herself from her boyfriend of three years—no need to rush back in. It was time for the new Sabrina, the one who lived, who did things, who didn't worry so much.

This good girl needed a break. The last few weeks had shown her that.

"You okay?" Eric said over the music.

"Yeah," she replied. A bug flew in her mouth as she did so, and she picked it out.

Was she okay? Her worries were still there, nibbling at the edge of all her thoughts. She tried to shut them out. That's what tonight was for. Breaking the spell of fear.

"Sure?"

"Just cold," she said.

That much was true. It was cool tonight, especially as the top was off the Jeep. She was only wearing shorts and a green Camp Wonder Falls T-shirt. Regular Sabrina would have been more prepared and brought a sweatshirt—new Sabrina was going to be cold. Eric wrapped his arm around her and drew her close. His blond curls tickled her nose as she leaned into his shoulder.

The Jeep pulled off the path and stopped off to the side,

under the cover of a small group of trees. The music cut out, and the four passengers stepped out of the vehicle.

"This is it?" Sabrina asked.

"Not here," said the girl in the passenger seat. "Close, though. We have to walk."

The girl's name was Diane McClure and she was a fellow recent graduate of Liberty High. Diane was a tall redhead, with freckles clustered all over her body. She and Sabrina had never been in the same orbit at school. Sabrina led the class in academics; Diane seemed to spend most of her time leaning against lockers and hanging out in the smoking lounge. She was the kind of person Sabrina's parents told her to avoid. But she wasn't a bad person. Sabrina had come to like her company. She was loyal, hardworking in her own way, and school wasn't for everyone. Diane was Todd's girlfriend, and probably Todd's only redeeming feature.

Sabrina climbed out of the back of the Jeep, which took a little doing, as they had packed it with several bags of supplies, several of which hampered her exit.

"It's this way," Eric said, taking Sabrina's hand in his. "Let me guide you, my dear. Never fear, never fear. Into the woods we go!"

Diane and Eric both had powerful flashlights, but their beams barely penetrated the dark between the trees. Sabrina had lived in Barlow Corners all her life and certainly had spent time in the woods, but never this deep in, and never at night. It was something you didn't do. The woods were dark and deep, full of creatures.

3

"How far?" she asked, trying to make her voice light.

"We're almost there. Trust me. I come out here every week. I know the way," said Eric.

"I trust you," she said.

"You sure you're okay?" Eric asked.

"I'm sure. Why?"

"You're kind of crushing my hand."

"Oh!" She released her grip. "Sorry."

"It's okay. I have two. Actually, I have three, but that's because the experiment went wrong. . . ."

She laughed. That's what was great about Eric. He could make her worries vanish. Eric knew something about living, something she wanted to learn.

"I won't tell anyone," she said.

"Oh, good. I can't let them shut down my lab, not when I'm so close. Soon my creation will come to *life*!"

He shouted that last word, causing something in the branches above to stir and fly off.

"Eric, you freak," Diane said, laughing.

"You say that like it's a bad thing," he replied. "Aaaaaand . . . here we are!"

The flashlight beams struck a small clearing. There were a few cut logs on the ground, rough seating around a stone circle.

"Okay," Eric said, setting down the bag he was carrying, "you guys do the setup. We'll go get the milk. This way, my dear. Just over yonder a few paces."

Eric took her hand once again to guide her through the dark. They reentered the woods on the other side of the clearing.

"So how do you pay for it?" Sabrina asked, picking her way along the tangle of roots beneath their feet. "What's the system?"

"If you continue to come with me on my magical journey, you will learn all, little Bilbo."

"Did you just call me Bilbo?"

"It's from *The Hobbit*."

"I know what it's from, you moron," she said, laughing.

"Never question the girl who works in the library," Eric said, bowing low. "I beg forgiveness."

Something crunched near them, and Sabrina let out an involuntary yip.

"It's fine," he said, shining the light around. "Lots of noises out here. They startle you at first."

Suddenly, she didn't want to be here. Her whole body flooded with anxiety. Eric seemed to sense this and stopped.

"It's cool," he said.

"There's something out there."

"There probably is. A raccoon. A possum. A skunk. But they don't come near the clearing or the fire."

"You're sure?" she asked.

"I come out here every week. I always hear something. It's the woods. Seriously, they don't want to come near people. They stay away."

"I know. I need to relax. I'm trying."

"Here's the thing . . . you're *trying* to relax. You're even pushing yourself to do that. You push yourself too hard."

"I know. I *know*."

The world slowly righted itself. Sabrina took a deep breath and straightened up.

"Keep going," she said. "I'm fine."

They continued on another fifty paces or so, until the flashlight revealed a small structure. It was a box in the woods, about eight feet long and four feet high.

"Here we are," Eric said, approaching it.

"What is this?"

"An old hunting blind," Eric replied, handing her the flashlight and lifting the large lid with both hands. "Hunters would hide inside while they were hunting deer. It's got little openings in the side they could look out of."

"Creepy," she said. "But I guess hunting is creepy by definition. You creep behind animals to kill them."

"True. Anyway, this one hasn't been used in a long time."

That much was clear. While not completely rotted, the box was on the path in that direction. The boards were weatherworn and bowed, and some of them were coming away. It was now most likely home to spiders and snakes and various other critters, so she cringed a bit as Eric climbed inside and started rooting around in a pile of discarded wood. She made a mental note to check herself carefully for ticks when they got back to camp.

"Where is it, where is it. . . . Ah. Here we go!"

He stood up and proudly held aloft a crumpled McDonald's bag.

"That's it?" Sabrina said.

Eric climbed out of the box and closed the lid.

"Shine the light," he said.

He set the bag down, opened it up, and removed a used Big Mac box, two hamburger wrappers, and a used cup, still with the straw.

"I can see you're not impressed," he said. "But behold. . . ."

He opened the Big Mac box. The container was brimming with fresh, fragrant marijuana buds. As were the hamburger wrappers and the soda cup. Sabrina had seen marijuana before—small amounts of it, usually in the form of joints—but she had never seen *this* much. This was an extremely illegal amount of marijuana. A scholastic-career-ending amount. A definitely arrestable, criminal record amount.

"No one looks at trash," Eric said with a smile. "Especially trash inside of something that also looks like trash, out in the middle of the woods. Pretty clever, wouldn't you say?"

"I guess."

"You *guess*? I'll have to try harder. Come on. Time to get to work."

Back in the clearing, things were looking much more inviting and cheerful. There was a fire going, and a camp lantern sat on one of the logs. Two sleeping bags had been unzipped and spread out as blankets, their soft plaid flannel insides resting upward. The portable tape player was piping more Led Zeppelin into the velvety darkness. (They were Diane's favorite band. Sabrina didn't like them at all, but if you hung out with Todd and Diane, you had to get used to it.) Todd and Diane were stretched out on one of the sleeping bags, munching on chips and staring up at the sky.

"Behold!" Eric said, brandishing the bag aloft. "Your milkman cometh!"

He cupped his free hand over his mouth and made the tooting sound of a triumphant horn. He and Sabrina sat down on the other sleeping bag, which had been opened up for them. Eric handed the bag to Diane, who set it down on a stolen dining pavilion tray. She moved the lantern a bit closer and dumped out the contents of the Big Mac box and picked through it expertly.

"And now, we roll," Eric said, grabbing a handful of chips, "for rolling is a part of the service. First ones are always for us. No one beats Diane. She's a machine."

Diane was working smoothly, plucking the buds. In the space of only a few moments, she had rolled the first joint, which she passed to Eric. She kept right on rolling, her movements hypnotic. Eric put the joint between his lips and lit it, then took a long inhale and passed it to Todd. Todd did the same, and then passed it to Diane, who didn't look up from her efforts as she took her hit. It ended up with Sabrina, who took it and held it. She could hear the gentle sizzle of the paper.

"You don't have to," Eric said. "Totally up to you."

She had asked to come out here. She wanted to try something new, and there was no way she wanted to get to Columbia and be the only person in the entire freshman class who had never smoked a joint. This was the perfect place to try. No one around, with people she knew. She put it to her lips and inhaled—and promptly coughed it all out in a gagging, reflexive manner. She expected them to laugh at her, but no one did.

"Happens to everyone the first time," Eric said. "Try again. Slower, hold it as long as you can."

She inhaled once more. The smoke was acrid, and it burned a bit, but she held it for several seconds before coughing it out again, though less violently this time. After a moment, she felt a little change. An easing. Her attention locked on to the music—she suddenly needed it to be different.

"Can we switch the tape?" she asked.

"Sure," Eric said. "What do you want to hear?"

"Fleetwood Mac."

"Can we change it?" Eric asked. "Put on *Rumours*."

There was a low groan of displeasure from the other couple.

"Come on," Eric said, smiling. "It's her first time. Let her pick the music."

Reluctantly, Diane dug around in the backpack and pulled out a cassette. She stopped the one that was playing and replaced it. The haunting jangle of the guitar and

9

the heavy, slow beat of the drum echoed between the trees, mingled with the crackle of the fire. Sabrina rested against the log and let the music wash over her. This was her favorite album. She'd listened to it thousands of times, probably. She knew the lyrics back to front, but tonight, they were especially clear.

Running in the shadows, damn your love, damn your lies

"Eric," she said.

He leaned over and looked down at her. He had a nice face. A kind face. It loomed over her like the moon.

"How you doing?" he asked.

"Damn your lies . . ."

"You got it."

Beyond them, out of the range of the glow of the fire—what was that thing moving between the trees? An owl? A raccoon? A witch that rang like a bell in the night, or a ghost, or . . .

No. It was a bit of the potato chip bag, which had caught fire and floated up.

"Excuse us," Todd said as he and Diane peeled themselves off the ground and pulled their sleeping bag away. They went off toward the trees behind them and vanished into the dark. Sabrina strained to turn around and watch them go, then she looked back to Eric.

"It's okay," Eric said. "There's no pressure like that. We'll just hang here, eat chips, listen to some music."

Sabrina eased and tucked herself under Eric's arm, resting her head on his shoulder.

"My throat is dry," she said.

Eric leaned up and retrieved a Coke, which he opened and passed to her. It was warm, but welcome, sliding down her throat, sticky and sweet, ungluing her lips. It tasted so good. She downed half the can in one go.

"What do you think?" he asked.

She responded by belching and bursting into laughter.

"There we go," he said. "That's what I like to hear. See? Everything's not so bad."

Things weren't so bad; they were inexplicably hilarious. She felt her muscles ease and she settled back into the gentle puffs of the sleeping bag.

"This is . . . stoned?" she said.

"Yes," he said. "Take it easy, listen to the music. Nowhere to be, and nothing to do. I'm going to take a leak. Back in a second."

He pushed himself up off the ground and headed toward the trees. As he walked off, he tripped dramatically over a log and did a staggered almost-fall—it was clearly a fake-out for her amusement, and she burst into laughter again. Then he stepped into the trees.

Sabrina leaned back, her head against the log. She was surrounded by the long shadows, the veil of smoke that oozed along with the music like honey. If she closed her eyes, she knew everything would spin and the world would cease to make sense. It barely made sense as it was.

The bass drumbeat on this song was like a heartbeat. *Thump. Thump. Thump.*

Break the silence, damn the dark, damn the light

It sounded so serious, being a member of Fleetwood Mac. She loved them. This album had given her so much solace this year, through all the terrible things that had happened. Things she was *not*, she reminded herself, going to think about now. She tried to focus her eyes over the corona of the campfire. Somewhere behind her, Diane and Todd were making a lot of noise, really getting into whatever they were up to.

Thump, thump, thump.

She stared at the tray full of little flecks of leaves and buds, at the bag of chips and the fire and the hook of a moon. So many things had been troubling her recently. Why had she let herself get so *stressed*? This was Barlow Corners, and the whole point of Barlow Corners was that nothing ever happened here. Right?

She realized the song had changed. Wait, this was "Gold Dust Woman." That was four songs into the second side of the album. She hadn't even noticed the songs or the time go by. How long had it been? Ten minutes? Something like that? Why was she still alone?

"Eric?" she called.

No reply.

"Eric!" she called again, louder this time.

There was nothing aside from Stevie Nicks singing about the black widow and the pale shadow and the dragon, the song increasing in intensity. Sabrina's body was heavy and the shadows were long, and when she tried to move, everything had a slow, syrupy quality. She elbowed her way over to the tape player and turned down the volume.

All around her was silence.

"Diane! Todd? Eric?"

No one replied.

One part of her mind tried to say that this was fine. Maybe Eric had gone back to the hunting blind. Diane and Todd were busy. The other, louder part of her mind told her that something was wrong, wrong, *wrong*.

She decided to listen to the second voice.

Sabrina pulled herself up to her feet. The ground was both too close and much too far away, and her eyes were confused from staring at the fire and then going into darkness. She blinked to refocus and reached for the lantern. It probably wasn't cool to bug Diane and Todd now, but she was going to do it anyway. She lifted the light and peered around, then took a few uncertain steps in the direction she thought they had gone. It took her a minute or two of fumbling in the dark, tripping over tree roots and stumbling over her own feet, before she finally saw them on the ground, pressed together.

"Hey," she said, stumbling forward. "Hey, Eric is . . ."

They didn't sit up when she spoke. They didn't move at all. There was something in the way they were lying there that was unnatural. Her heart was doing something very bad, pushing too hard, sending gurgles of air and confusion through her body that bottled up in her neck.

There were footsteps behind her.

She turned.

It wasn't Eric, as she somehow deep inside knew it wouldn't be.

THE STUDENT SLEUTH OF ELLINGHAM ACADEMY

By Germaine Batt

Most high school students have hobbies. Some play music. Some play sports. Some write, or draw, or make things.

Stephanie "Stevie" Bell solves crimes.

Stevie is a student at the exclusive Ellingham Academy outside of Burlington, Vermont—that storied institution opened by tycoon Albert Ellingham as a place of creative, playful learning. Ellingham has no tuition and no admissions policy; students are admitted by presenting themselves and talking about their passions, interests, and skills. Ellingham accepts students who want to *do* or *be* something in particular, and assists them in meeting that goal. This was the mission of the school when it opened in 1935. In 1936, it became the scene of one of the twentieth century's most infamous crimes, when Iris Ellingham, Albert's wife, and Alice Ellingham, their daughter, were kidnapped on one of the local roads. A student, Dolores "Dottie" Epstein, also vanished from the school grounds. Iris's and Dottie's bodies would be found in the following weeks; Alice Ellingham was never seen again. The case is a favorite of true-crime enthusiasts and the subject of countless articles, books, and documentaries.

Stevie Bell applied to Ellingham with the stated goal of solving this case. It was a bold and possibly unachievable goal, but the school accepted Stevie and allowed her to have a shot. Weeks after arriving at Ellingham, her fellow classmate, online sensation Hayes Major, died in an accident. Once again, Ellingham was the scene of tragedy.

Stevie Bell, the student sleuth, didn't think that Hayes's death was an accident. Two more people associated with the school would die in the weeks following.

That's a lot of accidents, and a lot of deaths. But Stevie was not deterred, even when the murderer projected a threatening message on her wall in the middle of the night. With the help of her friends, including the author of this article, she continued her investigation and discovered who was responsible. The culprit [log in to continue reading] . . .

1

MURDER IS WRONG, OF COURSE. STEVIE'S FUTURE WAS PREDICATED on that fact. She wanted to solve murders, not commit them. To solve them, you had to understand why they'd occurred. Motive. That was the key. It was all about *motive*. Understand the reasons behind the act. What pushes another human being to that point of no return? It has to be a strong impulse.

"I'll have . . . a pound of . . . is that . . . do you have . . . low-sodium ham?"

"Yes," Stevie said, staring at the woman on the other side of the deli counter.

"Which one is that?"

"It's the one marked 'low-sodium ham.'"

"Where?"

Stevie pointed at a round-edged rectangle of ham, the one with the card that read "Low-Sodium Ham."

"Oh. Okay. I'll have a . . . I guess . . . make it a half pound of that, and a pound of . . . do you have low-fat Swiss cheese?"

"Yes."

17

"Where's that?"

Stevie pointed at the cheese that was similarly marked.

"Oh." The low-fat Swiss cheese somehow disappointed. The woman bit her upper lip and consulted her phone. "The recipe says low-fat Swiss, but . . . do you have low-fat provolone?"

"No," Stevie said.

"Oh. Um. Hmmmm."

What were the murder statutes in Pennsylvania? Surely there had to be something in there about people who came to the deli counter and stood there asking questions about things that were clearly written on signs, making ten other people wait behind them. It was the Friday-evening shift, which meant people wanted their weekend lunch meat and deli stuff and they wanted to go home. And here was this woman, lost in the cabinet of wonders that was the deli counter.

"Do you have . . . ," the woman began.

Lots of murder weapons at the deli counter. So many knives. The most dangerous thing was the meat slicer, but it would be hard to turn that into a murder weapon. Too heavy, and it had a safety guard. It could probably be done, though. . . .

"I guess . . ." The woman peered into the glass. "I mean, I guess I'll take the Swiss. The low-fat Swiss. A quarter, no . . . wait. I'm probably going to double it, so . . . well . . . a quarter would probably be fine. Or . . ."

You'd have to get someone into the feeding side of the

slicer. Really hold them in there. You could take off their fingers. . . .

"Miss?"

Stevie snapped back. She had been staring at the slicer, shoving imaginary fingers into the opening.

"A quarter pound of the low-fat Swiss," the woman said again.

This was said with a bit of an edge to it, indicating that it was outrageous how Stevie had made this woman wait entire *seconds*. There was no recognition of all the time the woman had spent pondering her lunch-meatorial thoughts. She saw the woman give a side-eye to someone else in the line that said, *Can you believe the kind of person they hire here?* Stevie clenched her jaw and took the heavy brick of cheese from the refrigerated counter.

"Thin!" the woman yelled. "Thin!"

Stevie considered the slicer again. Not the most elegant weapon, but it could get the job done.

Fame is a fleeting thing. One minute, she was the student sleuth, celebrated on the internet for catching a killer at her exclusive boarding school. People wrote articles about her. She saw her face at the top of some news pages, her short blond hair that she cut herself sticking up at weird angles, her face too round for the camera but normal in life, and her vintage red vinyl coat looking good. She'd finished out the school year a celebrity. She'd kept her school open and safe. And, though the world at large didn't know it, she'd solved one of the greatest cases of the last century.

And then . . . the world moved on to the next shiny thing. Her name still popped up from time to time, but not as much, and then not really at all. Then she was home from school, back in the suburbs of Pittsburgh. Her Ellingham friends returned to their homes as well, all over the country. Her old job at the mall was filled, and she was super lucky to get this job at the grocery store, four days a week, from four to eleven.

Stevie didn't mind the job so much, really. The first part of the evening was the most annoying—the four-to-eight shift behind the deli counter. She liked putting things in order, filling containers, slicing, packing. Where the whole thing fell apart was when she had to deal with people. She learned a lot working with customers. She knew the person who would chat to her nonstop, the person who felt that they were entitled to her entire soul as she got them ham. She saw people stressing and straining, working out budgets in their heads. She learned that people really like American cheese, and that she wasn't sure what American cheese even was.

The second half of the shift was spent breaking down the salad bar. That was definitely the best part of the night. From that point onward, she usually didn't have to talk to customers anymore. While she technically wasn't supposed to wear earbuds while people were in the store, no one cared *that* much, especially if you were doing a job like this one, where you didn't have to deal with people. She had a full hour and a half of a true-crime podcast to listen to while she removed the steam trays, filled carts with the leftover vegetables and fruits, and cleaned up the weird gunk that was on the side of the industrial-size salad dressing bottles. She was in the middle of dumping out the bloody remains of a tray of pickled beets when her phone rang.

"Hey," she said quietly.

"How's my princess?" David said.

"Still working. You talk."

"Well, I'm here in . . . I don't remember the name of the town. We had dinner at Cracker Barrel. And now I'm at the local firehouse helping run a raffle for a group of candidates in this area. If you play your cards right there might be a basket full of lavender bath salts in your future. What do you have for *me*?"

"Do you like used potato salad?" she asked.

Stevie noticed her manager eyeing her curiously.

"Gotta go," she whispered. "I think they know I'm on the phone."

"Talk later. And remember, if these coasters I'm looking at are telling the truth, it's always wine o'clock somewhere. Think about that for a while."

At eleven, Stevie Bell, student sleuth and destroyer of salad bars, clocked out and stepped into the muggy night. Her mother's maroon minivan was there, waiting by the curb. Stevie did not have a car of her own; that was definitely out of the Bell family's financial reach. Every night, one of her parents came to get her.

"Have a good night?" her mom asked as she got in the car.

"It was okay. I got the cheese you asked for."

American cheese, of course.

"You talk to David tonight?" her mom asked as they pulled out of the parking lot.

"Uh-huh."

"How is he?"

"Fine," Stevie said.

"He's a good one."

Historically, Stevie and her parents had not gotten along. She wasn't what they expected from a daughter. Daughters were supposed to like prom dresses and getting their hair done and shopping. Stevie assumed those things were all fine and good, but she didn't understand them, really—at least not in the way that you were supposed to understand them. She never once in her life felt the desire to dress up, do her hair and nails, accessorize. She stared blankly at Instagram ads for new makeup palettes that looked, to her eyes, exactly like every other makeup palette. The only clothing item she really adored was her vintage red vinyl raincoat from the seventies. She wore a lot of black, because it suited her and it always seemed to go together. Sometimes she felt like she was missing a chip or a gene or something that made this all matter, but it never bothered her much.

Before Ellingham, Stevie's lack of daughterly graces was a sticking point, but there had been peace in the household for months now, and not because Stevie had solved a murder. No. It was because she had a boyfriend—and not just any boyfriend. Stevie's boyfriend was David Eastman, who happened to be the son of Senator Edward King. Stevie's parents loved Edward King. That Edward King had recently been the subject of a major scandal and had to withdraw his bid for the presidency did not diminish their love for him. Like any true believers, they felt that the more Edward King was accused of wrongdoing, the more right he must be, the more it had to be someone else's fault.

Her parents didn't know that David was the one who had gotten his father busted. They certainly didn't know that Stevie had seen the proof against Edward King with her own eyes.

David had been pulled out of school when his father found out what he had done. He finished the school year remotely, then left home to work with a voter registration campaign that traveled around the country. This was why he didn't know what town he was in tonight, and why he was standing around at a Cracker Barrel with baskets full of lavender bath salts and coasters.

The details of all this were largely unknown to Stevie's parents. They only knew that David had completed high school off campus, and that he was doing some kind of internship or work-study somewhere. All that mattered was that Stevie had a boyfriend—the perfect boyfriend, in their eyes—and therefore she had completed her mission.

It was the most infuriating thing that had ever happened, and it made Stevie want to scream all the time, but she also wanted to maintain this weird peace that had been established so that she could get back to Ellingham in the fall, and then to college after that.

But what then? She had gotten in with the stated purpose of solving the Ellingham case. She'd done that. It was impossible, but she'd done it.

What do you do for your next act after that? What would she study? Where would she go from there?

It hit her every night, this weird emptiness, usually as she unclicked her seat belt and got out of the car, still smelling of grocery store deli department, biting her tongue so that she didn't snap at her mom about the boyfriend thing.

As she climbed into bed, Stevie thumbed through her messages. Right after the Ellingham case broke, she had gotten many of them—media requests, strange influencer offers ("We think you'd be a great fit to promote our paleo meal kits"), creepers, and people who wanted her to help find their lost relatives or dogs. The media requests had been okay, but they had petered out. The bizarre influencer offers had stopped. Stevie had sympathy for people who had missing relatives or dogs, but usually there was nothing that could be done from a distance. So really, it was just the creepers now. They were loyal.

Tonight there was one note about a lost cat, two messages that said "hi" and nothing else, and a random picture of a teddy bear holding a heart. But right in the middle, there was a subject line that stood out: "Camp Wonder Falls."

There was only one Camp Wonder Falls.

Well, that probably wasn't true. There might be a lot of places called Camp Wonder Falls. But there was one Camp Wonder Falls that was related to true crime.

She opened the message.

> **Stevie,**
>
> **My name is Carson Buchwald, and I am the owner and founder of Box Box (you've probably heard of it). I've recently purchased a camp in western Massachusetts called Camp Sunny Pines. It used to be called Camp Wonder Falls. Yeah.** *That* **Camp Wonder Falls.**
>
> **I am making a true-crime podcast/documentary about the Box in the Woods murders. I read about what you did at Ellingham Academy. I like to think outside the box (which is ironic, I know, because I run Box Box) . . .**

(Stevie frowned at the screen.)

> **. . . and I thought of you right away. How would you like to come and work here this summer and look into the case with me? You could be a counselor at the camp, but mostly you could do what you need to do to look into the case. I can provide you with travel funds and pay you for your time. You can bring friends, if that sweetens the deal. It's a camp—there's plenty of room.**

**If you're interested, get back in touch with me.
I hope to hear from you.**

**Carson Buchwald
CEO and founder, Box Box
"It's what's inside that counts!"**

Well. This was a development.

July 7, 1978
7:30 a.m.

THE MORNING'S PA BLAST RATTLED THROUGH THE TREES, STIRRING the birds.

"Good morning, Camp Wonder Falls! Welcome to another beautiful day!"

Brandy Clark shoved her face into her pillow and pressed it against her ears, trying to block out the announcement, the light, the birds, the sound of ten kids waking and laughing. Too soon. Too much morning.

Just a little more sleep. Please.

Brandy had been up five times during the night with Claire Parsons. Claire was eight and scared of going to the bathroom by herself. The bathroom was outside, about thirty feet away from the cabin, and Claire had to pee more than any child alive. Brandy had tried everything—cutting off Claire's supply of bug juice after dinner, taking Claire to the bathroom three times before lights out, offering to give Claire something to pee into on the cabin porch so she wouldn't have to go out to the toilets. If you told Claire to go by herself, she would stand by your cot and poke you with a wet finger until you took her. (Why was it always wet? From what?)

Usually, Brandy split this duty with her fellow counselor, Diane McClure, but Diane had never come back from her midnight rendezvous with her boyfriend.

"We're going to have a beer and a smoke," Diane had said the evening before. "I'll be back by two. Promise."

Sure.

"This morning we have pancakes in the dining pavilion, and it's softball day, so everyone let's get up and at 'em!"

"Shut up shut up shut up shut up . . . ," Brandy mumbled into the pillow. "Shut up and die. Shut up and die."

"What?"

Brandy turned and looked up to see Bridget Lorde, another one of her campers, standing right next to her. The campers slept in the main part of the cabin; the counselors had a little privacy in the form of a plywood half-wall. The campers weren't supposed to cross this boundary unless they needed something. Most of them followed this rule, but not Bridget. Bridget was a natural narc with a nose for trouble, and she would quite literally get in your face to find out what was going on.

"Where's Diane?" Bridget asked.

"I don't know," Brandy said, rubbing her eyes.

"Did she stay out all night?"

As much as Brandy was annoyed at Diane right now, there was still a code around here: you didn't rat on the other counselors. If you wanted to go to the woods for private time, or skip out on a bunk inspection, or cut a few corners with any of the rules, everyone else would look out for you.

"No," Brandy replied, pushing herself out of her cot. "She probably went to get an early shower."

"Why?"

"More hot water. I don't know."

"I didn't hear her get up," Bridget said.

"So? Do you hear everything?"

"Kind of. One time I heard my sister *smoking*. In the *garage*. And I was in my *room*."

Brandy believed it. Bridget was terrifying.

"Well, you didn't hear her. Get your stuff. Come on. Shower time."

Bridget narrowed her eyes. She could smell Brandy's cover-up, but there was nothing she could do about it because she was eight and being eight sucks. You have no power. Someday, Bridget would have her revenge. The world would know her rage.

Brandy abandoned hope of a blissful five or ten extra minutes and shuffled into the main part of the cabin, not bothering to put on her flip-flops. The campers were all crawling out of bed. She made sure they had their bath caddies and towels and that they were all moving in the direction of the bathrooms.

"Where's Diane?" Bridget asked again, tagging along beside Brandy as they all got in line.

"I told you. She got up early."

"And went where? She's not in the showers. I looked for her stuff."

"Bridget, can you stop?"

She was going to kill Diane and Todd. Those idiots were going to ruin it for everyone.

Little Claire was the first one into the bathroom. She may have been a midnight pee-er, but she was mercifully quick in the shower. (There was no way she washed. She just turned the water on and off. Brandy knew this but did not actually care. Little kids were filthy. You accepted it and you moved on.) She ran out merrily in her little terry-cloth robe. In daylight, Claire was all butterflies and rainbows. She sang to herself and spun and skipped toward the edge of the woods. She reappeared seconds later and hurried back to Brandy.

"Someone's asleep on the path," she said.

This was all Brandy needed—one of her friends passed out in the dirt.

"They're all sticky," Claire added.

Great. Super great. Working alone? Check. Cleaning vomit off a passed-out person before even waking up completely? Perfect.

"Where?" Bridget asked, whipping around toward Claire.

Claire pointed toward the path. Bridget tore off in that direction, her whole demeanor screaming "*J'accuse!*" Brandy trailed behind her. This morning was the worst.

Beyond the cabins and the bathrooms, there was a parting of the woods and a slender dirt path that snaked back toward the archery grounds and the structure that was generously referred to as the "open-air theater." A few yards up the path, there was a figure, fast asleep, facedown in the dirt.

"That's not Diane," Bridget said, her voice dripping with disappointment.

Bridget was right. The figure on the ground wasn't Diane. It was a guy, a guy with a head of blond curly hair. That and the red jersey T-shirt told Brandy it was Eric Wilde.

"What's wrong with him?" Bridget asked.

"Go brush your teeth, Bridget," Brandy said.

"I want to see."

"Bridget."

Bridget narrowed her eyes but backed up as directed.

Brandy continued down the dirt path. She could see now why Claire had said he was sticky—there was something darkening the dirt all around him, some explosion of bodily emissions. This was going to be a bad one. That it was Eric was at least less trouble. She would be obligated to cover for Diane, help her shower. That was what bunkmates did. With Eric, though, the obligations were less arduous. Just shake him awake and get him moving. Not her problem after that.

"Eric, you moron," she called, stumbling down the dirt track in her bare feet. "What the hell?"

Eric didn't stir.

Now that she was closer, Brandy could tell something was off about his position—he'd fallen facedown, his arms and legs extended like he was in Superman position. Such a weird way to fall. His vomit—or whatever it was—dribbled all down the path to where he had landed and pooled out around him. The underside of his skin was faintly purple, and there was something wrong with his hair. It was darker than it should have been.

"Wake up," Brandy said, coming up to the unconscious figure and kneeling down. "Eric, come on. . . ."

His stillness was unnatural. He made no sound. There was only the soft birdsong and the sound of the trees and the chatter of the camp as it woke.

"Eric?" she said.

She rolled him over.

Someone was screaming. It took her a moment to realize it was her.

2

THE NEXT MORNING, STEVIE PLANTED HERSELF AT THE KITCHEN TABLE with a bowl of cereal and an Ellingham library book that she had been permitted to take home for the summer. This was one of the many perks of Ellingham, and of being on good terms with Kyoko, the school librarian, who had specially ordered it for her.

"What's that you're reading?" her mother said as she passed behind Stevie. She paused, leaning in to look, as Stevie knew she would. "Is that a dollhouse?"

"Sort of," Stevie said, flipping the page.

Her mother made a noise that sounded like a hamster being gently but persistently pressed until flattened.

The scene depicted was a kitchen lovingly crafted in miniature. The walls were papered in a cheerful pattern of deer and flowers. There was ironing on the small board, a pot in the sink, two potatoes on the draining board, each no bigger than a child's pinkie nail. From the curtains to the line outside the window pegged with bras and stockings to the pile of folded linens, everything about this scene was made with care. This included the unmistakably dead figure on the floor by the oven, a doll-size ice tray under her hand.

"It's called *The Nutshell Studies of Unexplained Death*," Stevie said. "They're dioramas made in the thirties and forties to teach investigators how to look at crime scenes. This one is called Kitchen. Look at the incredible level of detail. See these tiny cans on the shelves? Those labels are accurate reproductions. See the carefully printed tiny newspapers stuffed in the cracks of the doors? And all these doors have tiny, functioning keys. Everything in this scene has been made and put in here to be examined. It all means something. Did the woman stuff the paper in the door herself to gas herself? You can tell it's gas for sure. The jets are open on the stove, and her skin has been painted so you can see the blush you get from carbon monoxide poisoning. But did she do it herself or did someone knock her out, then stuff the paper in the doors and leave her in there? See, she's in the middle of taking things out of the oven. . . ."

Her mother stared at Stevie grimly.

"The woman who made these was named Frances Glessner Lee," Stevie went on. "It used to be that when someone died, there was no set method for examining the body and the scene. All kinds of people would be sent who had no formal training, and they'd move things, or they'd guess at what happened, or they'd contaminate the scene. Sometimes people would be accused of murder when it was an accident and the other way around. So this woman . . ."

Stevie flipped to the photo of the grandmotherly woman

with the old-fashioned glasses and bun who was peering lovingly into a skull.

". . . was the heiress to a tractor fortune, and she was friends with the chief medical examiner in Boston. He told her about all the trouble he was having with how bodies and scenes were being treated, and all of the things you could learn about a death from the scene and the body. She basically established forensics in the United States. Then she made these miniatures, each depicting an unexplained death. Each one is a contained mystery. They still use them to train detectives."

Her mother walked over to the counter, shaking her head. Stevie observed her surreptitiously.

"I wish you'd get another hobby, but . . ."

The sentence was left unfinished.

Stevie flipped back to the kitchen scene and let a few moments tick by while she waited for her mother to speak again.

"What are you up to this afternoon?"

"I was going to read," Stevie said.

"It's a gorgeous day. You could get some sun."

Stevie *hmmmm*ed and leaned in close to the picture of the death kitchen.

"I got a note," she said casually, "from a guy who owns a summer camp. He read about me, what I did at Ellingham. He asked if I wanted a job working there as a counselor. I guess he thought I'd be an interesting addition, you know, something extra for campers."

"A summer camp?" Stevie's mom said. "You?"

"I know," Stevie said. "Right?"

Stevie had never precisely been the outdoor type. They had camped once as a family, when Stevie was twelve and the neighbors down the street invited them to come on a week's trip to a state park. Stevie spent most of the week huddled under their RV awning trying to read, while her parents and the other family drank iced teas and beers and talked about television shows and what was "wrong with America." No one could swim in the lake because apparently there was some kind of brain-eating bacteria in it. Periodically someone would encourage her to walk through the woods or try out the mountain bike. Stevie viewed these offers with grave suspicion and declined. Stevie couldn't listen to anything or talk to anyone because her parents had taken her phone in order for her to experience some "offline time," which she had been anyway because they were in the middle of nowhere with no real signal and no Wi-Fi.

Camping sucked.

Stevie flipped to another part of the book slowly, to an even more graphic image.

"This is the most elaborate of the Nutshell Studies," she said. "It's called Three-Room Dwelling. Three rooms, three bodies. What's key in this one is the blood splatter . . ."

"Where is this camp?"

"Somewhere in Massachusetts," Stevie said. "Looks pretty, I guess. He even said I could bring my friends. Look at the blood on this blanket here . . ."

"What's it called?"

"What?" Stevie said.

"The camp. What's it called?"

"Oh. Um. Sunny something. Sunny . . . Oaks. Some kind of tree. Wait. I looked it up on my phone last night."

This was a careful calculation. Her parents had probably never heard of the Camp Wonder Falls murders, and the Sunny Pines website certainly didn't advertise the connection, but she couldn't risk them Googling it. She had it primed and ready to go.

Her mother looked at Stevie's phone while Stevie continued her contemplation of the blood splatter on the tiny kitchen floor.

"It looks nice," her mother said.

It did. Stevie had examined the site in detail. It was image after image of trees, kids leaping off a platform into a lake, kids playing instruments and making crafts, bonfires, cookouts, and toasting marshmallows.

"And they said you could bring friends?" her mom asked.

"Uh-huh."

Stevie flipped to another part of the book, to an attic scene that featured a hanging.

"And this is a real offer?" her mom said, eyeing the pictures. "From the real owner?"

"Yup."

"Let me see it."

Stevie blinked, as if this request was a surprise.

"Oh," she said. "Sure. I guess."

Stevie reached for her phone and pulled up a message, then passed it back to her mom.

Stevie,

My name is Carson Buchwald, and I am the owner and founder of Box Box (you've probably heard of it). I also own a summer camp in western Massachusetts called Camp Sunny Pines.

I read an article about what you did at Ellingham Academy, and I thought it was incredible. How would you like to come and work here this summer? You could be a counselor. I think it would be great to have someone like you on our staff! Our camp is in some beautiful woods. We have a swimming lake, falls, and a great little town nearby with some of the best ice cream in the country. It's a fantastic place with great kids!

You are welcome to bring friends, if that sweetens the deal.

If you're interested, get back in touch with me. I hope to hear from you.

Carson Buchwald
CEO and founder, Box Box
"It's what's inside that counts!"

"This sounds great," her mom said. "Wouldn't you rather do this than work in a supermarket and read books about murder dollhouses?"

"That seems like a lot of outside," Stevie said.

"Outside is good. You could use some sun."

"Skin cancer," Stevie said. "Besides, I want to get a lot of reading done this summer, and there's a free online course in forensic pathology starting in a week. . . ."

"Stevie," her mom said. "Don't you want to be social? Wouldn't you like to be with your friends?"

Stevie made a show of considering this point.

"I guess," she said after a long moment. "I'll think about it."

This little piece of magic had been achieved with relative ease.

She had recently been reading about Charles Manson, who used many popular persuasion techniques in order to form his murderous cult. One tip he had picked up from a popular self-help book was "Make the other guy think the idea is his." Stevie wanted nothing to do with Charles Manson's personal philosophy, but this passed-along tidbit was very useful and, it appeared, effective. (The only thing worse than saying "I want to go work at a murder camp" was probably "I have been studying the persuasive techniques of Charles Manson." So this was one she was keeping to herself.)

The new email from Carson was real. She had written back to him immediately the night before.

Carson,

I am very interested. But I can promise you this—my parents are never going to let me go if they think this is about investigating a murder. Could you write another note about how this is all about camping and doing healthy outdoor stuff?

Stevie

She had no idea if he'd go for it, but it turned out he did. The squeaky-clean new email had arrived with astonishing speed. All Stevie had to do then was prop herself up with her murder dollhouse book in the morning and wait. By midafternoon, the matter was settled. Stevie Bell was going to be a camp counselor at the most notorious camp in America.

More important, she was back on a case.

SUSAN MARKS WAS PROUD OF HER CLIPBOARD WALL.

There were twenty-six clipboards in all, hung from little screw-in hooks that she had put in herself five years ago, when she started running the camp. From this command center she made order out of chaos, organized hundreds of children and dozens of teenagers. There was a section for everything. Clipboards for every bunk, listing campers, counselors, contact numbers, known allergies. Another line of clipboards listed the activities for every week of the camp, which led to a different section of clipboards that broke down activities for every day.

For most of the year, Susan Marks ran the physical education and health department at Liberty High. During the summer, she ran the camp, and the job suited her very well. She woke early, when the camp was still asleep, and took a quick seven-mile run. She began on the camp side, running around the lake, then crossing over the dirt road that separated Camp Wonder Falls from the public campground on the other side. She continued her way around the lake there, where the paths were more rugged and rocky and the incline steeper. She went quietly past the tents full of sleeping tourists and waved to the fishermen setting out in their little boats. Up, up, up, working hard now as she ascended the hill at the far end of the lake. Here, the path left the lake edge and wound through the trees. Once she made it to the top, at the far end, she would pause at Arrowhead Point to catch her breath. The spot was so named because it resembled an arrowhead of dark stone, jutting seventy feet above the lake.

It was the best view you could ever hope to see. Below, Lake Wonder Falls stretched out, reflecting back the early sun. There was nothing like seeing dawn break from up here. After this moment of reflection, it was an easy trip downhill and back over to her cabin at Camp Wonder Falls for a quick (cold) shower. At seven thirty exactly, she picked up the clipboard with that day's activities and switched on the loudspeaker.

"Good morning, Camp Wonder Falls!" she said. "Welcome to another beautiful day!"

She meant it, too. The runner's high stayed with her for a while.

"This morning we have"—a quick glance at the clipboard that read "menus"—"pancakes in the dining pavilion, and it's softball day, so everyone let's get up and at 'em!"

She switched off the loudspeaker and ticked "announcement" off the daily to-do checklist. Even if you knew your routine like the back of your hand, a checklist was still important.

She ran down the rest of the day. The local stable was coming by and bringing five horses for riding lessons. There was a water safety test. Cabin 12 had developed a leak in the roof. Someone was taking a canoe out at night and she needed to find out who it was, and some other joker had put a snake in the girls' changing rooms at the junior pool. She would start by calling the stable and . . .

Then there was a scream. A single, unbroken scream.

Screaming was common at the camp. Campers screamed when they swam and played and sometimes simply for the sake of screaming. But this scream had a high, clear ring to it, and it did not break for almost ten seconds. It lingered over the water before it sounded again, this time louder, more insistent. She had never heard its equal, not when Penny Mattis almost drowned in the lake, or when that counselor a few years back fell out of a tree.

Susan did not hesitate. She grabbed her walkie-talkie from its charging base as she went to the small porch of her cabin to survey the camp. It was impossible to know exactly where the scream had come from, but it was certainly on the other side of the lake, from the direction of the cabins.

Her walkie crackled to life.

"Susan, did you hear that?"

It was Magda McMurphy, the camp nurse.

"Yes. Not sure where it came from." Susan was moving

quickly toward the footbridge. "I think it was over toward the edge of the woods, over by archery."

The scream came once more, and it stirred the whole camp.

"I don't like the sound of that," Magda said. "I'll meet you over there with my bag."

It didn't take Susan long to locate the source of the scream—the camp had all turned in its direction, many moving toward it. She made her way through, encouraging people to go back to what they were doing as she went. When she reached the edge of the woods, she found one of the younger campers, Claire Parsons, standing outside of her cabin in her little terry-cloth robe. She looked up at Susan and pointed toward the path into the woods.

"She went that way," Claire said.

"Who did?"

"Brandy."

"Go inside and get dressed, Claire," Susan said as she hurried off.

"He's asleep."

Susan had no time to try to work out what that meant. She moved faster. Behind her, there was the sound of a bicycle. Magda skidded up, hopping off the bike and then dropping it on the grass. Before them, the path bent gently to the left, going deeper into the woods, toward the camp's theater and archery range. They came upon a strangely calm scene. Brandy Clark, one of Susan's most reliable counselors, was kneeling on the ground, looking straight ahead. In front of her, maybe twenty feet or so, there was a figure on the path. Susan recognized the curly head of hair at once. Eric Wilde.

"He's there . . . ," Brandy said, sounding sleepy and distant. "I put him back."

Again, this made no sense. No time for questions. Susan and Magda continued on.

Eric was facedown in the dirt, like he was taking a nap. His shirt was mottled, ragged. There was something wrong with his hair—Eric was blond, but this hair was much too dark in places.

But the most telling thing? The flies. All the flies, buzzing around, landing in groups.

Magda made an odd noise, like a hissing tire, and broke into a run. She dropped down on the ground next to Eric and pressed her fingers to his wrist.

"He's cold," Magda said.

"I'll call an ambulance . . ."

"No point. He's gone." Magda looked at her watch. "I'm putting it at 7:46. What do you have?"

Susan blinked once, then consulted her own watch. "I have 7:44."

"I think we can call it 7:45."

Magda turned Eric over just enough to look at the underside of his body. Shock spread across her face.

"Susan, you need to come here."

Susan walked the few steps to what she already thought

of as "the body." The sight she saw then would never leave her.

"There are stab wounds," Magda said in a low voice. "And his head . . . Jesus, Susan."

Susan raised the walkie to her mouth, which had gone dry.

"Lake house," she said. "Pick up."

"Lake house," said a sleepy voice.

Shawn Greenvale. He was always reliable, and the lake house was one of the only other buildings with its own phone.

"I need you to call the police. Tell them to come right into the camp, to the path that leads to the theater. Say there's been a serious accident. No ambulance."

"What's going on?"

"Just do it, Shawn."

Behind them, campers were starting to congregate. They were getting louder, talking, crying, pointing. They didn't know exactly what was going on, but it was clear to them, as it had been clear to Susan, that something terrible had happened.

"Everyone," she said, "stay calm and back up."

Everyone did not keep calm. She needed to establish order, now. She did what came most naturally to her—she blew the whistle that hung around her neck. This startled everyone enough to shock them into silence.

"Get to the dining pavilion," she said. "Now."

She marched over to Brandy and helped her to her feet.

"Come on," she said. "Come on. Time to go."

Brandy let herself be led, but she was almost deadweight,

stumbling through her shock. Patty Horne, who had been staying in the nurse's cabin the last few nights as part of a house arrest, came running, breaking through the wall of campers who were reluctantly leaving the scene.

"Is that Eric?" she said.

"Patty, go get your campers and go to the dining pavilion."

"What about the others?" Patty asked. "Are they okay?"

Susan froze.

"Others?" she repeated.

3

Trains run through countless murder mystery novels. People are pushed off them or vanish when they move between the cars. When trains pass through tunnels, at least one passenger will get an axe in the face in the dark. People who seem to be asleep on trains are dead, victims of strange poisons in their tea. If you're not murdered on a train, you'll probably end up as a witness, seeing something out the window as you speed by—a man with a gun creeping toward a house, a strangling in a window. Train times always mattered. Jasper couldn't have been on the 7:14 from London because it doesn't run on Sundays!

Stevie had never actually taken a train anywhere. Her family went places by car only, as trains had a vaguely European and suspicious air about them. It turned out that the train was a pretty quiet and kind of boring tube where you mostly heard other people's phone conversations or smelled their sandwiches.

It had been a few frantic days. Once she got permission

to go to Sunny Pines, she had to scramble to gather up her friends, while Carson moved some things around and got them all jobs that suited their abilities.

At Ellingham, Stevie had lived in a small house called Minerva, with three students on the first floor and three on the second. By the end of the school year, this number was down to four, for various unfortunate reasons. Stevie was one of the four, as was David. The other two were Janelle Franklin, her next-door neighbor, and Nate Fisher, who lived upstairs.

She began with Nate.

Nate Fisher had written a book when he was fourteen, a fantasy novel that had gotten so popular online that a publishing company picked it up. The thing he created to keep himself away from people accidentally launched him into the world at large. The publisher wanted him to go on tour, to make videos, to smile and promote, and—most important—to write a second book.

Nate was always "working" on his book, which meant that Nate was never working on his book. He went all the way to Ellingham not to write his book. Nate would go to Mars if it meant that he didn't have to write his book. It was never clear to Stevie why he didn't want to write it; he must have liked writing in order to write a book in the first place. Sometimes she would try to get him to explain, but it always ended with him saying something like "That's not how it works" before windmilling his arms around and disappearing to his room.

49

She sensed it was something to do with performance anxiety, which she understood. Or maybe it was as simple as not wanting to do something that other people wanted you to do, which was also something she understood.

Nate was the only person in the group who would hate the idea of camping more than Stevie, but she was sure that when offered the chance to reunite with his friends and not write, he would leap at the chance. She was right.

Carson had found the perfect job for him. There was some kind of treehouse library at the camp that wasn't used very often. Nate could be the camp librarian, which wasn't really a position. He even arranged to quickly build a bunk space up there out of plywood so that Nate could stay up there all he wanted.

"I get to live by myself in a tree, doing some bullshit job for no one?" Nate said when Stevie told him. "This is my dream, Stevie. This is my *dream*."

So Nate was in.

Next was Janelle. Janelle was the person Stevie considered to be her best friend. She was the person Stevie could go to in the middle of the night when she had a panic attack. She was the person who pushed Stevie to acknowledge her feelings. She had met her partner, Vi, on the first day of school, and the two had been together since. Janelle was a budding engineer, a maker, a crafter—someone who was only happy when she had wires in one hand and a hot glue gun in the other. Whether you needed to build a miniature drone or make a dress, Janelle was your woman.

Unlike Nate and Stevie, Janelle was fine with the idea of camp but wouldn't be content with a pointless job with no responsibilities. Carson shuffled some things around and returned with the perfect gig—Janelle could be head of arts and crafts.

"It's going to be *a lot* of crafting," Stevie explained to her. "And there will be so many supplies to organize."

This gave Stevie her cover job. She would be Janelle's assistant. The two of them would share a bunk behind the art pavilion that usually went to senior staff.

Not everyone could make it. Vi, Janelle's partner, had gone to Vietnam for the summer to visit family. This was part of the reason Stevie thought Janelle would come—she was lonely without Vi, without her friends.

This left David. That conversation had not gone how Stevie had expected. Stevie thought he would accept. His campaign position, while not voluntary, was low paid. It was the kind of job that needed you more than you needed it, and it was clear that he and Stevie missed one another.

"I want to . . ." he said. Stevie felt her chest rising, but there was a weight hanging off the end of the sentence.

"But . . ."

"But . . . this work I'm doing now, it means something to me. I didn't apply to college yet. I've committed to this, and I . . ."

A strange constellation of emotions came upon her. There

was a damp rush of sadness—then an urgency of feeling, something like panic, but with a duller edge. Then a punch of soft-boiled anger. Back to sadness again, with a goose egg blooming in her throat. All of this happened in about five seconds.

"You there?" he asked.

She coughed softly.

"Yup. Yeah. No, I get it."

"I mean it," he said. "I really want to come be with you. It just . . . it feels like I'm repairing some of the damage my family has caused by doing this work. I really hate saying no. It *sucks* saying no."

Even though the answer still felt like a blow, there was a lot of feeling in his voice. She could tell he meant it. She picked at a small hole in her T-shirt.

"Sure," she said. "You have to do this."

It came out a bit dry, because Stevie didn't really know how to have sensitive conversations.

"Don't sound so sad," he said sarcastically.

"No, I . . . I do. I get it."

They hung on a moment in silence.

"But . . . ," he said. "I can take a little time off to visit. I'll be there. We'll camp. Oh, we'll camp."

And so Stevie found herself on a train heading toward the Berkshire mountains of Massachusetts. Camp Wonder Falls, or Sunny Pines, was located about an hour outside Springfield, not far from Amherst, in the green and rolling landscape dotted with lakes.

The camp had provided an exacting list of things to bring: a set of twin sheets, a pillow, a blanket, three towels—all with your name on them. Flip-flops, sneakers, sturdy socks that were at least as high as the ankle, either a one-piece bathing suit or trunks and a swim top, bug spray, bite cream, a high-powered flashlight, at least one pair of long sweatpants or similar exercise pants, a long-sleeved sports top, a hat . . .

Ellingham had also set a list of things to bring to school, but the specificity of this one spoke volumes. The sturdy socks at least as high as the ankle meant there was some kind of hiking in the future. The sweatpants and long-sleeved shirt had an ominous ring to Stevie, hinting at activities in wild places where protection would be needed, or maybe walks at night to go raccoon-poking.

She reminded herself that she was not required to poke raccoons. While she was technically going to be a camp employee, Carson had promised that her position was special. She would have the camp experience without the camp requirements.

In the rush to get ready to go, she had little time to learn about the Box in the Woods case. She knew the basics, of course—all true-crime fans did—but she didn't know the case in the way she had known the Ellingham Affair. She'd spent over a year researching that case before she wound up at Ellingham. She watched everything, read everything, participated in every message board, listened to every podcast, so that by the time she arrived at the scene, she could navigate without a map and quote half the books.

Not so this time. She powered through podcasts as she packed and read as much as she could at night. Her old friend anxiety started bubbling inside her, ready to party. This time, it was too much, too soon. She was going to fail, and that would mean she was a fail*ure*. She would never solve anything else. Never be a detective. Her life would go nowhere.

The texts from Nate came at a good moment.

Stevie.

STEVIE

THERE IS A TRAPEZE IN HERE

This confused her enough to defuse her internal situation.

When she reached Springfield (she had been lurking in the metallic vestibule of the train for two stops, paranoid she would miss it), she dragged her heavy, wheeled suitcase into the terminal.

Another text, this time from Carson, who had arranged to meet her.

Outside.

She stepped outside and saw a man, not much taller than her, leaning against the wall, typing furiously on his phone. He clearly worked out a lot—he had muscular arms and a six-pack that he showed off in a snug black T-shirt. The bottom half of his body was adorned in flowing yoga pants in a purple-and-green mandala pattern. His head was shaved completely bald. He had the word CARBON tattooed in huge letters down his left arm, and the word BASED down the right.

"Hey!" he said, waving to her as if they were old friends. "Stevie! Stevie!"

As she got closer she noticed that he reeked of burned sage. Not yoga studio levels—more like he'd been in a brushfire on a sage farm.

"My car's out this way," he said.

Stevie continued behind, dragging the bag toward the green Tesla that he was opening. The inside of the car was a creamy pale tan leather that was probably called "latte" or "toasted coconut" or something like that. A set of wooden meditation beads hung from the rearview mirror, and there was a pink crystal in the cupholder. The sage smell was much stronger inside the car, and Stevie found herself hungry for air.

"Barlow Corners is about an hour's drive," he said, pulling the eerily silent car out of the parking space. "Your friends are already here."

"They said there's a . . . trapeze?"

"Oh yeah. They're in the Bounce House."

Stevie could not bring herself to ask why it was called the Bounce House, and it didn't matter. She knew he was about to tell her.

"I call it the Bounce House because that's where I host all

kinds of creators and we bounce ideas around. We call them Think Jams."

She resisted the impulse to open the car door and jump.

"Tonight you'll all stay in the guest rooms there," he went on. "Tomorrow I can drive you through town and take you over to the camp. Might as well get in one night with air-conditioning and hot water, right? Also, no snakes."

Anxiety is very accommodating. Minutes ago, Stevie's anxiety was all about failure. It neatly converted itself into worry about places called Bounce Houses and not having hot water or air-conditioning. It was perfectly ready to bring the snakes to the party. It's a big tent. All problems are welcome.

"Snakes?"

"I mean, there are some around the lake, but not at the camp."

"The camp is on a lake."

"Yeah, but the snakes are . . . I mean, they're around, but over on the other side. No snakes at the camp."

There were for sure snakes at the camp. It was entirely made of snakes. Why hadn't she thought of the snakes?

"Tonight I thought we could have a meeting," Carson said, "to go over the details of the case. And tomorrow I have something really special planned."

The snakes slithered to the side of her thoughts.

"What?"

"A big event, sponsored by Box Box. See, I donated a children's reading room to the town library, so I'm having a big picnic to open it, with free food and entertainment. I've made sure lots of people will be there, including some who were there in 1978. You'll be able to meet some of the witnesses and even some of the suspects. We'll start our work off right. The Box in the Woods—finally solved!"

"*If* it can be solved," Stevie said.

"Of course it can. With everything available now? Someone just has to put some pressure on, get things moving, look into all the stuff that's been ignored for decades."

"But people have been doing that."

"Not people who own the camp," he said with a smile.

She had to admit, he had a point.

A ridge of gently rolling green hills appeared in the distance. Buildings became more scarce, and the land opened up like a blank page waiting for a story. He turned a corner between two sprawling fields. Every road got smaller and deeper into the trees. It reminded her a little of the drive to Ellingham Academy, except that drive was up, up, up. This drive was more gentle, the terrain far less imposing. Everything had the soft veneer of Americana—flags, farm stands, screened porches. There were thick green canopies of trees along the roads, under which people walked dogs or rode bikes or took purposeful runs while listening to headphones and squinting at an invisible finish line.

The first sign they had entered Carsonland was the stone Buddha next to the green mandala-covered mailbox. They turned up a short drive, past a trampoline, a pool, and a small field with three goats. Stevie stepped out into a peaceful place bordered by a burbling creek, nestled in the trees. There were piles of rocks out in the shallow water, delicately balanced on one another.

"This is the Bounce House," he said, pulling her bag toward a barn—or what had probably been an old barn at some point. Everything about it looked fresh and new, from the electric-blue paint to the massive windows with the hot dog mustard–yellow sills.

"That's my house over there," Carson said, pointing through the trees to a large purple house with an eye painted where the front of the house met the peak of the roof. It gazed down on Stevie sleepily.

The door to the barn opened. There was a high-pitched noise, and then Janelle Franklin came soaring over as if on winged feet and grabbed Stevie in an embrace.

"You're wearing your lemons," Stevie said.

"Of course! We're all here! Almost all here!"

Janelle loved lemons, and when she wore her lemon-print dress, it was a sign that she was happy. She had wrapped her braided hair in a matching yellow scarf and complemented the whole look with a sunny yellow eyeshadow that popped cheerily against her black skin. This is what Janelle was like—always dressed to express. She understood how things went together, how makeup was applied, how to be perfectly together and make it all look easy. It probably was for her. She did calculus in her head, for fun.

Behind her was Nate, his lips twisted into a wry smile. Even when he smiled, Nate's expression suggested that of an old-timey fisherman resignedly watching his boat being devoured by a sea serpent. His hair was always a bit scruffy, and his clothes a little too big for him. At school he usually wore beat-up cargo pants or corduroys—for his summer look, he had exchanged these for beat-up cargo shorts. He wore the same T-shirts that he had in school; this one read SHRIMP OPTIONAL.

"I'll let you guys catch up," Carson said. "I have evening meditation. I'll be back in an hour. Everyone good with vegan pizza?"

There was a polite pause.

"Or I can get some dairy pizza. See you in a few. Make yourself at home, Stevie."

"Oh," Nate said in a low voice, opening the wide barn door, "wait until you see home."

The first thing that struck Stevie was the vibrant orange color of the walls—it made her eyeballs wobble in her skull.

"Restful, isn't it?" Nate said.

There were no chairs or tables. Everywhere you looked there were fancy beanbags made of some NASA-quality foam that made you feel like you were floating and supported you in any position. Thick ropes hung from the ceiling with knots tied in them, so you could climb or swing. There were yoga balls, and regular inflatable balls, and a partially deflated human hamster ball in the corner.

"Welcome to the house that boxes built, I guess," Janelle said.

As reported, there was indeed a single trapeze suspended high up in the rafters.

"How do they trapeze in here?" Stevie said. "There's not enough room to swing, at least, not very far. And what if they fall?"

"We've been wondering about that for the last few hours," Janelle replied. "We think they use a hook to pull the trapeze over to the loft, then they must jump off really gently and kind of hang there. They probably use that to get down."

She indicated a large rolled-up tarp against the wall.

"So they just hang from the ceiling and fall into a tarp?" Stevie asked.

"Yeah. It's not really a trapeze as much as it's a . . . dangler?"

"He calls them Think Jams," Nate said, allowing himself to sink deeper into the beanbag. "Did he tell you that? *Think Jams*."

"I mean, the thing is, I don't hate it," Janelle said. "And that fact makes me hate *myself*."

Along the side of the main room there were hundreds of inch-square pieces of fabric, little flaps of them in a grid pattern, attached to the wall with tape. It wasn't art, Stevie was pretty sure.

"We have no idea what those are for," Janelle said. "Maybe he's really into quilting."

Stevie flopped into one of the massive beanbags, which

caught her in its space beads or foam or whatever was in it.

Funny how the world shifts when you're in the same space with your friends. The air is energized, the light is warmer. The two weeks they had been separated evaporated, and they began to talk as if they had finished their last in-person conversation moments before.

"I'm so ready for this," Nate said. "I love summer camp horror movies, so I rewatched a bunch of them last week to prepare. Do you want to hear about summer camp horror movies?"

"Nate . . . ," Janelle began.

"You cannot deny me this," Nate said. "This is a *murder story* at a *camp*. It's *how I want to go*. My favorite is called *Sleepaway Camp*. It makes the least sense. First of all, the campers in this movie are, like, eighteen years old. Not the counselors. The campers. Everyone in this movie is terrible. They spend pretty much all their time trying to have the sex. Obviously, though, in terms of the killer, Jason is still the best. He lives in a lake and commits murders in space."

"Are you done?" Janelle asked.

"Do *you* live in a lake?"

"Okay," Janelle said, getting up and smoothing out her dress. "I have to call Vi. I won't be long—we have to schedule because of the time difference."

"How's Vi?" Stevie asked.

"They're good. They like Da Nang. It's a lot of family stuff. They're mostly working on their Vietnamese, plus learning more Mandarin. It's . . . you know. Really far, though. I'll be right back in. Okay? Right back!"

"Do you have to make a romance call?" Nate said when Janelle was gone.

"No," Stevie replied. "We don't have a schedule."

"How is David?"

"Good," she replied with a shrug.

One of the things that made Nate and Stevie such good friends was their mutual hatred of sharing emotional things. Somehow, they managed to have a deeper bond by staying on the surface—as if they were snorkeling their feelings, floating along side by side, observing all of nature's wonders without getting close enough to be stung by something under a rock.

"So here we are again in Murder Town," Nate said. "Where you live."

They both gazed up at the trapeze, suspended from the ceiling. It was an innocent-enough object, meant to be fun, but in that moment it reminded Stevie of another Nutshell Study, one called Attic, which featured a hanging.

"What do you think?" he asked.

He didn't need to explain. Stevie knew what he meant, because he meant a lot of things. How was it to be back on a case? What did she think about this case?

"I don't know yet," she replied.

"I think it's going to be great," he said. "Murder camp, living in a tree, not seeing anyone. This is my summer. This is when I shine. I'm going to achieve peak me. And there are no tunnels here, so you probably won't get trapped underground. I feel good about it. I think?"

That Nate was feeling so positive should have served as a warning, but people rarely recognize signs when they appear.

July 7, 1978
8:05 a.m.

SHERIFF ELLIOT REYNOLDS AND HIS DEPUTY, DON MCGURK, TURNED down the drive into Camp Wonder Falls. Don tapped absently on the passenger's side window.

"What do you think it is?" Don asked. "Drowning?"

"I hope not," Sheriff Reynolds replied.

"Can't be someone dead. Eight in the morning at the camp?"

It didn't make sense to Sheriff Reynolds either. From the sound of the confused message he had gotten over the radio, something very bad had gone down. A serious accident, no ambulance needed. But, as Don pointed out, it seemed unlikely that there was a dead person at the camp on a sunny weekday morning.

Then again, since Michael Penhale, Sheriff Reynolds had felt something turn in Barlow Corners. Of course, accidents happened everywhere. But that business—it had tainted things, tainted his reputation. A barely perceptible but inescapable whiff of rot had taken over this once-pristine little corner of America.

Damn that business. Damn it to hell. Everything about it was terrible—but what was the point of ruining a young man's life like that? Who would it have helped?

No. He really did not want another dead kid in Barlow Corners.

Susan Marks was waiting for them by the camp entrance along with a weeping Patty Horne. The look on her face confirmed the worst. When he stopped the car Susan immediately opened the back door and shooed Patty inside, then followed.

"What's going on, Sue?" the sheriff asked.

"One of the counselors is dead. Eric Wilde. He's been murdered."

"Come on," Don said.

"I've just about been able to keep this place under control. He's up on the path toward the woods. Keep going and this road will join up with it. Hurry."

Sheriff Reynolds didn't have to be told twice. He started up the road with as much speed as he could manage without risking hitting a wayward camper.

"There's more," Susan said. "We have three more missing. Apparently they went out into the woods last night."

"Who's missing?" he said, glancing at her in the rearview mirror.

"Diane McClure, Todd Cooper, and Sabrina Abbott."

"Sabrina Abbott? And Todd Cooper?"

"Shit," Don said quietly.

The sheriff shot him a glance.

"Patty," Susan said. "Explain to them what you told me."

Patty burst into a torrent of sobs.

"Come on, Patty," Susan said firmly but not unkindly. "We can't waste any time. Tell them."

Patty heaved, then brought herself under enough control to speak. "They went out around eleven. . . . They go out . . . Eric gets the . . ."

"Gets the what?" the sheriff prompted as he turned the car slightly to merge onto the dirt path.

"I . . . I can't . . ."

"You can," he said. "I don't care what was going on, just tell me."

"He . . . gets the grass. In the woods. They went out for the grass."

"Shit," Don said again, but he managed to keep it under his breath.

"Stop here," Susan said. Don remained in the car to coordinate over the radio and watch Patty. Susan and the sheriff hurried down the path. The morning was eerily silent, the campers all gathered in the dining area. It was a stunning morning, soft and sweet, birdsong in the air. It made the sight of Eric's discolored and lifeless body all the more grotesque. Magda McMurphy, the camp nurse, was with him, though it was immediately clear that there was nothing she could do aside from shoo away the flies.

"He's been dead for some time," Magda said. "A few hours at least."

The sheriff squatted down next to the body.

"Let's turn him over," he said to Magda.

They rolled the body carefully, and the full extent of the carnage was now clear.

"What in holy hell happened here?" the sheriff said in a low voice.

"I can count six stab wounds," Magda said. "There may be more. It's hard to tell. He's also got a massive head wound."

Sheriff Reynolds took a long, steadying breath and sprung back to stand.

"Come on," he said to Susan, then broke into a run back to the car. Susan paced him easily. He threw open the back door to the cruiser, where Patty Horne sat with her knees tucked up to her chest, her long hair pulled over the sides of her face like she was trying to cocoon herself away from the horror.

"Patty," he said without any preamble. "Where do they go to get the grass?"

"In the woods. Up the road."

"You've been there?"

"Once." She nodded heavily. "I don't know where, it's just . . . in the woods somewhere."

"Do you walk or drive?"

"Todd drives. We take his Jeep."

"About how far up the road? How long do you drive?"

"I don't know," she said, still weeping but maintaining control. "Five minutes?"

"Stay here with Susan."

Patty slid out of the car, looking terrified.

"Keep all the kids together," he said to Susan. "I don't even want them going to the bathroom by themselves, got it?"

Susan nodded, and he knew she was more than up to the task. He got back behind the wheel, where Don regarded him in bafflement.

"What's going on?"

"We've got a dead kid with half a dozen stab wounds to his chest."

"Shit," he said. "Do we call the mayor if Todd's involved?"

"No," the sheriff said, stepping on the gas. "We're not getting him involved again. Keep him the hell out of this as long as we can. We call the state police and head out now, see if we can find the others. Get them on the horn."

They took the bumpy road through the woods at a good pace. It didn't take long to find Todd's Jeep. Patty's estimate had been correct—it was about five minutes up the road, parked off to the side on a slight diagonal. The sheriff pulled the cruiser up behind it. He retrieved his gun and holster from the locked glove compartment. Guns weren't usually required in Barlow Corners; he'd only pulled it once in his career there, during a suspected robbery that turned out to be a raccoon in the wall.

"Get the rifle from the trunk," he said to Don.

Once armed, the two men began to scan the area. There was nothing around to suggest a rendezvous spot.

"Todd!" the sheriff called. "Diane! Sabrina!"

There was no reply.

"Footprints this way," Don said as he scanned the dirt. "Looks like they went in this direction."

They tramped into the trees, pushing back branches, calling all the while. Birds scattered, but no one replied. They came upon a small clearing, with a blanket on the ground and the smoldering remains of a fire, now just a tiny smoking glow under a pile of smoked-out logs. There was a tape player sitting on one of the logs by the fire. The blanket was a sleeping bag that had been unzipped and spread out, and an open can of Coke sat on a log. Three unopened beers were on the ground nearby, along with a cafeteria tray that contained a McDonald's bag, some small papers, and some kind of green substance.

"Marijuana," the sheriff said, examining it. "They were here. I don't know why they'd leave this behind if they weren't in trouble."

He scanned the ring of trees around them. In a clearing like this, you were vulnerable. There were ample places to hide, and someone could approach from any direction. In the dark, this place would have been terrifyingly easy to attack a group of teenagers.

He pulled his handgun from its holster.

"Todd Cooper is a big kid," Don said, as if having the same thought. "He'd fight. So would Diane."

But there was no sign of a fight. The area was neat. It was as if they had simply walked away from their camp, leaving the fire, the tape player, and a significant amount of grass spread out on a tray.

The sheriff and Don made a slow circuit of the area, looking at the spaces between the trees, examining the ground.

"Here," the sheriff said. "Something's been dragged here."

They picked their way between the trees. Don reached for a branch with a piece of torn dark green fabric and a tuft of white filler clinging to it.

"Looks like it could have come from a sleeping bag," Don said.

They continued on, and about a minute later came upon a sagging hunting blind. Beside it, neatly rolled, was the sleeping bag with a tear in the side. The woods were velvety quiet as they approached the box. The sheriff opened it slowly. The smell hit first, seconds before his brain could process the hideous jigsaw that was before his eyes.

"Oh god," Don said. "What the hell . . . what . . ."

There was a single-word message, roughly painted on the inside of the lid in white paint. It read: SURPRISE.

4

It appeared that Carson had correctly read the room when he returned with a stack of pizza boxes containing every possible kind of cheesy, meaty pizza. The traveling, the reunion joy, and the sweet woodland air seemed to have stimulated all their appetites, and the pies were soon torn apart and consumed. For his own meal, Carson brought a giant cup of thick blue juice and regarded the pizza carnage like someone watching a nature documentary.

"So you own a box service, right?" Nate asked innocently as he reached for his fifth slice of pizza. "One of those get-a-box-every-month things?"

"Box Box," Carson said.

Nate knew all this already, which meant he was asking for entertainment, rather than information.

"What is it, though?"

"Every month you get a curated selection of boxes," Carson replied.

"What's in the boxes?"

"Boxes. It's a box full of boxes. We have themes, like bathroom boxes, or closet boxes, or gift boxes, kitchen boxes, garden boxes. Everyone needs boxes. We're starting a new thing in a few months. We're either going to call it Bag Box or Bag Bag. You get reusable bags. See all those fabric samples over there? Those are for the bags. I was Think Jamming them."

"Why?" Nate said.

"Why what?"

"Why would you want a bag full of bags? Or a box full of boxes?"

"It's environmentally friendly," Carson replied.

"How?"

"Because you get the boxes so you don't have to buy them. Same as the bags."

"Isn't it worse to send people a bunch of boxes they don't need and then have them get rid of some of them? Especially when you add all the packaging, and the transport and everything?"

"It's about convenience as well," Carson said.

"How is it convenient to get a bunch of boxes or bags?"

"People like it," Carson said, though more quietly. "We have over four hundred thousand subscribers. Anyway . . . we should get started."

Nate happily chomped off half a slice of pizza in one bite as Carson gestured them over to the beanbags and sofas in the center of the room. Stevie, Janelle, and Nate moved over, Nate taking a pizza box with him. Carson picked up a remote control. The lights dimmed gently and there was a soft whirring noise as a massive screen unfurled from the ceiling.

A title slide appeared on the screen.

THE BOX IN THE WOODS MURDERS,
JULY 6–7, 1978

"It's important to set a sense of this town, this camp, at this time, because these murders are very much of a time and a place. . . ."

Stevie could tell at once that Carson had written this line in advance and was proud of it. He was testing out his podcast script, for sure.

"The 1970s were a different era. For example, information and communication were more limited . . ."

"Well, yeah," Nate said. "That's why their slasher films work. No one knows anything and no one can call for help."

"Right," Carson said. "And the lack of communication impacted safety. This is a time when everything was loose. Your comings and goings couldn't be tracked. Everything relied more on word of mouth and who knew what. The world was smaller. The camp was an extension of the high school and the town—a closed loop. Everyone knew everyone. Which brings us to . . ."

BARLOW CORNERS

This slide featured a photo that Stevie had seen several times now; it was the image that pretty much every book or article or documentary on the case included. It was a color photo with a sepia tint, the colors washed out and overly bright at the same time. A group of people stood in front of an equestrian statue decked out in red, white, and blue bunting. Most of the people in the group were middle-aged. The men all wore Bermuda shorts with belts. The women wore dresses or pants that they would have referred to as "slacks."

"So this," Carson said, "was a picture taken at the Bicentennial, in 1976, two years before the murders. The town built and dedicated a statue to the town founder, John Barlow, a minor Revolutionary War hero. A local photographer took the picture and submitted it to *Life* magazine, and it ran in a special commemorative edition. There are a few people in this photo associated with the case. It says a lot about the town—a small place, all American, everyone knows everyone. And pretty much everyone was connected in some way to . . . "

THE VICTIMS

"We'll start with the basics," Carson said. "The four victims. All recent graduates of Liberty High. All residents of Barlow Corners. All four worked at the camp. This is Eric Wilde. . . ."

He brought up a picture of a boy with wildly curly light-colored hair and a goofy grin.

"Eighteen years old. Son of the town librarian and a teacher at Liberty. Generally well-liked but could get into trouble. Diane McClure . . ."

A tough-looking redheaded girl with a thin smile and a freckled face appeared on the screen.

"Daughter of the owners of the town diner, the Dairy Duchess. Academically unremarkable. Liked rock music and having fun. Your basic seventies teenager. She was girlfriend to this guy, Todd Cooper."

Fashions come and go, but jawlines are eternal. Todd Cooper had a good one, if a big one. His face was almost square. He had medium-length hair, in a seventies-style feathered cut. There was a thin, wry smile on his lips. His face exuded confidence—arrogance, even.

"Son of the mayor. Football captain. And a lot of trouble. More on him later. The real outlier of the group was . . ."

A photo of a girl came up. It was hard to say what made her seem different from the rest. The photo was the same quality, and her raven hair was in long seventies-style wings. She had big brown eyes, and a sincere smile. There was something about her, something in the way she looked at the camera. There was a bright spark there, something that connected to Stevie viscerally.

". . . Sabrina Abbott, the town good girl, daughter of a dentist. Top student at Liberty High. Volunteered at the library every week, reading to little kids. It's one of the enduring mysteries that surrounds this case—why did the town good girl go with three of the bad seeds to a drug buy in the woods? But let's get to it. . . ."

THE MURDERS

"Here are the undisputed facts. On the night of July sixth, Sabrina, Eric, Todd, and Diane left the camp somewhere around eleven at night in Todd's Jeep. They went to the woods to pick up the weekly pot delivery. Eric Wilde was the dealer at camp. Todd and Diane were a couple, and Sabrina Abbott was along for the ride, for whatever reason. The next morning, one of the campers found Eric Wilde, facedown on a dirt path through the woods that led to the theater and archery range. He had been struck on the head and stabbed six times. Five of the wounds were fatal."

He brought up a black-and-white photo of the scene, taken from a short distance. There was a sheet over the body on the dirt path, and a group of police officers standing around it, conferring with one another.

"The camp quickly figured out that the other three were missing, so the police rode out to try to find them. The Jeep was parked alongside the road. They found the campsite. . . ."

He brought up a picture of the campsite—a smoldering fire, a blanket, a camping lantern, a plastic tray with something all over it, some sodas, a backpack.

"No sign of a struggle," Carson said. "It looks like they

simply left the site. The police searched the area and found an old hunting blind. When they opened it up, well, that was the box in the woods. Pictures of the bodies aren't available to the public, just a description. Here's a diagram. . . ."

A creepy drawing of three featureless bodies in a rectangle, with dots and dashes to mark wounds and bindings. Stevie had seen these kinds of drawings before, but they always unnerved her.

"The bodies were arranged in the box neatly. Diane and Sabrina were facing one way, and Todd was turned the other, his head between the girls' feet. Todd and Diane both had massive head wounds, like Eric. Then they were each stabbed multiple times—Todd had sixteen stab wounds, and Diane had nine. Sabrina was the only one without a head wound. She was stabbed twenty-one times and had defensive marks on her hands, so she was probably facing her killer. The evidence suggested they were killed at the campsite and then moved to the box. The killer bound their legs and wrists in red nylon cord. There was a single word written in white paint on the inside of the box's lid . . ."

He pulled up the most famous photo from the case, one of the only crime scene photos that had been made available to the public—the word SURPRISE painted in rough, blocky letters. It was so comically ghoulish it seemed like it couldn't be real.

"There are three major theories about who did it," Carson said. "Let's do the least likely first. . . ."

DRUG DEAL

"The police first suspected that it was a drug deal gone wrong. Eric Wilde was the camp pot dealer, and the four of them were out in the woods that night picking up the weekly supply for the camp. So people thought—illegal activity in the woods, must have something to do with it. Also, Eric was found in a different location than the others. Sabrina, Todd, and Diane were in the box. Eric was almost at the camp."

"But this one is dumb," Stevie said. "They found all the pot at the crime scene, so the sale had gone through. There's no reason for anyone to get killed over a little bit of pot that no one even bothered to take."

"Agree," Carson said. "Basically, no one really thinks this had anything to do with it, but it was an easy explanation, especially then. Pot in the woods ending in multiple murders? Sure, why not. Now, the next one is more compelling and was the most popular theory for a long time. . . ."

THE WOODSMAN

"So the 1970s were kind of the golden age of serial killers. There were loads of them. There was one known to operate in the area at the time called the Woodsman. The first murder was in 1973, in New Hampshire. Then there were two in Massachusetts, one each in 1974 and 1976, and two in upstate New York in 1975. There were two more cases, in 1979 and

1980, both back in New Hampshire. The Woodsman stabbed his victims and left them in the woods, covered in sticks and debris, with their hands and feet bound in red cording. In all the cases, the word *Surprise* was written somewhere near the scene, usually on a tree. So it looks like the Woodsman, right? Now, here's the thing . . . the Woodsman's crimes were in the news. The local paper even covered the story in 1976."

Carson brought up a photocopy of an old newspaper article entitled "Woodland Killer Strikes Near Hawley."

"This murder happened about a forty-five-minute drive from here, so it was local enough. It's a real seventies kind of story. A nineteen-year-old girl named Becky O'Keefe was a free spirit who was spending the summer camping in the Berkshires. Her friends last saw her when she left to hitchhike to get to another campsite to meet a guy. She was found two days later. This newspaper article says that her legs and wrists were bound in red cord, and that the word *Surprise* was written on a tree. This is pretty much exactly how the bodies in the box in the woods were found. But the police kept some details out of the press: in all the Woodsman killings, the bodies were bound with torn pieces of silky red fabric ripped into pieces, and all the messages were written in chalk. So it seemed obvious from the start that someone was copying the details in the paper. This killer used white paint and red nylon cord."

"So it was a copycat," Stevie said. "Did they find out anything about the paint or the cord?"

"The white paint was found to be a common type that you could buy at almost any hardware store in the northeastern United States. The cord was a little more interesting. . . ."

A close-up photograph of a piece of red cord on a white background came up on the screen. There was a ruler under the cord, showing that this section was six inches long.

"This particular cord was sold in sporting goods stores, and it was commonly used in water-related sports in the area. Fishermen used it to secure boats and supplies. The camp used it to tie up canoes. The police tried to run down all recent purchases of the cord, but the best guess is that someone probably lifted it from a boat or a supply shed. It would have been easy enough to get."

"Can't they test for DNA?" Janelle said.

"Here's where things in this case get ridiculous—the police got rid of most of the clothing the victims were wearing."

"What?" Nate said.

"It's amazing, but it's true. They still have Eric's T-shirt, but all the rest? Someone just . . . got rid of them. They tested the shirt and came up with a profile, but it didn't match the Woodsman samples. Could have been the killer's. Could have been anyone's. There was nothing usable on the cord."

"Didn't they test the town or anything?" Nate asked. "Don't they do that, take samples from everyone?"

"What they found wasn't good enough to test everyone against. And now we come to the third. . . ."

REVENGE

"Revenge," Nate read in a low voice. "*Revennnnnge*."

He brought up a photo of a smiling young boy.

"The previous December," Carson said, "in 1977, an eleven-year-old named Michael Penhale was struck and killed by a car. No one was ever arrested or charged. It was written off as a hit-and-run. But it seemed to be common knowledge in town that Michael was run over by Todd Cooper. His brother, Paul, was friends with the victims and worked at the camp. The neighbors said that the Penhale family was home on the night of the murders, and Paul Penhale had someone who could place him at the camp that night. That person was Shawn Greenvale, Sabrina Abbott's ex-boyfriend. Sabrina had broken up with him a few weeks before. Some people speculated that either Paul or Shawn might have wanted to kill Todd or Sabrina, respectively, but they were also seen by Susan Marks, the head of camp. Also, nothing ties them to the case except for the fact that Todd probably hit Michael Penhale, and Sabrina broke up with Shawn. And that is pretty much that. The case was so badly handled from the start that it was dead in the water."

Carson hit the remote again, and the screen glided up to the ceiling, rolling itself snugly back to sleep. The lights came up like a sunrise.

"Our goal this summer," he said, "is to make some headway into a case that's been dormant for decades. It may seem difficult, but we have a lot going for us. I own the camp, so we can turn it upside down if we want. Lots of people who were alive then are still here in town. We have the internet. And we have Stevie. We have an early start tomorrow. I'll come get you guys at, say, seven?"

When Carson left, the three friends sat in their respective beanbags for a moment in silence.

"The murder camp thing is a little less fun now," Nate finally said.

5

Stevie tried to focus her newly opened eyes on the thing hanging from the ceiling. What the hell was she looking at?

Oh right. The trapeze.

Stevie had spent the night in a pile of beanbags on the floor of the main room. There were several guest bedrooms in the Bounce House, but she had fallen asleep here while talking to Nate and decided to stay. She would have been content to stay there for a while longer, floating on the foam or beads, drifting in and out of sleep, but Janelle was up and moving, and it sounded like Nate was in the shower. She pushed herself up and began getting ready for the day.

Carson appeared several minutes early, not bothering to knock as he came into the barn.

"Lots to do today," he said. "First, we'll drive through the town so I can show you all around. Then we'll go to the camp, get you settled in, give you the whole tour."

The drive from Carson's compound to the town was a sedate one. Every house had a front porch, often a screened one. Everywhere you looked there were flags, flower planters, green lawns, and shady spaces. This was the kind of town where everyone seemed to have a tire swing. There was one incredibly sharp turn along a wooded stretch, which then led them past a full-size blue billboard that read LIBERTY HIGH, HOME OF THE MIGHTY OWLS.

"Take it down a notch, sign," Nate said. "Why are you yelling about owls?"

The sign was ridiculously huge, almost as high as the trees around it, and it seemed entirely out of place along the road. The high school it announced was a modestly sized redbrick building, midcentury and fairly ugly compared to all the other places Stevie had seen along the way. The school and its sign were then left behind for another half mile of woods and streams, before they reached a traffic light.

"This is Barlow Corners," Carson said, turning onto a slightly busier street. "Population two thousand. This is the main drag here—all the businesses."

There were the kinds of places you see in every small town. A boutique full of local crafts, scarves, and bric-a-brac. A savings and loan. A place for takeout tacos. A yoga studio. There was the Dairy Duchess, the diner that had been owned by Diane's family.

He indicated a cheerful-looking coffee shop called Sunshine Bakery.

"That place over there is where we're going first," he said. "It's run by Patty Horne. She was friends with at least three of the victims."

The Sunshine Bakery was a painfully adorable

small-town kind of business, painted in a half dozen varieties of yellow, from a pale buttery color to a lemon, all the way to a near-orange that mirrored the namesake sun. It had several glass cabinets of genuinely astonishing cakes on display—real works of art, detailed and sculpted. Janelle was drawn to them at once like a moth to a flame.

Behind the counter was a woman with dusty blond hair pulled up in a messy bun. She wore loose distressed jeans and a blue apron. She looked to be somewhere in her fifties, and seemed lost in thought, examining a list.

"Morning!" she said, looking a bit surprised. "Camp already? I thought the counselors were coming tomorrow?"

"These guys are special," Carson said before anyone else could answer. "This is Stevie Bell. She was the one who solved those murders at Ellingham Academy back in the fall."

"Oh," Patty Horne said. Stevie could tell she didn't really know the story but was being polite and acting like she was trying to remember the details. "Wow. That's impressive. And you're . . . going to be counselors?"

"Yup!" Carson said quickly. "Here to grab some coffee and . . ."

He stared at the display of baked goods under glass as if he were looking at a collection of captive spiders.

". . . muffins? Or whatever you want. I don't drink coffee or eat sugar."

Stevie looked around the room, at the framed historical photos of Barlow Corners over the years, along with some portraits of an older man. Janelle was closely examining the bakery case, where three small cakes were on display. One was baby blue, with a delicate pattern of raised white edging, like Wedgwood china. There was one that was covered in butterflies, and a third that was in the form of an exploding volcano.

"Your cakes are beautiful," Janelle said. "The detail is incredible."

"Thank you," Patty said. "Those are samples I did for a wedding this week. They came out really well, so I've left them up for display."

"How did you even make those butterflies?"

"They're sugar," Patty said. "Are you interested in decorating cakes? Here. I'll show you up close."

She removed the cakes from the case and set them on the counter.

"For this one here," she said, indicating the blue cake, "it's designed as a replica of a Wedgwood plate the bride's grandmother got for her own wedding."

"How did you get that detail?"

"For that one, I made silicone molds of the actual plate."

Janelle's eyes almost glowed at the words *silicone molds*.

"Oh no," Nate said quietly. "She's getting a new craft."

There was no denying it. Janelle Franklin had never met a craft that she didn't love.

"With the butterflies, I made them separately," Patty went on, "but you see the vine work here . . . actually, I goofed this up a bit and had to fill in a mistake with more leaves.

86

You can cover up a lot of things with icing. Most people work from the middle out when decorating a cake—set your main element in the middle, then go toward the edges and down the sides. It's true that this helps in terms of not disturbing any edge work by accidentally hitting it as you go. But I've always preferred working from the outside in."

"Like a crime scene," Stevie said. She didn't mean to say it out loud. The words slithered out on their own.

Patty looked over the edge of the cake.

"A crime scene?"

"She does this," Nate explained.

Stevie quickly surmised that this was one of those cases where she sounded weird if she explained, but far more weird if she did not.

"What I mean is that crime scenes are processed from the outside in," Stevie said. "First, they set up a wide perimeter, closing off the entire area, to make sure the whole scene can be looked at for things like footprints, items, tire tracks, whatever. Then they move closer in toward the body or . . ."

Patty began turning the cake aimlessly, like you might do if a random teenager popped up in front of you and told you your elaborate cake was like a crime scene.

"She does this," Nate repeated.

"I'm not sure I'm going to look at my cakes in the same way again," Patty replied.

* * *

"I think she's going to remember you," Nate said as they stepped outside with their coffees and muffins. "You have a way."

"It just came out," Stevie said.

"Those cakes are really impressive," Janelle said, her thoughts still back in the bakery. "I'd love to make silicone molds. Maybe we can do it in the art pavilion? Maybe we can do a cupcake decorating session? Kids would love that, right?"

She pulled out her phone and started taking notes.

"She's so pure," Nate said, watching her and smiling again.

"I'm not sure I like this happy you," Stevie replied.

"Get used to it. Or don't. Because no one is going to see me once I get in my tree."

On the town green, Carson was speaking to a crew that was unloading long poles from the back of a truck. In their life at Ellingham, Janelle had built a Rube Goldberg machine for a national competition. Stevie had many fond memories of Janelle dragging her poles around the workshop, welding and building and generally being a badass. The machine had come to a bad end, but that was not Janelle's fault.

"Are you going to reenter next year?" Stevie asked, gesturing to the poles.

"Probably not," Janelle said, understanding at once. "I'm looking for a new kind of project. I'm thinking robotics right now, but I have a few weeks to decide."

Carson saw them and waved them over.

"Setting up for tonight's event," he said as they approached. "To dedicate the Sabrina Abbott Children's Reading Room. Let me show it to you, since we're here," Carson said.

He marched them toward the library next to the green—a classical building painted a prim white, with two columns supporting the front portico. The library was small and a bit out-of-date, but there were several people inside, and the displays looked well-curated. Carson walked straight through the building to the more modern structure at the back. Only one person was inside—a woman in a blue wrap dress, sorting and arranging a long shelf of picture books.

This could only be Allison Abbott. The resemblance to Sabrina was unmistakable—she had the same big brown eyes, the same determined look. She looked to be in her midfifties, with short, dark hair, graying only at the temples. She looked at the coffees and muffins in Stevie's, Janelle's, and Nate's hands and opened her mouth to speak.

"Sorry," Stevie said.

"Oh, that's okay, it's fine," Carson cut in. "You can drink in here."

Allison bit her lower lip but said nothing.

"This is Stevie Bell—from Ellingham Academy," Carson said, in what Stevie realized was going to be the standard way she would be introduced around the town. Janelle and Nate were not introduced.

The walls were painted a happy sky blue. There were

89

lights suspended from the ceiling in the shape of fluffy clouds, and Carson proudly demonstrated the various effects he could achieve with them—bright light, pink clouds, a rainy day effect. There were readying stations with beanbags (this man loved a beanbag maybe more than anyone had ever loved anything), a fake indoor tree with a small treehouse, long, low tables for games, and racks and racks of books.

"It's a beautiful room," Allison said. "The kids are going to love it. We already have loads of events scheduled—story times, board game afternoons, writing classes."

Carson nodded absently and continued fiddling with the controls for the cloud ceiling fixtures.

"My sister," Allison said, turning to Stevie, Janelle, and Nate, "she worked here, in the library. She passed away."

"We were going to put in a mural of Sabrina," Carson added. "But—"

"It would be difficult," Allison cut in. "I think the room is the perfect tribute to her, especially this."

She indicated a giant turtle in the corner that contained bench seats and a little table, perfect for children to sit in.

"She loved turtles," Allison said. "She would have loved that—kids reading in a big turtle."

"Looks like we're all good for tonight's event?" Carson said. "Lots of people coming?"

"I think it's going to be well attended."

"Good! Good." He nodded. "Well, have to get over to the camp. See you tonight at the picnic!"

Stevie took every step carefully, not wanting to spill a

drop of coffee on the floor.

"So that," Carson said as the group got back into the Tesla, "is Barlow Corners. Allison is one of the most vocal family survivors. She really keeps the case alive—stays in touch with the police, that kind of thing."

"That's really nice what you did," Janelle said. "Building a reading room like that for her sister's memory."

"Yeah," Carson said, pulling out onto the road. "It helps me get the town on my side, for the show. I spent a few hundred thousand—but if I play it right, the show may be worth in the millions."

Janelle cast Stevie a sideways glance.

"Charity runs both ways, right?" Nate said from the back seat.

6

CAMP SUNNY PINES WAS A FEW MINUTES' DRIVE FROM THE CENTER OF town, on a road that ran alongside a low and slow-moving creek. The sign was made of brown wood, with the camp named burned in and painted white. The road wove through the trees for a moment, then opened up into a wide expanse of fields and low buildings. Carson parked and the trio got their things out of the back of the car. They followed Carson to the large dining pavilion, hauling their suitcases and bags over the gravel of the parking area. Stevie's cheap suitcase had even cheaper wheels, which gave up once they got a stone stuck in them. She dragged the bag the rest of the way, scraping it along the concrete floor of the pavilion and leaving grass and skid marks as it went. Inside the pavilion, a woman was supervising a small crew that was assembling welcome packages while fielding phone calls.

"That's Nicole," Carson said in a low voice. "Agree to everything she says. We'll work it out later."

This was an ominous statement.

Nicole looked up and noted their arrival with a nod but

no smile, and came over while she continued her conversation, which turned out to be about septic tanks. Nicole was a tall woman, probably about six feet, with her hair tied back in a brown ponytail. She wore long swim shorts, a fitted running top, and a whistle around her neck. Stevie could see many things in Nicole all at once. Whatever time you woke up, Nicole woke up earlier than you, when the day was young and the sun just born. She made a complete breakfast, which contained protein, fruit, and maybe even a vegetable. She accomplished things that she'd put on a list the night before. She stretched in the fresh air. She forged a trail. She punched into the future with a mighty fist. She knew who she was, where she was going, and why she was better than you. But go ahead, whine about how tired you are. She will listen. She will crush you with her eyes. You will emerge smaller from the encounter because she has compressed your spine.

Or something like that. She had a whistle, anyway.

After the first general round of introductions was made, Nicole took a long nasal inhale and gazed across the picnic table at the assembled.

"Just so we're clear . . . ," she began. "This is a camp. It's for kids to have fun over the summer. It's also part of a community. Sunny Pines is not about what happened in 1978. That's in the past. Terrible things have happened at a lot of places. You move on. It's not a *murder mystery* thing."

She stared at Stevie for a long moment. Stevie wanted to politely reply that it was kind of a murder mystery thing, what with the murder, and the mystery. But Stevie did not say this, because she did not want to eat a whistle.

"So when you're at this camp, you work for the camp," Nicole said. "That means you do your job and take care of the campers. A few basic rules that you'll hear again in the main orientation, but hear them now as you'll be here for a few days. No swimming on this side without a lifeguard present. No night swimming. No jumping off the rocks, ever. No open fires that aren't a part of authorized camp activities. No smoking or vaping. No alcohol, and no use of marijuana products. Violations of these policies will result in your dismissal, even if you are here with Carson."

Carson was fingering a set of meditation beads and staring at the ripples on the lake.

After that, there were forms to sign, conduct policies to read. They were all given welcome packs, sets of information, maps, and a list of emergency numbers to put into their phones.

"I'll give them the tour," Carson said. "I know you're busy."

Nicole gave him a long look and returned to whatever she had been doing. They left their bags at the pavilion and followed Carson out into the grassy fields that surrounded it.

"She's the head of the good times committee, huh?" Nate asked.

"I liked her," Janelle said. "She's a strong woman."

"I'm afraid of everyone," Nate reminded her, and Janelle nodded in acknowledgment.

"You have your tree," she said.

A blissful smile crossed Nate's face once again.

Camp Sunny Pines was a collection of brown-timbered buildings around a lake, interspersed with large pavilion structures. At the center of it all was Lake Wonder Falls, which seemed like a weird name now that she looked at it. There were no falls in sight, and very little wonder. It seemed like a nice and ordinary lake, the water a brownish color, and still enough to reflect the clouds and sky above. Little docks jutted out all around it, and there was a floating dock in the middle for swimmers and divers.

"The lake is sort of shaped like an hourglass," Carson said. "This part down here is smaller, flatter, and shallower. Then it gets really skinny—the road goes over that part. The other side is open to the public. It's higher, with the big rocks, and it's a lot deeper. It's really like two separate lakes with a little channel between them. This is the child-friendly side."

On this side of the camp, the lake was about a hundred feet across, surrounded by a narrow edge of beach, with some swampy, reedy areas (snaketown) cutting into it. There was a swimming pool, tennis court, fields, and a large assembly area with a firepit in the middle. Carson showed them all around, pointing out the racks of canoes, the rows of communal bikes, and a yoga and dance pavilion. They worked their way around to the tidy wooden bunkhouses that butted up against the woods. They were built on raised concrete platforms, probably to protect them if the lake flooded its banks. Stevie noticed that while all the windows had screens in them, they also had metal latticework. She suspected this was installed in the wake of the murders, to ensure no one could get in from the outside.

"This"—Carson pointed at a cabin with the word PUMAS painted over the door—"is the cabin Brandy Clark was in the morning the bodies were discovered. As you can see, it's close to the tree line. The first body was found this way."

He led them down a wide grassy opening in the trees, which narrowed to a path about eight feet wide, surfaced in cedar wood chips.

"Eric Wilde was found right about here," he said, taking his tablet out of his messenger bag and pulling up the black-and-white photo he had shown them the night before. "You can see that he was lined up more or less with that tree there with the double trunk."

Stevie took the tablet and compared the spot. Eric had been found facedown, with his head pointed in the direction of the camp.

"It looks like he was heading back," she said.

"It was a dirt path then, so they had a footprint trail for at least part of it. What seems to have happened is that he was attacked and injured probably at the primary site, and he ran through the woods to escape. He must have largely stayed off the path to keep away from his attacker. He was almost back to the camp when the killer caught up with him. He almost made it."

The landscape and the path looked very much the same. Standing here, she could see that the path veered around the performance area, meaning there was no clear line of sight to the camp. Eric had been close, but not close enough.

"Now," he said, "ready to go to where the main event took place? We'll need the car for that one."

Nate mouthed the words *main event*.

They got back into the car and drove over the short bridge that spanned the narrow of the lake. This route continued back past the camp buildings and into the woods. It was startling how quickly things went from manicured and inhabited to entirely forested and overgrown. The canopy of trees was so dense that the woods were dark in the bold light of day. The road bent gently to the left and merged with the dirt track they had seen earlier. It was a narrow, bumpy trail, more holes than solid ground. The Tesla handled it but was clearly used to more refined surfaces, and the group bounced up and down in their seats like popping corn. After a few minutes, Carson pulled over and stopped the car on the side of the road.

"This is it," he said. "Blink and you'd miss it."

They stepped out into the woods. The air here had a rich smell of leaves and plant life, and the sun occasionally poked through the cover in a thin finger of light, but mostly it was subdued and soft. Their footsteps fell silently on the dirt and soft pine needles underfoot.

"This is like being inside of a meditation app," Nate said, looking around.

Carson pointed at a small stake in the ground by the path

with a black ribbon tied to it.

"People come here and mark the spot where you should stop your car. The parks department takes the stake out all the time, and someone puts one back in."

He cheerfully marched on, into the trees. Stevie was about to follow, but Janelle put out her hand, which held a bottle.

"Tick spray," she said. "There are going to be so many ticks in here, and Lyme disease is no joke."

Ticks. Snakes. This is why camping was bad. This and every other reason.

After spraying themselves, they followed Carson down an indistinguishable path, a random and winding walk through the trees, full of roots and snags and branches that reached out to grab hair and clothing. They shortly arrived at a small clearing. The only thing that indicated anything at all might have happened here was a small ring of stones where a fire had been, with a few melted-down candles in the grass.

"This is it," he said. "People come here, as you can see. It's a big murder tour and goth hangout."

The first thing Stevie noticed was that the spot was so . . . unremarkable. When she'd read that this occurred in a clearing in the woods, she expected a wide-open space. This was a spot between some trees, maybe a little larger than most, but it wasn't special.

"I've worked out all the spacing from studying the photos," Carson said. "Many of the trees are still here. That fire pit is about right. People have been coming here long enough to mark the spot that they basically made the campfire area permanent."

He stood on a spot to the left of the stone circle.

"There were log seats there, and there. Everything here at this site was left in an undisturbed state. No sign of a fight of any kind. There was a blanket that would have been about here, the tray of grass was on it. The box was this way. . . ."

He continued on, back into the woods.

"He's creepier than you," Nate whispered to Stevie. "How does that make you feel?"

"Honestly, pretty good," she replied.

The path this time was much thicker, harder to walk down. Stevie had to press back branches with every step. This was where the wild things were, quite literally. When Carson stopped again, there was barely a clearing—just a narrow space between trees.

"It was right here," he said, leaning on a thick oak tree. "The infamous box. In actuality, it was a hunting blind."

"What exactly is a hunting blind?" Janelle asked.

"Basically a place to hide," Carson replied. "It looks like a box. It has a slit open in the side, just big enough to see out of. Hunters sit in the blind and look out and wait for animals."

"That seems fair," Nate said.

"And literal," Stevie added. "In this case. Do we know what happened to it?"

"The police took the lid," Carson said. "Souvenir hunters

took the rest, years ago."

"So the crime scene walked away," Stevie said.

They tramped back to the clearing. As she stood there on the spot of a notorious quadruple homicide, Stevie had a strange feeling—and not the strange feeling that you would expect to get on the site of a notorious quadruple homicide. The sun was bright overhead. A soft summer breeze came through the trees. Everything smelled soft and fresh. This spot was . . .

Nice. It was a nice, normal spot. A good spot for a picnic, or to hang out under the stars with your friends. Its remoteness almost added to the feeling of security. It was padded by woods—a nook. A little oasis. Sabrina, Eric, Todd, and Diane had come here, set up their blankets and music and snacks, set about their rolling and talking and having fun. Someone had waited, perhaps behind one of these very trees, for the right moment.

"What are you thinking?" Carson asked.

What was she thinking? What was the feeling? What was it, this little sensation, like a finger tracing its way up her spine?

"I knew it was out in the woods," she said, "but I guess I thought it was closer to the camp. This is remote. And it's so . . . it's not a place you'd stumble upon. You'd have to know where to go. There were four of them. Four teenagers. One was a football captain, but it sounded like they were all physically fit. So a lone murderer, or even a pair, they'd be outnumbered. How do you subdue four young adults in a remote place like this, that they may know better than you do?"

"Gunpoint," Carson said. "That's one way."

"But they were all stabbed. If you have them at gunpoint, you shoot them."

"And there were drugs in their systems, but they weren't sedated or anything like that," Carson said.

"So they're maybe high or drunk, but they're conscious—conscious enough that Eric could run four miles in the dark. Probably not gunpoint. Maybe you separate them, or they've separated themselves. You go two by two. Lots of killers have taken on couples."

"Like Zodiac," Carson said a little too eagerly. "Make one tie up the other."

"*Creepy man, creepy man*," Nate sang under his breath. "*This is a creepy, creepy man*."

"Another thing," Stevie said. "There were no other tire marks, right?"

"Right."

"So this person or these people probably came on foot. That's a lot of night hiking in the woods. Whoever it was came with supplies. Someone went to a lot of trouble to kill four camp counselors. Who does that?"

"Besides Jason Voorhees," Nate said.

"This is my question," Carson said. "There's something messed up in Barlow Corners, something no one's ever gotten to the bottom of. Someone has to know something. The answer is here, if we look for it. I'm a disrupter. I like to make things happen. We're going to disrupt this situation and crack it open."

"Oh my god," Nate said in a low voice. "I gotta get in my tree."

July 11, 1978
6:00 p.m.

NOTHING HAPPENED IN BARLOW CORNERS. OR, NOTHING WAS SUP-
posed to happen in Barlow Corners. It was the kind of place
where things were always okay—not great or terribly exciting,
but okay. There was a gentle hum of boredom that teenagers
hated and adults came to love.

You could get everything you required on the main strip
along Beechnut Street and Maple Avenue. There was the
Ben Franklin five-and-dime and Unity Hardware for all your
basic household needs. The Dairy Duchess, the local diner
owned by the McClure family, was good for a quick bite or a
family meal. Anderson's Grocery and Deli provided day-to-
day food items. For your bigger weekly shop, there was the
A&P grocery two miles down the road. There was even a nod
to the younger crowd in the form of a boutique called Zork's,
where the teenagers bought their T-shirts, posters, and lava
lamps.

On a fine summer night like this one, most of the town
would stroll along with an ice cream or a Popsicle, the kids
would ride their bikes, and there would be horseshoes on the

green. But it was not a normal summer night. When faced with a tragedy of this proportion, the residents of Barlow Corners did the only thing they could think to do—they threw a town-wide potluck picnic.

Four days after the murders, every business in the town closed at three in the afternoon. Large folding tables came out from the fire department hall and the church basement and the high school events supply closet. These were set up on the town's main green space—the square next to the library. The citizens of Barlow Corners came together under the blue twilight and the long green shadows of an early summer evening with their folding garden chairs, lawn blankets, and coolers.

Everyone brought something for the picnic tables. Indeed, people seemed to be trying to outdo themselves by bringing more than one dish. Tupperware of every size clustered on the tables, heaped with potato salads and coleslaws. Multiple families brought along their grills, and an assembly line was created to distribute hot dogs and hamburgers. There was much fussing over the arrangements of the condiments and the rolls and salads. Did someone have an extension cord to plug in this electric covered dish of baked beans? Was there a way of keeping the bees out of the relish? On the dessert tables things were stacked two deep: peach and blueberry and strawberry pies, lemon bars, Jell-O molds, banana pudding with Nilla Wafers, fruit salad, angel food and chocolate cakes. As everyone placed their food down, they had a look in their eye, a look that said that every item was an offering, thanks to have been spared. The angel of death had visited Barlow Corners again, and again gone past their door.

Nothing on this scale had been seen in the town since the massive festivities for the American Bicentennial, two years prior, when they had unveiled a statue of John Barlow, for whom Barlow Corners was named. John Barlow was a minor figure in the American Revolution who had stolen a British general's horse and slowed him down on the way to a battle. The town was on the site of his farm and massive property, so when a town was established on the spot, it was named in his honor. On that night, two years ago, the mood had been jubilant. All of America exploded in fireworks, and everything was draped in red, white, and blue. Barlow Corners was the perfect American small town, unveiling the perfect American small-town statue of their own local Revolutionary War hero.

Tonight, there were no fireworks, no sparklers, no bunting or clusters of red, white, and blue balloons—just people quietly keeping busy, filling the Chinet paper plates, putting tape labels on the Tupperware containers to make sure they were returned to their owners. The smaller children, unaware or unaffected by the gravity of the moment, chased each other around the grass as the fireflies started their evening rounds. A few biked or Big Wheeled around the sidewalks that bordered the green.

Everyone watched everyone else.

Around the edges of the green, strangers lingered. There were several news vans from New York City parked just out of view. There were other strangers as well. Some of these were law enforcement—local, state, and probably a few FBI. And then there were simply the people who had come to gawk. Everyone watched everyone watching everyone while the Big Wheels and bikes went around and around.

An hour or so into the picnic, Mayor Cooper, father of Todd, parked his Coupe DeVille in front of the library and walked quietly across the green. People nodded in his direction and greeted him solemnly as he approached his friends, Arnold Horne and Dr. Ralph Clark. Both were pillars of the community—Arnold the president of the local bank and Dr. Clark the main physician. Both men had daughters who had been touched by the events and even seen one of the bodies. They would normally have been joined by Dr. James Abbott, the town dentist, but the Abbotts did not come out that evening—their grief over the loss of their daughter was too great. Mayor Cooper, Todd's father, had only come because he was the mayor, and the mayor had to show up.

Mayor Cooper accepted a beer that Dr. Clark offered, and then the men exchanged the polite, subdued pleasantries that were expected.

"How's Marjorie?" Arnold Horne asked.

"She's . . . been in bed the last few days."

A nod of understanding from the two men.

"I can prescribe her something," Dr. Clark said. "To help her rest."

"That might be useful."

"I'll have Jim open up the drugstore. I'll go over with him

and get it and drop it by your house later."

"Very good of you," Mayor Cooper said.

They communed silently for several minutes, sipping their beers and watching their neighbors pretending not to watch them. The children made repeated runs to the dessert table, snatching brownies and lemon bars.

Mayor Cooper cleared his throat softly.

"People are going to talk," he said, keeping his focus on the dessert table. "About what happened in December."

His companions were silent.

"It had nothing to do with this, of course," Mayor Cooper went on. "Todd had nothing to do with that, anyway."

"Of course not," Arnold Horne said.

Perhaps without meaning to, all three men looked over at the Penhale family, who sat off to the side on their plaid blanket. Many people in town thought Todd Cooper had run down little Michael Penhale. It was certainly true that Todd had been a reckless driver. Teenage boys often were, especially when they'd had a few beers. And what teenage boy didn't have a beer now and again? Things happen. Besides, no one knew for sure, and no one would ever know for sure.

"Of course," Dr. Clark added.

On a different part of the green, Brandy Clark sat with her older sister, Megan. Brandy hadn't slept a full night since she had found Eric's body. She tossed, she turned, she paced. She put on her headphones and sat on the carpet by her record player and cycled through her albums. She brushed the cat and rearranged the figurines on her bureau and cried and paced some more. She could sit here at the picnic as well as anywhere else, and she didn't want to be alone.

"You need to eat something," Megan said.

"Not hungry."

"How about a lemon bar?"

"I'm not hungry," Brandy repeated.

Megan sighed and stared at the row of hydrangeas that bordered the library. In the falling daylight they took on an intensity that was hypnotic—violently saturated raspberry and indigo blue. Above them, the ever-horsebacked figure of John Barlow stood sentry over a town that was bleeding, and all the macaroni salad in the world was not going to heal the wound.

But she had to try.

Megan got up and walked over to the bank of coolers. She lifted the lids one by one, pawing through the contents, which bobbed around in the melting ice water. She plunged her hand into the water and grabbed a root beer and an orange soda. She might be able to convince Brandy to have a few sips of one of them. This was about all she could do for her sister now: get her soda. She returned to their chairs and held the cans out to her sister.

"Take one," she said.

Brandy wordlessly reached for the orange soda and popped it open. They sat and drank for a few moments, before Brandy finally spoke.

"Who could do this?" she said.

"I don't know," Megan said quietly. "Someone evil."

"Maybe they'll come back."

Her voice carried on the breeze, and a few people turned.

"No," Megan said. "They're long gone."

"How do you know?"

"No one would stick around after doing something like that."

"They would if they lived here. Or if they were planning on doing it again. I feel like they're here, watching us."

"Come on." Megan stood and took her sister's hand. "Soda's not enough. You're going to eat something."

Reluctantly, Brandy stood and followed her sister to the folding tables that were groaning under the weight of all the food. She allowed her sister to make her a plate of seafoam green ambrosia salad, watermelon, and cake. She allowed herself to be reassured.

The thing was, Brandy was right.

7

THE GREEN TESLA SNAKED ITS WAY DOWN THE VERDANT BACK ROADS and into the center of Barlow Corners as day was falling and the shadows were growing long. Nate was absorbed in reading something on his phone, and Janelle was texting Vi. Everyone in the car seemed to be somewhere else. Looking out the car's window, Stevie noted how different the place looked at various times of day. In the morning, the trees glowed with halos of sunlight, and everything had a freshness and vibrancy that could not be denied. In the heat of the afternoon, the trees were a welcome umbrella from the sun, which still wiggled its way between them. As the sun began to set, however, things took on a strange quality. The spaces behind and around the trees stood out in sharp contrast to the bright places. They were holes, places where things could vanish or emerge into the tranquil town. Doorways.

She wrinkled her nose to dismiss the thought. This is how she had learned to release some of her anxiety—thoughts may come, but she didn't have to follow them everywhere they wanted her to go.

They pulled up to the curb by the library. The poles and other materials they had seen on the green earlier were now replaced with several marquee tents, linked together into rooms. There were string lights all around the square. People had already gathered and were sitting at the tables. There was a sound system set up, and a DJ pumped out a standard wedding mix of songs that any crowd could tolerate.

"I have to check on a few things," Carson said. "Go get something to eat and meet me back here. Keep your eyes peeled."

Stevie had no idea what, exactly, she was supposed to keep her eyes open for—and that felt like both a fair confusion and a personal failing at the same time. She was working this case now, which meant she had to take everything in, but part of working a case is knowing what to take in and not getting distracted or overwhelmed by the hugeness of the world and its innumerable rabbit holes.

Carson didn't skimp on the food. There were a dozen food trucks parked along the street, serving up tacos, lobster rolls, vegan bowls, corn dogs, and ice cream.

"How much money is in the box business?" Nate said, looking around at the tents and food trucks.

"Enough," Janelle said. "People like boxes, I guess."

"But this is weird, right?" Nate went on. "Building an addition to a library, throwing a party, all to get a town to like you enough to talk to you for your podcast?"

Janelle shrugged in a *Nate makes a good point* kind of way.

"A lot of things work that way," Stevie said. "Albert

Ellingham used to throw big events to get Burlington to support his academy. Companies do it all the time—'Forget about how we're destroying the environment, here's a free hat.' That kind of thing."

Janelle gave another *This is also a good point* gesture.

"I'm still going to eat a lot of tacos," Nate said. "But I'm going to do it judgmentally."

They wound around the trucks and were soon carrying more food than they could reasonably hold. As they made their way to a table, Stevie noted Carson supervising the unloading of some video equipment and directing where he wanted the cameras to go. He came over and joined the group.

"I've got almost everyone here who was associated with the murders who still lives in town or nearby," he said in a low voice. "Right ahead of us, blue T-shirt, with the man in the green shorts—that's Paul Penhale and his husband. He's the town veterinarian. It was his brother, Michael, who got run down by Todd Cooper seven months before the murders."

Paul and his husband were talking with Patty Horne, from the bakery.

"You met Patty before," he said. "And Allison. Over there, white T-shirt and white baseball hat . . . that's Shawn Greenvale, Sabrina's ex-boyfriend. It took a lot to get him to come. He owns a water sports business—kayaks and canoes and things. I sponsored a bunch of free rentals, so he had to show up. That older woman sitting in that group over by the trees? The one with the striped top and the short hair? That's

Susan Marks, the head of the camp in 1978. And that . . ."

He waved to a woman in a gray linen suit, which was out of place with all the shorts and light dresses.

"Hang on," he said. "I have an important introduction to make."

He stood and signed to Allison, who was coming out of the library. She approached the table.

"Allison!" Carson said. "It's going pretty good, huh?"

"It is," Allison said, looking out at the festivities. "It's very . . . My sister would have appreciated this. We already have a crowd of kids in the reading room playing games and picking up books."

The woman in the linen suit had reached the table.

"Oh, this is Sergeant Graves," Carson said. "You know each other, right?"

Allison shook her head.

"I know you," the woman said. "Or of you. I'm a cold case detective, and I've been assigned . . ."

The unfinished bit of the sentence indicated that she had been assigned to this case: the Box in the Woods.

"Nice to meet you," Allison said, shaking the woman's hand formally. "You know, we get someone new every year or two. It never comes to anything."

"I'm aware of that. It must be very difficult for you. But I want you to feel free to reach out to me anytime at all. Here." She reached into her bag and produced a business card. "Anytime. I'm happy to talk, to answer any questions I can, whatever you need. Consider me a resource."

Allison took the card and looked at it for a long moment.

"That's kind of you to say," Allison replied. "I don't hold out a lot of hope, but there is one thing you could do for me."

"Name it."

"My sister had a diary," Allison said. "It was very important to her. She had it with her at the camp, but when they sent her things home from her bunk, it wasn't there. I know her things from that night are still in evidence. We've asked before if her diary was there—maybe it was in her bag. We've always been told it wasn't. But it has to be somewhere. Could you look through the paperwork or boxes again? Maybe it was misplaced?"

"I've never seen anything in the files about a diary," Sergeant Graves replied. "But I'm not about to pretend that things were handled well back then. I'll go through everything and look for it. I'll start tomorrow."

"I would appreciate that," Allison said. "It's the one thing of hers I really, truly wish I had."

"No problem. Good to meet you. Excuse me—I'm going to get something to drink."

"I always ask about the diary," Allison said when she was gone. "They always tell me they'll look to shut me up. I guess they mean well. I don't know."

"I think it's about time to do the honors," Carson said to Allison, "if you're ready."

Allison nodded, and Carson got up and took his position behind the microphone. The DJ faded out the music, and

Carson called out to the crowd to come gather around.

"Thank you for coming out tonight!" he said. "I'm Carson Buchwald, founder of Box Box. We're here to dedicate the Sabrina Abbott Children's Reading Room. And to do that, let's have Allison Abbott come up. . . ."

Allison took the microphone and said some remarks about her sister, which got warm applause. Stevie scanned the tent. Most of the people there wouldn't have been alive during the murders, or if they were, they had probably been children. It seemed a bit gross to use an occasion like this to gather people associated with the case in one place, but the truth was, it was also very effective.

Allison handed the mic back, and Stevie expected Carson to conclude the remarks, but things did not go that way.

"Now," he said, "I'd like to tell you about something special I'm working on. Let me bring someone up here I want you to meet. Stevie? Can you come up here?"

"What?" Stevie whispered. "What's he doing?"

"Stevie!" he said again.

Stevie put her taco back on the plate, wiped her hands on her shorts out of nervousness, and joined him.

"This is Stephanie—Stevie—Bell. You may have read about Stevie recently in connection with the events at Ellingham Academy in Vermont."

The vast silence punctuated only by someone asking for a hot dog indicated that they either did not know or did not care.

"That case was famously cold until Stevie came along

and helped to partially solve it . . ."

(Stevie had, in fact, entirely solved it, but that was not public. She ground her jaw.)

". . . and I knew she was the person I had to partner with on my new venture. Obviously, you have a cold case here in Barlow Corners. Well, I want you to know, we're here to make sure it doesn't stay cold. Stevie and I have teamed up . . ."

Stevie saw Nate rub his hand all the way down his face, trying to block out what was happening. She felt her abdominal muscles tense and flex.

". . . to make an investigative podcast, taking a fresh look at what happened here, and I'd like to get everyone in Barlow Corners involved . . ."

Total, muffled, deadly silence. Even the lightning bugs seemed to sense that this was a bad scene and flew out of the tent.

". . . and together, we will get to the bottom of what happened at Camp Wonder Falls."

He paused and looked around in a way that absolutely indicated that he expected some applause to follow.

It did not follow.

"So," he went on, "we're going to be here and working. If anyone wants to contact us at any time, you can reach me on Twitter, or Instagram, or you can message me on Signal. Everything you say will be completely confidential. So thanks, and please enjoy the evening!"

Stevie half wondered if he would blow a kiss and drop

the mic. Instead, he gestured to the DJ, who deemed "Single Ladies" to be the correct jam for this particular car crash of a moment.

"Okay," Carson said to Stevie, smiling. "I think that went great!"

Stevie wobbled a moment in bug-eyed horror, then tried to move back to the table, but Allison Abbot stepped forward, accidentally blocking her egress.

"What is this?" she said.

"A podcast," Carson said eagerly. "Maybe a limited series. I've been talking to some producers—"

"This!" Allison said, gesturing around her.

Carson looked around the tent in confusion. "A picnic?"

"Is this some kind of publicity thing?"

"No, it's to—"

"Buy our participation," Allison said.

"No. No! See, I want to help. I want to—"

"You don't want to help," she said, her voice like a dull blade. "People always come here to write a book or make a TV show or a podcast or whatever. But you . . . you give us a room for children at the library, all as a way of *buttering us up*?"

Allison was directing all this at Carson, but Stevie was there, curling up inside, as the entire town of Barlow Corners turned to watch Allison remove the bones of Carson's spinal cord one by one. The most charitable of the expressions showed embarrassment; most were cold and disgusted. Stevie felt herself getting a bit faint. She considered simply dropping to her knees and crawling away, under the picnic tables, out of the tent, across the green, into the woods, never to emerge. Nate and Janelle watched from maybe ten feet away, helpless. They may as well have been on the other side of a moat full of alligators.

"I'll tell you what you can do," Allison said. "You can take your picnic and your food trucks and your podcast, and you can shove it."

"I really just want to dialogue. . . ."

Allison gripped the plastic tablecloth of a nearby picnic table, and Patty Horne hurried up to her.

"Let's go," she said to Allison. "Let's get out of here."

"I'm fine," Allison said, her voice dry.

Allison lowered her gaze from Carson and looked at Stevie for a long moment. Stevie couldn't read her expression, but whatever it meant, it propelled Stevie backward and away from Carson and out the side of the tent. She quick-walked across the green, not looking back. She could hear footsteps behind her, and Nate and Janelle caught up.

"Yiiiiikes," Nate said. "Wow. *Wow.* Wow."

"You okay?" Janelle asked.

"Fine. I just . . ."

"Yeah. We saw. Everyone saw."

They stopped once they reached the statue of John Barlow. The base was large enough for all three of them to sit, and they could hide around the back. Looking at it up close, Stevie could see that it wasn't a particularly good statue—it was slightly formless, a generic figure of a man on a generic rendering of a bored-looking horse.

"It's ugly, isn't it?" said a voice from behind them.

Patty Horne had left the tent and come to join them. She walked up, hands tucked in her jean pockets.

"I remember when they unveiled it," she said. "They pulled off the cloth and everyone was quiet for a moment. My friends and I burst out laughing. And . . . don't worry about Allison. She doesn't mean it."

"It definitely sounded like she meant it," Nate replied.

"Well, she probably meant it for him, not for you. We get . . . *tired*'s not the word. . . . We get inflamed, I guess, when people come back and try to make something of the case. It's like we heal and then the wound opens again. It was hard enough for me, but Allison lost her sister. It doesn't matter that it was in 1978."

"I'm not here to inflame, or . . . anything like that," Stevie said.

"I know you're not. You're a kid." The slight was inadvertent, Stevie felt, and she didn't take it personally. "Some days it still feels unreal, like a story about someone else. Other times, like tonight actually, it feels like it just happened. I can remember so much about it—how it felt. It was warm like tonight. We would sit here on the green or go down to the Dairy Duchess for ice cream. I still go there sometimes and half expect to see Diane waiting tables."

She seemed lost in thought for a moment, looking up

at the strange metal head of John Barlow, then she snapped back to the moment.

"Want to come over to the bakery with me?" she asked. "Have some cake and relax while whatever's going on over there blows over?"

She did not have to ask twice.

8

THE TINY BELL ON THE DOOR OF THE SUNSHINE BAKERY TINKLED AS the group entered. There was a crepuscular quality to the bakery, lit only by the distant streetlights outside and the faint purple twilight. The cakes were dark figures in the glass case.

Patty turned on one of the overhead lights, which elongated the shadows. It was a cheerful kind of creepiness. It turned out that the lingering smell of cake was different, and maybe even better, than cake in the oven. Someone needed to turn it into a scented candle, pronto.

"Pick whatever you like," Patty said as she lifted up the leaf in the bakery counter to step behind it. "I've got some leftover red velvet, a golden vanilla, and double chocolate."

"Red velvet for me, please," Janelle said. She was back at the counter, examining Patty's work.

"You should come back in someday," Patty said. "I'll show you how I make the silicone molds. You seemed interested in that."

Janelle's head shot up upon hearing this.

"She's like the Hulk," Nate explained. "But instead of transforming when she gets mad, it's when she sees crafts. And she doesn't turn big and green. She just makes crafts. So not like the Hulk, really."

Patty blinked slowly.

"Chocolate, please," he added.

Stevie walked around the bakery and looked at the photos on the walls.

"This is your dad, right?" she said, pointing at one of the pictures.

"That's him," Patty replied, carefully lifting out a massive piece of chocolate cake for Nate. "Well spotted. How did you know?"

"He was in the group photo of the statue unveiling."

"Oh yeah! My dad was in it, and the mayor and the sheriff and Mrs. Wilde, and I forget who else. Someone took the picture for a local guide, but they submitted it to *Life* and it was accepted. It was a huge deal. My dad *hated* having his picture taken. That picture and the one you're looking at, those are really the only two good ones I have. He was a private guy, hardworking. Greatest Generation type. What kind for you?"

"Oh—chocolate?"

Patty chopped off another massive hunk of cake.

"Allison seemed really hopeful about the diary," Stevie said. "But then, she said everyone just humors her?"

"She asks every new detective about that diary," Patty said, passing the cake to Stevie. "If they haven't found it by now, I don't think they're going to turn it up at this point, but it gives her something to hold on to, I guess. I don't know if it's better for her to have hope about that or let it go. It's complicated. You said red velvet, right?"

Janelle nodded. Another heroic slice was produced.

Patty made herself a cup of tea and sat down at the table with them. She pulled the tie from her ponytail, letting her dusty-blond hair fall over her shoulders.

"So this is about a podcast, huh?" she said. "You want to know our stories? I'll tell you mine, if you want."

"Do you mind talking about it?" Stevie asked. "Even now?"

Patty shook her head. "It's nothing I haven't said before. I'm lucky to be able to tell the story. I would have been there that night. Todd, Eric, and Diane were my friends, my gang. The only reason I wasn't there was because I was in trouble. I have survivor's guilt. It feels like my duty to talk about it."

Having said she was willing to talk, Patty drifted into silence for a moment. Stevie, Janelle, and Nate looked at each other and ate cake for a moment until Patty stirred herself.

"What is it you want to know? The usual stuff? Who, where, when?"

Put like that, it felt dirty and low. Stevie felt herself contract internally. This was what it felt like to talk to real survivors—it was something she would have to get used to, if not get comfortable with.

"What were your friends like?" Stevie asked. It seemed like the best way to ease into the nitty-gritty details.

"Fun," Patty said without hesitation. "A lot of fun. Most of them. I'm going to sound like I'm a million years old, but it was such a different time. Everything was loose, free. A lot of it was really irresponsible, but we had a good time. Back then, I didn't think about the future. In high school, I was . . . unfocused. Spoiled, if I'm being honest. I was terrible." She smiled and shrugged apologetically. "My mother died when I was eleven—she had cancer. It was so horrific. My dad took care of me, but he didn't talk much about anything. He was a war hero, actually. Military intelligence. He did something important in the war, behind enemy lines, in Germany. Serious stuff, the kind people write books about. It made him tight-lipped and stern. He made a good living, and between his salary and a little life insurance from my mom's passing, we were very comfortable. He tried to care for me by giving me anything I wanted. I had fashionable clothes, whatever was the latest. I got all the records I wanted. I had horses. I got a car when I turned sixteen—a little MG convertible, which was *very* cool. We had the house with the big pool. I was *that* kid. While everyone else was thinking about their education and job, I was never thinking further than the next party, the next drama, the next new thing. I didn't apply to college. That's when my dad and I started to argue. We had some blowup fights my senior year. He wanted me to make a plan for my life, and he wanted me to stop hanging out with deadbeats. That's what he called my friends."

She took a long sip of her tea.

"You asked what they were like," she said, refocusing.

"Eric was sweet. Funny. A genuinely nice guy. Smart, too. A lot of people have made a big deal about the fact that he sold pot, but you have to understand . . . this was some low-level, high school, late-seventies stuff. He would have gone on to really good things if he had gotten himself together, which I think he would have. I miss them all, but I think about Eric a lot for some reason. Diane was one of my closest friends, but I can't say I ever knew her well. Her parents owned the Dairy Duchess—it's the diner down the street. She was tough, loved rock. *Loved* it. Especially Led Zeppelin. Loved going to concerts. I did too, but Diane was a real music person. She was Todd's girlfriend, and Todd was . . . "

Stevie saw Patty wrestling with her thoughts.

"I have a hard time reconciling this one," she said. "Todd was not a good person, and I knew it, and I still liked him. He was the big man on campus—son of the mayor, captain of the football team. He felt like a big deal, which is ridiculous of course. At the time, though, it seemed so important. It's so easy to get sucked in when you're young. I should have stopped hanging out with him after Michael Penhale died, but I didn't."

"You think he had something to do with Michael Penhale's death?" Stevie asked.

"Oh, he did it," Patty said. "I'm sure of that. I was in his Jeep all the time—I knew how he drove. Fast, drunk, high. Someone *saw* him that night, and the police did nothing at all to investigate. And I saw the change in him after Michael Penhale died. He was always cocky, but after that he was unbearable. I could stand it because I was on the inside of the circle with him. I think I tried to tell myself it was just a terrible accident on a dark road. Todd didn't mean to do it. I justified it in my mind by thinking that because it wasn't intentional, it was . . . not okay, but not something that needed to be pursued? I'm not proud of any of this—I'm just telling you how it was."

Janelle had stopped eating her cake. She was not the kind of person who could listen to a story like that and keep chowing down. Nate could multitask. Stevie was in the zone now, her mind moving through the facts.

"How did Sabrina fit into all this?" Stevie asked.

"I was never clear on why she started hanging out with us," Patty replied. "She started sitting with us at lunch at the end of senior year. I think Diane brought her over, but I never knew why. Sabrina was kind of the queen bee of Liberty High."

"Did you like her?"

"I think so," Patty said. "It's hard to say. I didn't *dislike* her. We maybe made fun of her a little for being perfect, prissy. But she was nice. Didn't seem to have a mean bone in her body. I wasn't close to her. But it was Sabrina who inadvertently caused me to miss the trip into the woods that night." Patty inhaled deeply and drummed her fingers on the table. "At that time, my life revolved around my boyfriend, Greg. We started dating early junior year. I was completely, totally, and utterly caught up in it. I barely thought about anything else. He was very handsome, but honestly, that's all he had going for him. I built him up in my mind as this bold, interesting free spirit. What he was, in reality, was the town drug dealer until Eric took over and did a better job. Greg couldn't even do *that*. He messed around with other girls. I knew it. We fought about it constantly, but I wouldn't break up with him. At some point, he kissed Sabrina. She came and told me, which was decent of her. This was a few days before the murders. I was so upset I left camp, went home for a day, and cried and moped around. But honestly, it was boring being at home when everyone else was there. So I went back the next day. Greg apologized, so I forgave him, as usual. It was one of those teenage things—you fight and you kiss and make up. It was the Fourth of July, and we snuck into the woods and were . . . making up. I don't need to say more than that. We were caught by the deputy head of camp and got put on house arrest. I worked with the kids during the day, but at eight o'clock each night I had to sleep in the nurse's cabin and help out there if she needed it. At the time, it felt like the end of the world . . ."

She shook her head.

"So that's where I was the night it happened," she said. "That's why I didn't go with them into the woods. I was bored out of my mind in the infirmary. I couldn't even sneak out because the nurse had insomnia. She sat up all night in a rocking chair, embroidering. All I remember was waking up the next morning to someone screaming across the lake, then the nurse grabbed her things and started running. I ran too, because I wanted to see what was going on. And that's when

I saw him. Eric. It was . . . I can't describe it. You don't ever want to see anything like it."

This, Stevie understood from personal experience. She had discovered two dead bodies at Ellingham. They had not died in the same manner, but it was something that did not leave you. Sometimes, especially when she was trying to sleep, Stevie's mind went back to those moments—seeing a pair of feet, a figure on the ground, the stillness, the . . .

She felt herself turning inside, the start of anxiety spiral. Janelle, being aware, pushed Stevie's cake closer toward her and nodded, indicating she should take a bite. Sometimes, this was enough. Leave the thought for a moment; break the cycle just long enough to get off the anxiety train.

"All I remember were people asking me questions," Patty said. "I told the police the others had been out in the woods as well. Then my dad came and took me home. We all went home. Everything stopped—camp, life in general. The only thing that happened after that was a big gathering in town. Some of us met up on the football field at school. I was there with Greg. He was drunk and high, so the usual. We fought, which was also usual, and he got on his motorcycle—no helmet, of course—and rode off. There's a sharp turn up the road from the school—a really nasty one. There are accidents there all the time."

Stevie remembered the turn from that morning's drive. It was almost ninety degrees, bordered on one side by a large wall of rock.

"He knew the turn well," Patty went on, "but everything

was so confused that week. He was too drunk, or too stoned, or just distracted . . . I don't know. But he crashed. He died on the way to the hospital. My friends were all gone."

Patty spread her hands on the table and looked at them.

"If therapy had been more common, my dad would have put me into it," she said. "As it was, all he really understood was hard work and business. He talked me into getting serious about baking, since it was the one thing I really liked to do. He pushed me into culinary school, and it helped. I threw myself into it completely. You work long hours in bakeries and kitchens. You sweat it out. Mentally, I recovered by chopping and mixing and standing in front of stoves and ovens. I changed. My father fronted the money for me to open this place. I'm glad my dad got to see my business get off the ground before he died. That's why I keep his picture up in here—he was my angel investor. He believed in me. I tried to make something good come out of the horror of it all."

After a polite pause to let the gravity of what had been said settle, Stevie picked up her questioning. "What did you think happened?" she asked.

"I know there have been questions about the Woodsman, but that's the only thing that ever made sense to me. That guy, or someone copying him. I don't know if you watch much true crime, but there were a lot of serial killers back then. . . ."

Nate actually guffawed. That was the only word for it. This confused Patty for a moment, but she disregarded it.

"I think some sicko went into the woods and killed my friends, and we'll always be replaying the events. We're always going to be the town with the murders. It'll never stop. After you, there will be someone else. It's our story, and we have to live with it. But I try to make something beautiful here—something people can enjoy. I called this place Sunshine Bakery because that's the vibe I want to give off. The truth is, this is a nice place, and the camp is a great place to spend the summer. I had so many good times there, before . . . you will too."

It was clear from her body language and tone that Patty was done talking. She insisted on giving them a bag of muffins and brownies to take with them as they left. They stepped back out into the muggy night. The picnic had fizzled while they were inside. The food trucks were gone, and the square had mostly emptied out. Stevie could make out Carson, sitting alone at a table under the marquee, looking at his phone. A queasy feeling came over her—the burning shame of Allison's upset.

Somehow, she had to manage this situation—the case, Carson, the feelings that were barely under the surface. The pain was so immediate for Allison and Patty. The past was not in the past for them, not really. The emotional current was alive and well, and the questions still lingered in the air.

She looked down the street, at the peaceful storefronts of Barlow Corners. This really was the perfect small town, with flower baskets hanging from the lampposts, everything tidy and quaint. She felt an internal quiver again, but this time, it wasn't anxiety; it was something akin to excitement, edged with fear. As long as the case was unsolved, the phantom that haunted Barlow Corners remained—restless, waiting for someone to dispel it. As stupid as she felt being connected to Carson, maybe she really could be the one to bring this to a close.

Now Carson was up on his feet, and he was doing yoga by himself in the empty tent.

Stevie's confidence vanished as soon as it had come. She was a teenager, saddled with a tech bro, trying to solve something she knew little about.

9

"So," Nate said, "what did we learn from tonight, class?"

They were back at camp, sitting on the gently bobbing dock, watching the moonlight spill over the water. They had a second dinner of brownies and muffins while millions of mosquitoes descended upon them, despite the best efforts of Janelle and her many sprays.

"Well," Stevie said, brushing one from her arm, "people don't love it when you come to town saying you want to donate a library, and then they find out that you actually want to make a podcast about a local tragedy."

"Very good. And what did *you* learn, Janelle?"

Janelle looked up from her phone. She had been texting with Vi. Stevie could tell this without seeing the texts, because Janelle had a particular expression when communicating with Vi—a focus, but also a softness. Her shoulders dropped.

"That people love to put up statues of people who owned other people," she said. "This guy John Barlow? I just looked him up. He had eight enslaved people on his property. *Eight*. And he has a *statue*."

Oh. Not texting with Vi then. Stevie was way off.

"So what happens now?" Nate asked. "Do you think this whole thing is still going to happen? Mr. Think Jams isn't going to be put off by criticism or public scorn, but I don't know what that means for the podcast or whatever he's doing."

"I think people are going to be pissed," Stevie said. "But I think it will still happen. It also sounds like Todd Cooper killed Michael Penhale. That's a pretty good motive for wanting him dead. But it doesn't make any sense to punish him for killing an innocent kid by killing three other innocent people along with him."

"Does it need to make sense?" Janelle asked. "Does sense matter in murder?"

"Not always," Stevie said. "But I think it does when you have one this carefully planned. Someone researched the Woodsman. Someone brought supplies. Someone chased Eric Wilde through the woods for miles. Why do all of that if you just wanted Todd Cooper dead?"

There was no answer to this question.

"You know what Patty is, right?" Nate said after a moment. "It just hit me. She's the *final girl*—that's what you call the survivor in horror movies. It's almost always a girl, and . . ."

"Nate," Janelle said.

"No, hear me out. This whole thing is ticking a lot of the horror movie boxes. Murder at a sleepaway camp. A serial killer. A final girl. A kid who died because some teenagers were being irresponsible."

"But this is real," Janelle said.

"I'm not denying that," Nate replied. "I'm just telling you the tropes."

"Does this mean you know who did it?" Stevie asked.

"Jason Voorhees, and like I said before, he lives in a lake. And he's been to space."

They let this profound insight linger in the space between the moon and the surface of the water. A gentle drizzle began to fall, and there was a rumble of thunder in the distance.

"We should probably go inside before it pours," Janelle said.

The trio walked up the dock and back into the campgrounds. Stevie and Janelle walked Nate to the treehouse, then continued on to their cabin behind the art pavilion. Stevie had become accustomed to the dark of the woods at Ellingham Academy—winter nights in the mountains of Vermont are very long, and very dark indeed. But at Ellingham, there were always lights in the windows or a fire in the hearth, and the walls of the buildings were made of brick and stone, built to keep out the elements. Here at the camp, the veil between the outside and the inside was much thinner. There was a thick moistness to the air, gluing everything together.

And, of course, these were murder woods.

Stevie shook off the thought and followed Janelle inside their cabin. There was one overhead lamp inside, which seemed to cast more shadow than glow. They each had a small reading lamp at their bedside. It wasn't a lot of light. They set to work unpacking and setting up their cabin. Janelle removed a stack of citronella candles from one of her bags and began placing them around the room in what seemed to be a ritualistic fashion, though they were more likely to be in the places insects could access the bunk, including under the screen with the hole in it. Stevie arranged her medications on the top of her bureau. She had learned from her Ellingham experience that sometimes she needed something to help her rest when she was in a new place or things were especially stressful. She took a pill, washing it down with the warm remains of soda in the can. She dumped her suitcase out onto her bed and shuffled through the contents, stuffing them in drawers. Janelle opened the drawers of her dresser one by one, testing them for sturdiness and sniffing them.

"These can use some freshening up," she said. "I'm letting these air out overnight. Tomorrow I'll make some scented liners."

"You can make scented liners?" Stevie asked.

Janelle looked at Stevie as if she had asked her if she could spell her own name.

"I couldn't bring my full tool bench with me, or my sewing machine, but I figured since we have a whole art pavilion to use, that would be okay."

Janelle sat on the edge of her bed.

"I'm tired," she said. "Today was weird."

Stevie nodded in agreement.

They changed for bed and lay down to rest. Janelle cracked open her computer, and Stevie got out her tablet.

Outside, there was the chirp of cicadas and the occasional hoot of an owl. They cranked the fan on high, but it barely penetrated the thick air. The rain began to fall in earnest—a fresh summer rain that turned up the soil and drummed on the roof of the cabin. There was low, rolling thunder. The air was sweet with ozone and earth.

Carson had sent Stevie his entire collection of files on the case. There were over eight hundred documents, organized by subjects like SUSPECTS, CRIME SCENE, ARTICLES. She scanned through these, then opened one of the excerpts in the file marked SABRINA. It was from a book on the case.

Of the four victims that night, Sabrina Abbott's presence in the woods is the hardest to explain.

Sabrina Abbott was born in 1960 to the town dentist, Dr. James Abbott, and his wife, Cindy. Cindy Abbott was a self-described homemaker, and the Abbott household had a squeaky-clean feel to it. Theirs was a house where there was always a casserole or a pie in the oven, where Mrs. Abbott did the dusting and the grocery shopping while Dr. Abbott saw patients. Sabrina and her younger sister, Allison, played horseshoes together in their large backyard. Allison was twelve when her eighteen-year-old sister graduated high school. They'd roller-skate together in the street or at the local rink.

"Even though I was younger, she never complained about having me around," she said. "Sabrina loved me. She let me come into her room whenever I wanted. She helped me with my homework. She was the perfect older sister and I worshipped her. I really did."

Perfect is a word often applied to Sabrina.

Sabrina was at the top of the graduating class of Liberty High in 1978 and was valedictorian. She had an unbroken 4.0 grade point average, was a highly proficient pianist, and was the editor in chief of the Liberty High School newspaper, the *Trumpet*. On weekends, she volunteered at the local library, reading to small children. She was the kind of person the teachers could count on to take tests down to the office, or to watch over a class for a moment. Sabrina was never known to say an unkind word about anyone. She was the quintessential goody two-shoes but seemed to have been widely liked.

Her boyfriend for most of high school, Shawn Greenvale, was a similarly dedicated student, though his accomplishments were not as great as

Sabrina's. At Liberty High, Sabrina was known for being talented at everything, and for being good in general.

She set the tablet down and stared up at the ceiling for a moment.

"You okay?" Janelle asked.

"Yeah," Stevie said. "It's just . . . the Ellingham case felt really far away. It *was* really far away. There was no one left to . . ."

Stevie couldn't quite finish the thought, so Janelle stepped in.

"Feel any pain?"

"Yeah. Allison is still so raw. It's never stopped for her. And here I am—I'm at this camp, trying to work it out. Do I have any right to do that?"

Janelle considered this for a moment as the rain strummed its fingers on the roof.

"I think it's good that you're wondering that," she said after a moment. "It means you know where your priorities are. You are also the person who worked out what happened at Ellingham Academy in 1936."

"Am I?"

"Yeah. You really are."

"So why do I feel like a fake?"

"Because most people feel like fakes," Janelle replied. "Impostor syndrome. It's a thing."

"Do you ever feel that way?"

Janelle considered this.

"No," she said. "But what I do is different. I make things. If they work, I can see them work. If they don't work, I take them apart until they do. I have science on my side. You're making things you can't see."

It was good to have smart friends.

"The only times I feel it are when I think about Vi," Janelle said. "Not . . . like, not about us. But now that they're so far away . . . I can't think sometimes. I only think about them. I think about the next text message, the next chat, the next picture. I should be more serious. I should be thinking about my project for next year, or college, and I am . . . but then I check my phone to see if they texted."

"Isn't that normal?" Stevie said.

"I guess. But I don't want to be normal."

"You love Vi," Stevie said.

"Yeah. I do."

"And Vi loves you."

"Yeah," Janelle said with a little sigh. "They do."

"So I guess you have to ride it out."

"I . . . I want Vi here. Vietnam is too far. September is too far."

A silence settled over them, full of rain.

"Can you imagine how much Nate would hate this conversation?" Stevie finally said.

Janelle's laughter rang out like a bell.

"I'm going to put my headphones in," she said. "I listen to music to go to sleep."

She switched out her light, and after a moment, Stevie did the same.

For the first time in months, Stevie felt complete again. She was working a case. She was with her friends. Janelle was breathing gently in her sleep. The fan ticked away like a heartbeat.

For a few moments, her mind swirled with the faces of the victims of the Box in the Woods: Sabrina, Eric, Todd, and Diane. The raven-haired girl. The boy with the blond curls. The guy with the light-brown shag. The redhead with the long, straight hair and all the freckles. They had been here, all those years ago. Slept in this place. Whatever happened to them, the answer was here somewhere. She would find it. She would pin it down. She would . . .

She slipped into sleep with the images still flowing through her mind, blending with the sound of the rain. She stirred only to swipe away some insect that was trying to fly up her nose. The next thing she was aware of was Janelle yelling her name. Stevie blinked awake. It was a moist, almost sweaty dawn. A soft light came in from around the edges of the curtain, and Janelle was standing by the bed, gazing in Stevie's direction in horror. Stevie pressed herself upright in a second to face her friend, her heart already racing.

"What? Are you okay? What?"

Janelle pointed at the wall above Stevie's bed. Stevie

craned around, then jumped up when she saw what Janelle was indicating.

About four feet above where Stevie had been sleeping was the word SURPRISE.

July 11, 1978
9:30 p.m.

WHEN THE GATHERING IN THE CENTER OF TOWN DISBANDED, THE adults and the younger children all retired to their homes, to their television sets and bedrooms. To safety. To normality. But in the middle of the town, the teenagers, the ones who had come closest to the beast—they were awake.

They needed their own gathering, one that wasn't powered by Jell-O salads and burgers and polite talk. The parents of Barlow Corners allowed them to go, but only in groups, and only if they promised not to leave the football field. Because if they did not let them go, they would find another way—they would sneak into the woods to talk. Better to let them go as a group, in the open seclusion of the field, where no one could sneak up on them.

So they gathered, coming from dozens of cars in the parking lot. Some arrived singly, and others in groups. Someone went into the school and switched some of the outside lights on, but these did not penetrate the middle of the field. All around, the dark curtain of the woods penned them in. Everyone knew what had happened—and yet no one knew what had happened. Just enough information had leaked to make a mess of the facts. As the days wore on, the story had whipped around in ever-wider loops, taking on new and strange qualities with every pass. You could hear all these stories passing from one person to another:

"I heard all their fingers were cut off."

"There was a message written in blood on a tree."

"I heard they found Sabrina's head in a McDonald's bag."

Patty Horne had come with three other girls. They had been dropped off by her friend Candice's father, who leaned against the hood of his car and watched them. Because Patty had been close to the victims, she had pride of place at this strange gathering. She sat, the understood queen of a large circle of people who spoke quietly and looked respectfully in her direction.

"What about Shawn?" she heard someone say. "He was freaked out about Sabrina. I bet he did it. He's not even here. . . ."

Was this how it was going to be? People talking about severed heads and fingers and guessing who may have done it?

Apparently.

Candice passed her a cigarette and she accepted it. She reached into her fringed purse for some matches. Look how normal it all was—sitting here in her flip-flops and her yellow halter top and white shorts, getting grass stains on her ass and mosquito bites on her arms, smoking and talking with everyone from Liberty High here in the dark. What was real, even?

Then she saw a figure approaching, one she had been

expecting. Greg Dempsey, her boyfriend. His dark shaggy hair was blown all over, which meant he had come on his motorcycle. He wore cutoffs and a beat-up Led Zeppelin T-shirt. That felt like a tribute to Diane, who'd loved the band with all her heart and soul.

Without a word, the group all shifted to make space for him next to Patty. He opened the bag he was carrying and pulled out a six-pack of Miller beer and cracked one open for himself, leaving the rest in the grass, an open invitation to Patty and really no one else.

"Your dad here?" he asked.

"No. He's still working with the cops."

"Doing what?"

"Patrolling or something."

Patty's father was a little older than most of her friends' parents. He was one of the town's illustrious war heroes. No one ever talked about it, but everyone knew that Mr. Horne had been a spy or something. He wasn't a cop, but he was the kind of heavy guy who could help out when you were looking for a murderer. The town had a posse now, rolling slowly through the streets, watching the darkness at the edge of the woods.

"You want to get out of here?" Greg said quietly.

"Not allowed," she said, nodding to Candice's father. "He's watching, and he's taking us home at eleven."

"Who cares? Let's go."

"Seriously," she said.

Greg shook his head. He was almost nineteen now, and

out of high school. He had never really answered to his parents before, and he definitely didn't now. He shook his head and reached into his pocket, producing a handful of joints.

"Last ones," he said. "Last of Diane's rolls."

Candice looked over at Greg as he lit one of the joints.

"They're *watching*," she said, indicating the cars and silent forms of the parents on the edge of the field.

"So? They can't see. Looks like a cigarette."

"What if they smell it?"

Greg took a long drag and passed it to Patty, who declined. Greg exhaled hard.

"So is this how it is now?" he said. "Who cares what they see?"

"If my dad saw me with a joint he wouldn't pay for my college," Candice replied.

He looked to Patty for an answer.

"You're not going to college," he said. "What's your excuse?"

"Excuse? I live with him."

"For now. Are you going to live with Daddy forever? Do what he says?"

"Until I get my own place."

Greg let out a short laugh. "When are *you* going to get your own place?"

Patty looked down. She had no plan, really. It was possible that, yes, she would live with her father forever and do what he said. She hadn't thought about what would happen to her life much beyond this summer, and now this summer, while not over, was forever changed. Life would be different now.

An uncomfortable silence fell as the joint made its way around the circle. Greg pounded the rest of the beer and opened a second.

"They think maybe it had to do with drugs," Candice finally said. "That's what we were talking about before. Whoever Eric was buying from must have done it."

Greg said nothing.

"You were selling before Eric," Candice said.

"Yeah?"

"So who were you buying from?"

"That's not important," Greg said.

Patty plucked some blades of grass and crushed them between her fingers.

"But they think maybe that's who did it," she said to her boyfriend.

"That's not who did it."

"How do you know?"

"Because I know," Greg snapped.

"How can you *know*?"

The rest of the group fell into wide-eyed silence, and there was a general quieting all around.

"This is bullshit," Greg said. He dropped what was left of the joint into the beer can and stood up to leave. Patty jumped up as well and followed him toward the parking lot. Greg had parked his motorcycle at the end, as far away from the parents as he could, leaving them a long walk.

"Hey," Patty said. "*Hey.*"

He stopped and turned.

"I'm not doing this," he said. He had that tone he got when he wasn't quite sober, a random loudness.

"My friends are *dead*," she yelled, "and you're being an asshole. . . ."

"*Our* friends," he shot back. "God, you're always like this."

"Like *what*? You're the one who hooked up with Sabrina. You cheated on *me*."

He muttered something under his breath and got on his bike.

"Greg!" she screamed. She was losing it. It was all too much. Hot tears burned in her eyes. "Greg, don't. You're drunk. . . ."

He revved the engine to drown out her yelling and made to pull out. She stood in the way of the bike, so he walked it backward and turned out of the parking lot. She ran after the departing bike, yelling his name. She followed him all the way to where the parking lot met the road, crying and waving her flashlight. By now, everyone around was staring as she watched his bike disappear into the darkness.

Greg was barely a mile away when he left the road and went right into the trees and a wall of rock.

10

"WHAT THE HELL?" JANELLE SAID. "THE *HELL*?"

It was a good question.

Stevie turned first to the door, which was shut. She walked over and rattled it. It was still locked from the inside. She went over to the window, stepping onto a chair to examine it. The screen and the internal safety grate were intact. There was nowhere for someone to be, but they still looked under the beds. Janelle examined the screws of the window guards up close and found that they were tight, and that there would be no way to remove or replace them from outside. Since the cabin sat on a concrete base, there was no way to come from under the cabin. The only thing that was even slightly open was small hole in the screen, maybe an inch and a half in diameter, which was large enough to let in the mosquitoes, but certainly not large enough to allow a person through.

In short, someone had done the impossible.

They sat on the cold concrete floor and looked at each other.

"Well," Stevie said, "someone's been reading about me."

Not long after Stevie had arrived at Ellingham Academy and announced that she would be working on the long-cold Ellingham murder case, someone projected an image onto the wall of her room in the middle of the night—a terrifying version of the Truly Devious letter but rewritten to reference Stevie. Stevie had long kept this to herself, with only Janelle and David knowing most of the details. But after the case was over and Stevie was getting press, she had talked about it with Germaine Batt, Ellingham's resident student journalist. Germaine had helped Stevie solve the case, and Stevie owed her an exclusive.

So someone knew about messages appearing on Stevie's bedroom wall at night.

"But that one was projected," Janelle said. "That's *paint*. Someone painted our wall, while we slept, when there was no way in."

"So what does that mean?" Stevie asked. "It means it *didn't happen*."

"But it did happen."

"No," Stevie said. "It means that there's a message on our wall now. But it had to have been there before we came in last night, because there's no other way it could have gotten there."

"It wasn't there," Janelle said. "We would have seen it."

"How can you make something like that appear?"

Janelle fell silent in thought for a moment, then got up

and returned to the wall. She climbed up on Stevie's bed and examined the word up close, scratching at it with her nail and testing the residue with the tip of a finger.

"That's really dry," she said. "No tackiness to it at all. There are paints that go on one color and dry another, but . . . say that someone came in when we were out at the picnic and painted that on the wall. One, we would have smelled it. Paint stinks. And two, we were still awake for a while and paint dries quickly, at least initially. I don't think it would be *that* dry, though."

Stevie stood up and faced the wall.

It wasn't that Stevie had no fears. Stevie had a lot of fears and anxieties. There had been times when they had ruled her life. Someone was playing a game. Someone had presented her with a locked-room puzzle. And this wasn't scary as much as it was perplexing. If she had a mental puzzle to work on, her fears took a back seat.

Face the problem. Look at it hard. What did she *see*?

The message was painted on the top third of the wall, not the eyeline. The word was painted in blocky, sloppy capitals. The paint had run a bit, like a spooky horror font. She climbed back up on the bed next to Janelle and looked at the brushstrokes closely. There was something weird about how the paint ran down the wall.

"Look at how the drips all cut off at the same point," Stevie said, pointing. "Like a clean line."

Janelle leaned in to look. "Someone wiped the paint," she

said. "You can see the trace where they wiped it to keep it from dripping too much. How considerate."

Stevie gave a long exhale and stepped down. "Let's check under the bed," she said.

They pulled the camp bed away from the wall. Stevie got down on the floor, examining it with her phone's flashlight, looking over every inch. She found two dead flies, a small piece of used tape, a leaf, a spiderweb, and then . . .

"Here," she said, pointing to a small spot of white paint. "Look."

Janelle got down next to her.

"So the bed wasn't there when that message was painted on the wall," Janelle said.

"Exactly. This didn't happen last night, unless we can sleep so soundly that someone can drag my bed away from the wall, set up some kind of stepladder, paint a message, and then push me back again."

"That makes it a little better," Janelle said, nodding. "At least someone wasn't in here with us. So what do we do now?"

"Well . . ." Stevie sat on the edge of her squeaky camp bed. "We can't tell Nicole about this. She doesn't really want us here, and she's definitely not going to like this, especially on the day the other counselors are coming. She might tell Carson we have to leave."

"But I think we should make sure this place is secure. What if Carson could get us some plug-and-play cameras?"

Stevie pulled out her phone to text him.

"He'll be thrilled about this," she said grimly. She took a few pictures of the message and sent the texts. His reply came within a minute.

Will be there as soon as possible with cameras. Have something to show you.

"Cameras are coming," Stevie said. "You shower and I'll stay here. Then I'll go."

Janelle quickly gathered up her shower basket, towel, and clothes and headed off to get ready. Stevie went outside to sit on the tiny concrete porch of the cabin, hanging her legs over the side and letting her bare toes tickle the dirt. It was early, but she needed to make a phone call.

To her surprise, David answered right away.

"You're awake?" she said.

"Long drive today," he said. "We left at six. How's camp treating my princess?"

"Could be better," she said. "Someone wrote the word SURPRISE above my bed last night."

"Is this . . . some kind of sex joke?"

"No. Someone painted a message on our wall. It's the thing that was written at the crime scene in 1978."

"Okay," David said, sounding maybe not so okay. "First of all . . . are you all right?"

"It's fine," Stevie said, shielding her eyes from the bright morning sun. "Just a prank."

"Some fucking prank. What happened? They went into your cabin when you were out, or . . . ?"

"It's sort of more complicated than that," she said. "We don't really know when they did it, except it wasn't while we were asleep. Somehow they did it before and we only saw it when we woke up."

"What?"

She shook her head. It was complicated even if you were there, looking at it, and felt impossible to explain over the phone.

"Someone's playing a game," she continued. "Maybe someone knows about me, about how at Ellingham someone left a message on my wall."

"I don't want to keep bringing up what happened last time, but last time? That person was a murderer."

"This feels different," she said.

"Oh good."

"We're getting some security cameras. I don't know what happened, but I'm going to find out."

"Yeah, I hate this," he said. "How does this keep happening to . . . Scratch that. I know exactly how this keeps happening to you."

If Stevie was being completely honest with herself—and she preferred not to be—David's concern felt very good. He was really worried about her, possibly more worried than she was about herself. He cared. It sent warm bubbles of pleasure through her system.

Then a voice broke through the haze of romantic bliss.

"*Welcome, counselors!*" Nicole said over the loudspeaker.

"Please bring your things to the dining pavilion."

"I have to get ready and get going," she said.

"Okay, but text me. Call me. Both. Let me know what's going on, okay?"

"I promise," she said.

She couldn't help but break into a smile as she said it.

When Janelle returned, dressed in a flowing blue sundress, Stevie grabbed her things. The bathroom area was only a few yards away. The toilets and sinks were in a concrete and wood building (with no doors, so the air and flies could get in without difficulty). The showers were wooden stalls outside of this main structure, with no ceilings. It was basically a fancy hose in an open box, raised slightly off the ground to allow for drainage. Stevie would have much preferred it if the shower had been flush with the ground, because it seemed like a low, dark space under a shower would be an ideal spot for a family of snakes. *Something* had to live under there.

She tried not to think about it.

Though no one could see inside, it felt weirdly exposed to be able to see the sky and the trees above her as she undressed and showered. The water wasn't cold, but it wasn't warm either. It was already so muggy that it made no difference. She washed quickly, barely taking the time to rinse all the shampoo out of her hair. There were definite advantages to having short hair you cut yourself—all she needed to do was rub it a few times with her hand to dry and style it. She tugged on a shirt and a pair of black shorts, stuffed her feet back into her flip-flops, and took a leap out of the shower box to make sure the imaginary snakes couldn't bite her heels.

When she returned to the cabin, Nate was there, sitting next to Janelle on the concrete step.

"I heard," he said grimly. "It's not a party until someone writes you a threatening message, is it?"

"You have your treehouse," Stevie pointed out.

"I liked it better before you told me this, but yeah, I do."

"We should go," Janelle said. "I wish we could do more than just lock the door."

Stevie responded by reaching down and snapping off a blade of grass. She took it over to the door and slid it gently between the door and the frame, so that if the door was opened it would be displaced.

"People really do that?" Nate said.

"It works," she said. "It'll do until we get the cameras."

Camp Sunny Pines was springing to life. The parking lot was full of cars, and their fellow counselors were unloading bags, greeting each other with big hugs and squeals, and taking pictures. It reminded Stevie of watching the second years at Ellingham greeting each other when she first arrived, a new student, knowing no one. She had Nate on one side of her now, and Janelle on the other. With them, and with David, she could do anything. Even figure out how someone had snuck into their cabin and left a magically appearing message.

Nicole and her assistant were greeting counselors and staff and checking them in. She gave them a terse nod and presented them each with a bag containing a reusable water bottle, sunscreen, a mini first aid kit, and a shockingly white camp T-shirt that she would never wear. Stevie was pleased to see that breakfast was being served, and soon had a plate filled with pancakes, bacon, and sausage. Nate and Janelle got the same, but Janelle also accepted the cup of fruit, because she cared about things like balanced meals.

They had just sat down at a picnic table when Nicole approached them.

"Fisher," she said.

Nate looked up from his sausage.

"Small change of plan. One of the counselors got sick. He's going to be delayed by a day or two. I need you to sub in until he gets here."

"What?" Nate said, blinking.

"It's the Jackals, cabin 12. The kids are nine years old. You'll be working with Dylan and staying in that cabin until the other counselor gets here. Can you go join him over at that table when you're done eating? And you'll be needed at group orientation this afternoon."

She indicated a guy who was two tables over who wore what looked like high-end surf clothing in bright yellow and blue. He was taking multiple selfies with a group of girls, lowering and raising his sunglasses for each one.

"You two," she said to Janelle and Stevie, "can begin setup in the art pavilion. You don't have to go to the afternoon session. That's for counselors working in bunks. You'll go to the campfire this evening."

She strode away, leaving a shell-shocked Nate.

"Oh no," he whispered dryly. "No. How did everything fall apart so quickly?"

"Sounds like it's just for a day or two," Janelle consoled him.

"A lot can happen in a day or two," Nate replied.

Considering how the morning had gone, Stevie was inclined to agree.

11

STEVIE SPENT THE MORNING NOT PAYING ATTENTION TO THE RULES and safety walk and talk. She did not learn what to do in the case of a fire emergency at the campfire pit area. She did not learn where the lifeguard stations were along the lake. She paid no attention to where the first aid boxes were. As she walked, she mentally turned their cabin every which way, trying to work out how the message could be there and also not be visible. By the time the group headed to the dining pavilion for lunch, Stevie somehow managed to know less than she had when she'd started out that morning.

"You didn't hear any of that, did you?" Janelle asked her as they headed for lunch.

Stevie shook her head.

"Me either. Have you worked it out? I haven't."

She shook her head again.

Carson texted as they entered the dining pavilion, so Stevie peeled off and went to meet him in the parking lot. He was standing by the Tesla, shifting nervously from foot to foot.

"You weren't the only one who got something," he said. "Look at this."

He popped the trunk, which opened slowly. Inside, there was a plain cardboard box, about the size of a shoebox, with the words OPEN ME, CARSON written in black Sharpie. He opened the lid, revealing three dolls—one raven-haired girl, one plasticky boy, and one girl with red hair. They were bound in red string and had red slashes of paint all over them, and they were positioned exactly as Sabrina, Todd, and Diane had been found. They were all dressed in approximations of the clothes they'd been found in. The word SURPRISE was written inside the lid.

"I found this on my morning run," he said, rubbing his hands together nervously. "It was in the middle of the path. It was on my property, but out of the range of the cameras."

"Someone's done their homework," Stevie said. "I got a message on my wall, like I got at Ellingham. And someone knows where you run and where the cameras are."

"Yeah. And I'm the Box Box guy who owns the camp where the Box in the Woods murders were, so they sent me a box."

By the last *box*, the word had lost all meaning for Stevie.

She reached into her backpack and pulled out a nitrile glove. She had always been in the habit of carrying a few. It was probably a mockable trait until the Ellingham case, when they had come in handy on several occasions. She had actually brought them to camp in case she had to touch something gross. She snapped on a pair and carefully lifted the Sabrina doll out of the box. The shirt had the old Camp Wonder Falls logo painted on, and the hair had even been cut to resemble Sabrina's shoulder-length style. It wasn't a close match, but it was a good effort.

"Someone's trying to stop us from making this show," Carson said.

"Or someone's being an asshole," Stevie replied. "Still."

"I don't think we go to the police with this," he said. "I don't know if these things are crimes, or if they are, they aren't serious ones. Criminal mischief or something. Is criminal mischief a thing? It sounds like a thing. Anyway, I don't think it's the kind of thing anyone is going to take very seriously. I think I pissed someone off last night. Here."

He handed Stevie a reusable bag in a very realistic fish-scale pattern. Inside, there were half a dozen doorbell-size cameras.

"Put them somewhere that Nicole can't see them," he said. "Otherwise she'll start asking questions."

"Can I keep this?" she said, indicating the box of dolls. "I want Janelle to look at it. She's the craft expert."

"Sure," he said. "But be careful about . . . what am I saying? The police aren't going to dust this for prints."

"Probably not," Stevie said. "Unless one of us dies, I guess."

Carson's eyes grew wide.

"Kidding," she said.

He went into the back seat of his car and produced a box full of reusable bags in dozens of different patterns and colors, all bundled into tidy little pockets.

"Take one to carry it," he said. "Or take as many as you want. I have a lot of bags."

Back at the dining pavilion, Janelle was being social and chatting with a group of people at one of the tables. Stevie headed for her.

"Taking lunch to go," she said to Janelle. "Cameras to put up and something to show you."

Stevie went to the food line and grabbed a hot dog and a soda. Ellingham had an ever-changing menu of organic, often vegan meals, with seltzer water on tap and maple syrup in every possible form. Sunny Pines did not have this kind of elegant variety. The menu appeared to consist of boiled hot dogs, boiled veggie dogs, hamburgers, veggie burgers, chicken nuggets, and a sad and lonely salad bar. As the former caretaker of a salad bar, Stevie felt for it, though it was not as complete as at the grocery store. This was some iceberg and salad mix, shredded carrots, and ranch dressing. There was milk, water, soda, and sugary red bug juice to wash it all down. This was actually fine with Stevie. She would happily eat a hot dog every night for the entire summer, and she would guzzle bug juice and soda until all her teeth fell out of her head. Nate looked over anxiously as she passed by, like a drowning man. He was seated with Dylan, the other counselor, and a group of other new people. Stevie held up a hand of greeting and pointed, indicating that they were going back to their cabin.

"Bag of cameras," she said, handing it over to Janelle when they got back to their cabin. "How quickly can we get these up?"

Janelle examined the packages.

"Give me twenty minutes," she said.

"There's more," Stevie said, presenting the other bag to Janelle. "Carson found this when he went out for a run this morning."

"Oh god," Janelle said. "*What?* Stevie . . . this is messed up."

"It's crafty, though. Anything you notice about them?"

Janelle grimaced but peered inside the box, then removed the Sabrina doll and examined the clothing.

"Well," she said, pinching the material and looking at the stitching, "looks like a pretty well-made doll outfit."

She examined each doll in turn, checking cuffs and seams, looking inside and out.

"No labels," she said. "I think these are custom-made."

"So someone would have to know how to sew."

"You can buy them," Janelle said. "Off Etsy or other places. People sell doll clothes. It would be easy enough to ask for a few outfits. The logo looks like it was painted on the shirt with fabric paint, and not very well. You could probably source all this stuff pretty easily. But why would you do this to us, and also to Carson? Has to be the podcast."

There was a tinge of anger in her voice now.

"You seem mad," Stevie said.

"I am mad! We need to find the freak who did this."

"Cameras," Stevie said, taking the box of dolls and closing it up. "And you have to hide them as best you can so Nicole doesn't see them."

Janelle picked up the bag and got to work. By the time Stevie had eaten her hot dog and drunk half her soda, Janelle had gotten out some industrial sticky strips and had the first camera attached under the light fixture by the door. She placed another one on the inside of the window with the hole in the screen, tucked in between the wrought iron guards. She got up on top of a dresser to put a third high up near the ceiling, pointed toward the inside of the door. She downloaded the app and had most of the setup complete by the fifteen-minute mark. She brushed off her hands and examined the feed for a moment, walking back and forth in front of each camera to ensure she was satisfied with the placement.

"That should cover all the angles," she said. "It's got smart detection, so we'll know if anyone comes in. Most of the other counselors are doing orientation games. We're the special ones, so we get to spend the day unpacking art supplies and setting things up. Apparently supplies just arrived."

They headed over to the art pavilion, where Janelle stopped short.

"Oh my god," Janelle said when she saw the many piles of boxes. "So much to unpack and put in order."

The joy in her voice couldn't be hidden.

"Do you need a moment alone?" Stevie asked.

"*Maybe?*"

Janelle set about her dream job, while Stevie set about to work on the problem.

Stevie took the dolls out of the box and set them on the little table in front of her. Doll Sabrina. Doll Diane. Doll Todd. All slashed with red paint. This was easy and direct enough. The message on their cabin wall was different, clever.

Since she didn't know how the latter had been done, she switched over to asking why. *Why* leave the message? *Why* leave a box of murder dolls on Carson's running path? What would these things do?

Well, cause fear. That seemed like the obvious answer.

It would have taken time to get the dolls, time to make the outfits, time to do whatever it was that was done to their cabin. These things hadn't been knocked together in the short space of time between Carson's announcement last night and when they got back to the camp. Someone had been planning this for a few days, at least.

So someone knew *she* was coming and had taken the time to look her up.

It was entirely possible that some people in town had gotten wind of Carson's plans before he announced them. Did they think this would stop the podcast from happening? There was no message attached to these things, nothing that said *stop making your podcast*.

Maybe it was a question of how. But the how still eluded her. How did you paint a message on a wall well in advance and have that message be invisible? She spent the next hour look-ing up paints, dyes, and invisible inks, but absolutely nothing turned up that explained how the thing could be done.

"It had to be something with the paint, right?" she said, coming up behind Janelle and startling her as she was orga-nizing pipe cleaners by size and color. She pulled out her earbuds, leaking music out into the art pavilion.

"The paint," Stevie said, sitting down on the concrete floor opposite her. "It had to be something with the paint. But I can't find any paint online that would do what we expe-rienced. I think it was meant to freak me out."

"And me," Janelle added.

". . . *us* out. But I mean, it also feels like a gift to me? It's an impossible puzzle. It's the kind of thing I'll obsess over."

"Maybe you have a fan," Janelle said.

This had something to it. A fan? Some true-crime creep who wanted to mess with the student sleuth. It didn't explain what had happened with Carson and his box, but it made a lot of sense in terms of the cabin.

"A fan," Stevie repeated. "Someone wants to play? Then we'll play."

"Oh god, no."

Stevie's phone buzzed, and she checked her texts. There was one from Nicole.

COME TO THE DINING PAVILION, it read.

"I've been summoned," Stevie said. "If I don't come back, avenge me."

She walked over to the dining pavilion with a vague sense

of dread. Nicole was working on her laptop at a picnic table at one end.

"Someone wants to talk to you," she said. "She's over there."

Allison Abbott sat alone at one of the picnic tables at the far side, pensively tapping her chin with her fist. When Stevie approached, she looked up and straightened. Stevie braced herself. The relative of a victim had come here to chastise her. She felt sick but walked on and sat down.

"Hey," Stevie said.

"Stevie," she replied. "I wanted to apologize for last night."

Stevie could not hide her surprise at this turn of events.

"People always talk about this like it's some lurid slasher movie," Allison went on. "I lost my *sister*. Some bastard took my *sister* from me. I feel like Carson used her memory, gave us that reading room, to try to worm his way in. He can go to hell. But I didn't mean to catch you in the crossfire."

She leaned back a bit, taking Stevie in. Stevie was unsure what to do or say now that this announcement had been made. There was a heavy pause, full of the scent of boiled hot dog water.

"Why did you come here?" Allison asked.

"Because I got a message that—"

"I mean here, to Barlow Corners, to this camp. Carson clearly brought you here specially, which is why you were at the event last night and why he keeps introducing you to everyone as the girl from Ellingham Academy and as his partner in this project of his. I know what he wants. Why did *you* come here?"

Stevie considered her words carefully.

"Because . . . I want to . . . because people need answers. Because someone should do something."

Allison cocked her head very slightly to the side. For a moment, she said nothing at all. Stevie felt a clammy nervousness brewing.

"You know," Allison said, "I remember so much about her. So many little details. I remember sitting outside that summer, eating cherry twin pops. I rode bikes with her all over town. She drove me to the roller rink and skated with me. She helped me with my homework. And one of the last things I remember about that summer, right before she went off to camp . . . I remember sitting next to her in her room one afternoon while she played me Fleetwood Mac albums. She got up and wrapped a long scarf around herself and started doing a Stevie Nicks dance. She loved Stevie Nicks. She would have loved your name."

"My name is Stephanie," Stevie replied. "I've always been called Stevie. I don't know why. But I prefer it anyway."

"Well," she said, "she would have loved it. If she had lived, she would have been great at whatever she did. She would have done it all. She was one of those people, full of life. She was a force of nature."

She tapped her fingers on the plastic tablecloth.

"As it happens, I know Kyoko, your school librarian. We met at a library conference. I got in touch with her last night, and she told me about you. She told me about what you did at Ellingham. I read up about it last night and this morning. It sounds like you do the work, like Sabrina did. I talk to Sabrina all the time. Well, I mean, I imagine talking to her. I think about what she would tell me to do. She would have said to give you a chance. I have to get back to the library. I'm busy all this week after work, but why don't you come over tomorrow morning? I have some things I'd like to show you."

"Sure," Stevie said. "Definitely."

"I live on the far side of the lake. You can walk the path around, which takes awhile, or if you take a bike, it's about fifteen minutes. Here . . ."

She wrote her address on a napkin from one of the dispensers.

"Come at six thirty," she said. "We'll have breakfast. I leave for my run at seven thirty. You're welcome to run with me as well."

Stevie had not been expecting a six thirty in the morning meeting time, but she nodded confidently as if that was how she always started her mornings. Allison gave Stevie the address and left. Nicole watched this from the other end of the dining pavilion.

"Everything all right?" she asked as Stevie passed. Her tone suggested that there was no way she thought that was the case.

"Fine, actually," Stevie said, herself surprised.

Nicole seemed a touch disappointed.

When Stevie returned to the art pavilion, she saw that Janelle had made a display of paint jars on the shelves. She had been joined by a sweaty and defeated Nate, grass stains on his shorts, his hair sticking up on top and slicked around his face with perspiration. He was resting on the smooth concrete floor and staring up at the ceiling.

"What was that about?" Janelle said.

"Allison Abbott came to apologize. She wants me to come to her house in the morning to see some things. Are you alive?"

"No," Nate said. "And I heard your creepy message situation is now a creepy doll situation. Have you worked it out yet?"

"Not yet," she replied. "I will. It'll come to me."

It did not come to her. It didn't come to her that afternoon, or over hamburgers around the campfire. Instead of socializing, she watched the feed from the cameras and picked at the problem in her head, finally going back to the cabin early. She approached with care, finding that she was unnerved by the shadows. She opened the door quickly, to surprise anyone who may have been inside, but there was no one, as the cameras told her. She sat in the middle of the floor and looked up at the message, three-quarters of the way up the wall, with its neatly wiped paint. She stared at it until her eyes went blurry, then she groaned out a loud sigh and called David.

He picked up immediately.

"I've been waiting for you to call," he said. "Everything okay?"

"Basically," she replied, rolling onto her stomach. "Still no idea who left the message, but whoever it was also left a box of creepy murder dolls outside of Carson's house, so I have that going for me."

David was quiet for a moment.

"You there?"

"Yeah," he said. "I know this is what happens to you, but I really don't like this. Are you okay?"

"I'm annoyed," she said. "I can't figure out how it was done. It's not possible."

"I was going to wait to take my time off," he said, "but how about I do it now? I'll ask for the week and then I'll go there. I could be there in a few days. There's a public camping side. I'm going to stay over there and camp. Do some swimming. Get in touch with nature."

Stevie felt a light, floating feeling rising up from her heels, shooting through her spine and out the top of her head. David was coming. David was going to be here.

"Seriously?"

"Yeah, seriously."

"When will you be here?"

"Couple days," he said. "A friend of mine is going to lend me her car."

"A friend? Who will lend you her car?"

"Jealous? You should be. She's hot. She's also sixty-three and has two grandkids. Does yoga every day. She'd put my back out."

A feeling like warm, spreading sunshine crept over Stevie's body.

She had a cold case, she had a locked-room mystery, she had her friends, and now, she would have David.

In that moment, it was possible that Stevie had never been happier.

12

Stevie had an indifferent relationship with bikes. She knew how to ride one. At one point in her childhood she had owned one, but she never really rode it and the tires deflated, so her parents sold it at a yard sale. Bikes, however, were now her main mode of transportation.

Allison Abbott may have been able to do the ride in fifteen minutes, but for Stevie it was a sweaty forty-five-minute ride around the dirt trails that said they were excellent for biking but were actually uneven and pitted and unexpectedly narrow at times with surprise rocks. Also, where Allison lived at the far end was almost entirely uphill. By the time Stevie arrived, it was almost seven in the morning, which felt to her like a win. Judging from Allison's face when she opened the door, she did not feel the same way.

"I thought you would be here a bit earlier," she said, holding the door open for Stevie to come inside.

"Took . . . a while."

"Would you like a drink?"

Stevie nodded heavily, sweat running down her face.

Allison got her a large glass of water. As she gulped it back, Stevie took in her surroundings. This was a clean kitchen. It was more than that—this was a *precise* kitchen. The handles of the mugs on the shelf all faced the same way. The stainless steel fridge had no marks on the outside, and the inside, which Stevie saw momentarily, looked factory-pristine. There was nothing extra on the counter, no weird piles of stuff, no random pieces of paper or notes. The dish sponge sat up straight like a soldier, drying in the optimal manner. There were clear containers of things like cereals and grains in an open pantry. This place had shades of Hercule Poirot, who always needed things to be of perfect size and in the right place.

"I wanted you to come here because I have something to show you," Allison said. "This way."

Stevie followed Allison into the hallway, which had dozens of carefully framed photographs of family and friends. At least a dozen were of Sabrina. Not one was crooked or unevenly spaced. Stevie followed on, up the carpeted stairs, past more framed photos. The house was like a gallery. There were Allison and Sabrina sitting side by side on a step, a black-and-white dog between them. Sabrina and Allison, the latter with a gap-toothed smile, opening Christmas gifts by a tree. Sabrina and Allison squinting into the sun at the beach. Sabrina and Allison by the lake. A whole wall of Sabrina Abbott, with her raven hair and big brown eyes, her wide, open smile. Sabrina was beautiful, there was no question about it. There was a brightness to her, a determination that shone through the decades and the poor seventies photo quality that tinged the world in sepia.

They passed by the open door of an immaculate if slightly impersonal master bedroom and went to a closed door near the end of the hall. Allison opened this, and Stevie followed her into a darkened, smaller room that seemed to be a guest bedroom, except there was no bed. The walls were lined with packed bookshelves, and there were dressers and a rocking chair, but nowhere to sleep.

Allison opened the curtains, and the room was suddenly airy and bright.

"Light can damage things," Allison said. "That's why I keep it so dark."

With the sun pouring in, Stevie had a better look at where she was. While this room was neat as a pin, nothing here was curated or impersonal. Every surface was absolutely full of old paperbacks and textbooks, yearbooks, notebooks, photo albums. One entire set of shelves was filled with vinyl record albums, and a small portable turntable sat next to them. There were white archival boxes, and colored and clear bins, and wicker bins—everything precisely labeled: MAKEUP, HAIR SUPPLIES, JEWELRY, SCHOOL SUPPLIES, MISCEL-LANEOUS DRESSER CONTENTS. . . dozens of these. Sitting around and among these things were knickknacks: a stuffed Snoopy doll, a pink rotary telephone, a small figure of a monkey, a lumpy pottery bud vase. And all over, there were turtles—a large stuffed one; a pillow; a print; an oversize ceramic figurine of one, as big as a stuffed animal.

"My parents kept all of Sabrina's things in boxes," she

said. "They tucked them away in the attic. When I got them, I brought them out and gave them a space of their own. I know it may be odd to keep these things, but it comforts me. I come in here sometimes to sit and read. I feel close to her in here."

This room was Sabrina Abbott, right down to her hairbrush and her erasers. She looked at the spines of the books. Sabrina was certainly a serious reader—there were two shelves of paperback classics, textbooks on psychology and history, with a few romance novels sprinkled in for good measure.

"Part of me has always wanted to organize them by color and size," Allison said. "But I'm a librarian. I can't do that. Here . . ."

She indicated the top shelf of one of the bookshelves, which had about half a dozen small notebooks. She took one of these down carefully. There was a picture of Snoopy and Woodstock on the cover, along with *1977* in large cartoon print.

"Her last diary," Allison said, opening it with care. "The last one I have, anyway. Look at this."

She laid a hand over the actual entry, leaving a list exposed at the bottom of the page:

Piano: 1 hour 15 minutes
Calc: 50 minutes
German: 45 minutes
Physics: 30 minutes
History: 45 minutes

"She wrote it down every night," Allison said. "How much homework she did that day. I've read these diaries so many times I have them memorized."

She withdrew the book and set it back in its place on the shelf.

"You were asking the police about the last diary," Stevie said.

"It's my holy grail. I'd do anything to get it back. It would be a picture of her during those last months. It would feel like talking to her again."

"And it wasn't with her things?"

"We got everything from her bunk, and it wasn't there. If the police don't have it—I mean, I still think they may have had it at some point and lost it. The investigation, if you can even call it that, was a mess. But if they don't have it, my guess is that she hid it somewhere and it was lost. She told me that the kids in her bunk were nice, but they went through her things, played with her makeup, things like that. She may have stashed it somewhere that the kids couldn't get to it."

A small but bright light illuminated Stevie's mind. She would have to return to it later. There was still much to take in in this room.

"Here's something else," Allison said, removing a small blue plastic box from one of the shelves. She seemed to appreciate the fact that Stevie had a genuine interest in Sabrina's belongings.

"These are interlibrary loan slips. I found these at the library at the bottom of an old file cabinet. Look at these books she requested. You can tell a lot about a person from what they read. Even after she graduated, she was still requesting books, getting ready for the fall semester. The last two she requested were in June: *A Woman in Berlin* and *The Rise and Fall of the Third Reich*. This was my sister's summer reading when she worked at a camp. She studied German and she was pretty good at it, and she always wanted to know why people behave the way they do. She was deciding between majoring in psychology or history. She wanted to work for justice.

"I keep anything at all I can find of Sabrina's. Sometimes her friends from high school turn up something—a note from class, a picture, anything at all. They know I collect them. It's like I'm putting together a puzzle, but there are an infinite number of pieces."

She put the slips back in the box.

"I'm also an archivist," she added. "I come by it honestly. But you see what I mean. Sabrina worked. She studied. She volunteered. I became a librarian because she loved the library. She took me there, and it always felt like home to me."

She consulted her smartwatch.

"Almost seven thirty," she said. "If you want to keep talking, you have to come running with me."

Stevie absolutely did not run, but she had a lot more to ask, so it seemed that this morning was the day she took it up. She was dressed in black shorts and a black T-shirt, which seemed fine enough. It wasn't the moisture-wicking, professional-grade outfit Allison had on, but it would do.

"Great," Stevie said. "Would you mind if I took some pictures? Just for me? Not for Carson. I promise."

Allison considered for a moment, then nodded. Stevie photographed the room from several angles, getting various shots of the shelves. When she was done, Allison closed the curtains before leaving, shrouding Sabrina's things back in protective darkness.

"Partially I cope by running," she explained as she stretched against her outside steps. "I started running when I was a teenager, and I've never stopped. It makes me feel clear, like I have some control. I run the lake every morning. It's a beautiful view."

Allison set off, her gait even, and Stevie followed. It took her all of two minutes to become winded and so sweaty that she thought her body would lose every drop of moisture it contained, but she attempted to keep up.

"Is . . . there anything . . . you remember . . . about that night?" she asked.

Allison puffed out easy, even breaths.

"I remember everything," she said. "But nothing relevant. I was at home. I was twelve years old. We got a phone call. After that, it was like a nightmare that never stopped."

"But . . . you never . . . left town?"

"When something horrific happens, you sort of feel like you have to stay? Until justice is done. Which it never was."

Stevie found it hard to ask any more questions for a moment, as they started circling the lake. She tried to keep up with Allison, who was very obviously slowing her pace for her benefit. They continued on for another ten minutes or so, Stevie staggering alongside Allison, until she finally slowed to a stop in a break in the trees. She stepped forward, onto a lip of black rock that jutted out into the air.

"This is Arrowhead Point," Allison said. "It's the best view of the lake. I stop here every morning to take it all in—well, when the weather allows for it. You have to be careful in the winter."

She stepped out onto the point. Stevie hesitated behind her. While the point certainly seemed stable and it stretched out about ten feet, it wasn't very wide, and it had a gentle downward slope as it narrowed to its tip. Stevie took a few careful steps out onto the rock. Once she did, she could see why Allison stopped there. It was a stunning spot, the lake spread out below, winking in the morning sun. The trees wrapped around, like a hug. All of Barlow Corners and the camp stretched out below, partially visible through the trees. Allison rolled her shoulders, and Stevie managed to catch her breath enough to continue her questions.

"From everything I've heard," Stevie said, "it seemed like Sabrina was kind of the odd one out that night."

"That's what everyone says," Allison replied, sitting down on the rock to stretch her legs. "That's the standard line. 'What was good girl Sabrina Abbott doing out there?' But that part never confused me. She was having fun, that's all. She'd earned it. She was an incredibly hard worker, but she was also an eighteen-year-old kid in the 1970s, which were a really loose time."

"She broke up with her boyfriend right around then, right?" Stevie asked.

"She did," Allison said. "Shawn."

"Why did they break up? Do you know?"

"It was a normal teenage breakup," Allison replied. "Shawn was the kind of person who might go somewhere for college, but then he'd come home, get married, do exactly what his parents did. Sabrina was moving to New York City to go to Columbia in the fall. She was so excited about her new life. Looking back on it, I can see what happened. He was *always* around. Always really nice, but around . . . a lot. He was like an older brother to me. I was really upset when they broke up."

"Did you ever think that—"

"It wasn't Shawn," Allison cut in. "It's true that Shawn never gave up. I think he was convinced that Sabrina was going through some phase and that she would come back. He wasn't supposed to be working at the camp that summer. His family had an outdoor sports business—they rented canoes and kayaks, things like that. He was supposed to be working there, but when Sabrina broke up with him, he got a job at the camp. That really wasn't weird. Everyone worked at the camp. If he wanted to be with his friends, that was the place to be. It was an unwelcome surprise for Sabrina, but he never bothered her. Shawn was a lovesick kid, but a nice one. He wouldn't have touched a hair on her head. And he was in all night with Paul Penhale, anyway."

"Do you think Todd Cooper hit Michael Penhale?"

"Absolutely," she said without a moment's hesitation.

"Why would your sister hang out with someone who did that?"

Allison sighed deeply.

"I think she must have thought he didn't do it. Sabrina was really principled, and really smart. Maybe it was too horrible to believe that someone you knew could have done something like that. Sabrina was smart, but . . . she was also young, and she thought the best of people."

"Do you think what happened to Michael Penhale had anything to do with the murders, though?"

"That," she said, "I don't know."

Allison stretched out one last time to reach for her toes and stood.

"I'm going to finish my run," she said. "I don't know if you . . ."

"I may walk back to your house," Stevie said as casually as she could. "Get my bike. To get back to camp."

Allison smiled and nodded, then continued on her way, picking up her pace. Stevie was unsure what to make of her morning with Allison, but at the very least, she now had an idea about how to focus her time here.

She had a plan.

13

AFTER ANOTHER HOT AND EXCEEDINGLY SWEATY BIKE RIDE, MUCH OF which was down the edge of the road while cars whipped past her, Stevie turned down the drive to Sunny Pines. She dropped the bike in the bike rack, wiped her face on the edge of her T-shirt (possibly flashing some other counselors in the process), and hurried over to the dining pavilion for breakfast. It was good that most of her T-shirts were black—they hid the heavy sweat marks all over her torso. Unlike Ellingham, which was up in the mountains of Vermont and in session during the cooler months, everything about camp was moist in the heat. Her body—moist. Her clothes—moist. Her shoes practically stuck to the ground. Her towels were always damp. Her hair was never really dry. The constant tackiness gave the bugs something to stick to.

The first thing she noticed was that the camp as a whole seemed to have vanished. There was a man on a riding mower preparing the fields, and a few people were in the dining area cooking, but otherwise, no one. This was good for her current purposes, which were getting to her cabin and getting a shower before anyone saw her, or more important, smelled her. The cabin was still secure. The camera app alerted her that she was approaching, so that was working. The big SURPRISE was there to greet her in the morning sunshine.

"Surprise," she said back to it.

She pulled off her disgusting clothes and tossed them into her empty suitcase that she decided would serve as a hamper. (Janelle had brought a pop-up laundry basket for this purpose, because she was Janelle, and Janelle planned her moves in advance.) No shower had ever felt as good as the fresh-air shower she had that morning, despite the fact that something was definitely moving around under the stall. When she emerged, clean and fresh, the camp was still silent but for the birds and the mower in the distance. She walked over to the art pavilion, where Janelle was up on a chair, hanging a mobile from a beam.

"Where is everyone?" Stevie asked.

"They went on a hike around the lake. I thought about going, but I need to get this done."

Stevie looked around the art pavilion. It was a concrete shell structure, with three walls and a peaked roof, full of tables and chairs and cubbies and shelving for art supplies. The only private area was a room in the back to secure things when they were out of use. Janelle had already transformed it from the blank, rough space it had been to a cheerful, Insta-ready fantasia of crafting glory. She had made sample crafts of many types—jars full of colored sand, pot holders, woven bracelets, hanging ornaments made of colored beads—and had set up all the necessary supplies around them like a fancy store display.

"There was chalkboard paint," Janelle said, hopping down from the chair. "I got permission to spray the back door and use that as a bulletin board. I'm doing that this afternoon. This morning I was organizing the back office. There was a ton of crap in there."

"You don't have to do that," Stevie said. "You know you have a problem, right?"

"I can quit anytime I want. How was it?"

"Weird," Stevie said, sitting down in one of the child-size chairs. "But informative. But weird. Allison has a kind of museum of her sister's things. She kept everything of Sabrina's. Everything. Brushes. Little slips of paper. But I get now why she wants the diary so much. So I've decided to focus on getting the diary for her. I'm not sure it gets the case anywhere, and it's a long shot. But I guess finding diaries is kind of my thing."

This was true. At Ellingham, Stevie had located the diary of a student from the 1930s, which was hidden in a space in the wall.

Something that Stevie said made Janelle lift her chin in interest. She turned on her heel and walked into the room in the back. Stevie could hear her shifting boxes along the concrete floor. She emerged a minute later holding one, which she set on one of the tables.

"This one has loads of old paperwork in it," she said,

removing the lid and pulling out handfuls of loose, dog-eared paper in a variety of colors and conditions. "Just order forms and things like that, but I feel like I saw . . ."

Janelle shuffled through the box until she found what she was looking for and passed it to Stevie. It was an old pink piece of paper.

"It caught my eye because of the name," she said. "But I put it back because it's nothing."

Stevie took the paper and examined it.

```
EXTRA SUPPLY ORDER FORM
REQUESTSED BY SABRINA ABBOTT
JUNE 20, 1978

Paints: waterculors, acycilcs ($60)
Pencils and brshes: ($50)
Ceramics: ring boxes, earring stands, cats,
dogs, cookie jars; trash cann, turtle,
teddy bear, roller skate ($ 28)
String: leather, cloth ($18)


TOTAL: $156
```

"So much crafting, so cheap," Janelle said wistfully. "I mean, adjusted for inflation it's more, but I want to imagine it is this cheap for a second."

Stevie examined the piece of paper in her hand. It was

nothing special—a faded old supply list from a box of useless paperwork.

"How did they do anything with typewriters?" Janelle went on. "When they made a mistake, it was like, *I guess that's just how it's going to be*. Everything must have taken forever. Anyway, do you think Allison would want it?"

"Yeah," Stevie said. "I do."

"What about our problem?" Janelle said. "Any brain waves on that?"

"No." Stevie shook her head. "But whoever it was has been leaving our cabin alone, which is good."

Leaving our cabin alone . . .

The cabins were empty right now. Everyone was out. Stevie took out her phone and pulled up the digital files that Carson had sent to her.

"Map of the camp in 1978," she said. "It's in here somewhere."

She flicked through the folders and documents before finding what she wanted.

"Carson, you magnificent weirdo," she said. "You scanned everything. Where's the camp map, map, map . . ."

They had been given printed copies the day before in their welcome bags. She had folded hers up and shoved it in her bag. She pulled it out and compared the two.

"Sabrina was in the Sparrow bunk," Stevie said, glancing between the documents. "Sparrow bunk was . . . fourteen. What is it now? Here . . . Pandas."

If there was ever a good time to have a look in another bunk, this was probably it. She knew where all the counselors were, and there were no kids around yet. Everything was quiet.

"I'll meet you over at lunch," she said to Janelle.

The cabins were all identical, and there were over twenty of them, so even with the map things got a little confusing. She soon found herself at the Panda bunkhouse. She bounced up the four concrete steps to the doorway. The heavier door was open, and the screen door was unlocked. She could see there was no one inside and no one around. She entered the cool cabin, which was considerably larger than where Janelle and Stevie were staying. Eight camp beds were all lined up and ready to go, with colorful cubbies and hooks for the campers' supplies. An overhead fan beat the afternoon heat away without much enthusiasm, but this cabin was under tree cover and cool enough without it. Like Stevie and Janelle's cabin, the screened windows here were high and covered by the same metal grates, attached from the inside. At the back of the room, there was a plywood wall; there was a doorway in the middle marked by a green privacy curtain. Stevie stepped into this area, which was darker and smaller. The counselor who would be staying here had dropped off a red suitcase and a large gym bag, along with several shopping bags' worth of supplies. Stevie maneuvered around these, careful not to touch them. She felt the thin partition wall. It was a single layer of wood. She ran her hands along the outer walls, felt around the cubbies. Nothing.

She took several pictures, getting the bunk from every angle.

The floor was slightly more interesting. This cabin had a wooden floor. It felt to Stevie like there was nothing between the planks and the solid concrete the cabin rested on, but she got down on the floor and knocked, making sure all was solid. She crawled around, knocking and checking, picking at the boards with her fingers. Nothing gave.

"What are you doing?" said a voice.

Stevie jerked her head up and saw a redheaded girl standing in the doorway of the partition wall, a phone clasped to her head and a horrified look on her face.

Stevie could hear the person on the other end of the phone saying, "What? What?"

"There's someone crawling on the floor of my bunk," the girl said into the phone. "Hang on."

"Oh hey," Stevie said. "Sorry, I'm . . . looking for something."

It was true, and she had no other excuse ready at hand.

"In my bunk? On the floor? Who are you?"

"I'm Stevie, I . . . I got here yesterday and I . . . came in here by accident and I dropped my . . . um, a key?"

"Hang on," the girl said into the phone. "Hang *on*. So you were in here and you lost a key?"

Stevie nodded lamely.

The girl clearly didn't believe her, but at the same time couldn't seem to figure out why Stevie might be lying. She looked at her things, which had not been disturbed.

"It's not here," Stevie said, getting up and brushing off her knees. "Sorry, I . . . got the cabins mixed up before and . . . I must have dropped it somewhere else. Sorry to bother you. I'll see you later."

Stevie left as casually as possible, which was really not casual at all. She felt the girl's eyes on her back. Her lie had been okay at best. What was she supposed to say? *Don't mind me. I'm just a weirdo who creeps into your bunk while you're gone and crawls around on the floor by your bed. Why am I doing this? Oh, because of the murders.*

She decided to skip lunch, even though she was hungry. She didn't want to immediately face the redheaded girl again. She texted Janelle and asked her to bring a hot dog and soda to the cabin, where she was going to hide for a while with the door closed.

The red hair made Stevie think of Diane McClure, who in many ways was the least-documented victim. She wasn't as bad as Todd, as good as Sabrina, or the well-meaning drug dealer who almost made it to safety. She was simply there, the girlfriend, the fourth victim. Stevie flopped onto her bed and picked up her tablet, paging through the files until she got to the very short one allocated to Diane. There was an excerpt from a book on the case about her:

Very few people had much to say about Diane McClure. Her school records show that she was a middling student, barely passing many of her classes but not quite failing out. She belonged to no clubs. Her yearbook photo shows a black-and-white image of a heavily freckled girl with a strange smile that looks neither happy nor sincere. Her thick red hair is long and straight, but the photo cannot capture how vibrant it was in life.

Diane was the daughter of lifetime Barlow Corners residents Douglas and Ellen McClure. Her parents met at Liberty High in the 1950s, marrying in 1956. Her brother, Daniel, was born in 1958, and Diane was born in 1960. In 1965, they purchased the Dairy Duchess, a local diner, from its owners. They would run the diner well into the 1990s. Diane worked there in the evenings and on weekends.

"Diane liked to have fun," said friend Patty Horne. "She loved Led Zeppelin and Kiss. She loved going to concerts. She pretty much always wore a shirt from some band or other. That's so much of what I remember about her—her red hair and her T-shirts from concerts. She had really strong feelings about which albums were acceptable listening. She was passionate. God, she loved Led Zeppelin so much."

This was a time when high schools had smoking lounges, and Diane spent a lot of time in the one at Liberty High. Some of the only photos of her in the 1978 yearbook show her leaning out the window, cigarette in hand.

Diane began dating Todd Cooper early in their

junior year, and by the end of senior year, they were considered one of the leading couples of Liberty High. But they were not king-and-queen-of-the-prom material.

"Diane was too much of a badass for that," said another friend. "When I think of what happened that night, one thing that I always think is . . . Diane must have put up one hell of a fight. Whatever happened, she went down swinging."

Stevie stared at the ceiling for a moment. Had Diane gone down swinging? Had any of them? She paged through the file that detailed the injuries. (Carson might have had some unfortunate quirks, but he put together a solid set of case files.) She got to the diagrams of the bodies, with the detailed notes. Todd, Diane, and Eric had head wounds. Todd was stabbed sixteen times. Diane nine. Only Sabrina had no head wound, and Sabrina was the only one noted for having defensive marks on her hands.

What this seemed to mean to Stevie was that Diane, Todd, and Eric were all struck, possibly to incapacitate them. In Eric's case, he wasn't struck hard enough, and he managed to run. Sabrina, again, was the odd one out. Maybe this was because she was the least threatening and didn't need to be hit on the head.

Whatever the case, one of these things was always not like the other. Sabrina Abbott, again, the perfect girl, the special one—reaching up, fighting back the knife. . . .

Stevie jumped as the cabin door opened.

"Look who I found," Janelle said, coming in with Nate, whose shirt was soaked through with sweat. She passed Stevie a hot dog and a Coke.

"I'm not going to be popular," Stevie said. "Don't ask questions."

Neither of her friends seemed surprised.

14

THE REST OF THAT AFTERNOON WAS A FREE ONE, AND ACCORDING TO Nate, most of the counselors were going over to the public side of the park to go swimming and cook out. Nate and Stevie attempted to dodge this, but Janelle managed to convince them that some kind of effort had to be made to ingratiate themselves with the people they would be spending the summer with.

The counselors of Camp Sunny Pines set out in a formless parade, people walking in random groups toward the road that separated the camp from the public park. Once you crossed, there was a thick wall of trees and a great deal more shade. The ground was gnarled with roots, so in places the path was raised up on slatted wooden walkways and tiny bridges, before twisting and splitting into dirt and wood-chip paths, staked with trail markers. Janelle, Nate, and Stevie followed along as the group meandered down the path marked in red, which led down and around the water's edge. Stevie found that she was getting a bit winded from the walk and realized they had been going up a slow and steady incline, which then dipped down sharply to get to the water's edge. The trees opened up, and there was a big parking lot in the distance, fairly full of cars. Some RVs and tents dotted the area. The journey ended at a small sand and dirt beach, bordered by rocks and reeds.

On the Sunny Pines side, the ground had been cleared for the camp. Here, all was still wild, and the trees and reeds clustered around the lake like a halo. The lake was wide here, and Stevie finally saw the falls that gave it its name. It wasn't quite a wonder, but it was impressive enough. This side of the lake was the real deal; their little lake below was the spillover, the children's pool. On this side, the green-and-blue dragonflies ruled the waves, or the ripples. They buzzed the water's surface like drones. Stevie wasn't sure if dragonflies bit, so she shirked away when they landed nearby, twitching their many wings.

This was definitely where the snakes hung out.

Across the lake, a rock jutted up like a big, angry tooth, high above the water. It looked like something Jurassic, or like one of those views from exotic vacations where people would dive into crystal waters below. Except, in this case, any jumpers would have gone into the brackish water of Lake Wonder Falls, or perhaps into one of the smaller rocks tucked in below it.

The heat was thick and humming, enough that the lake looked inviting, despite the lily pads and dragonflies and thousands upon thousands of snakes Stevie was certain were slithering around them. Many of the other counselors had brought over inflatables, which they pumped up and used to float out on the water. Others jumped off the short dock. Only a few lingered on the side like Nate and Stevie. Janelle, being a social creature, immediately started chatting with two girls who had brought a large inflatable unicorn raft. She took off her coverup and got into the water with them, her bright yellow bathing suit making her easy to spot.

Dylan, Nate's new co-counselor, was having someone take pictures of him doing backward falls off the dock into the water.

"He's trying to become an influencer," Nate said grimly.

"It's nice that you guys have something in common," Stevie replied.

Nate gave her a long side-eye.

"It's only for a few days," she said.

"Easy for you to say."

Stevie sighed and looked around, debating with herself whether to try to swim. Her relationship with swimming was much like her relationship with biking—she'd done it as a kid. In the case of swimming, she'd never learned how to do it properly. She didn't have a solid crawl, and she didn't do laps. Her move was a kind of doggie paddle mixed with a fervent thrashing and treading, but it kept her afloat.

Still, it was too hot not to at least try. She got up and pulled off her T-shirt, revealing the old bathing suit she'd gotten at Target a year or so before. It was a hair too small, riding up her butt and cutting into the tops of her thighs. At first, the water was pleasant, and the ground sandy under her feet. By the time she got knee-deep, she felt the first wave of chill. She braved a bit farther, because running out of the lake when you were in up to your knees was a bad look. The ground dipped away and was replaced by a tangle of slime. The temperature dropped at once, and she was suddenly up to her mid-torso in cold swampland. She flailed a bit, her feet finding only slimy rocks. Her head filled with images of underwater snakes and strange creatures. She felt something brush her ankle, and that was the end of that. She lurched back in the direction of the beach, which was only about ten feet away. It made her struggle to return less than heroic.

"That looked fun," Nate said as she flopped down next to him.

"So you don't like to swim?"

"I swim," he replied, not looking up from his phone. "I'm really good at it. Captain of my junior high team. Varsity my freshman year."

"Shut up," Stevie said, reeling.

"It's true. I stopped because I don't like competing, but I swim really well. But that . . ." He nodded out at the expanse of lake in front of them. "Looks cold and gross. I like pools. They're *managed*."

"How come you never mentioned this before?"

"Never came up," he said.

"We once spent the night in the pool house at Ellingham."

"Not to swim, though," he replied.

The concept of Nate the Athlete was so astonishing that

Stevie found she had nothing more to say. People could be surprising, and that unnerved her. She wanted to believe she could see to the bottom, spot the hints. But she had never so much as suspected that Nate was a secret champion swimmer. She had failed this one.

Dylan and some others came out of the water and sat down not far from them. The gesture was entirely normal and friendly; they were making an effort to be social. Stevie knew this, and even appreciated it on some level. On another level, though, and one closer to her surface, she shied away from such approaches. She was never sure why. It's not like she had trouble talking to people. Maybe it was more the fact that her parents had always pushed her in that direction, told her to make friends, as if the quantity of friends somehow determined your worth. She already had friends—Nate and Janelle. She was with one of them now.

So instead of looking at the new people, she looked over at the imposing rock on the other side of the lake.

"That's Point 23," Dylan said, following her gaze. "They call it that because twenty-three people have died jumping off of it."

"It wasn't twenty-three people," said a girl. "People have died, but not that many."

"It's twenty-three," Dylan repeated. "Why else would they call it that? I jumped it last summer. It was awesome."

"You're an idiot, Dylan," the girl replied. "Besides, if you get caught jumping off that rock, they kick you out of camp." She snapped her fingers dramatically. "Like, you're *gone*."

"Raptured?" Nate said in a hushed whisper.

The girl wrinkled her nose, indicating that the joke was not all it could be. It was time to turn the conversation to something more Stevie's speed.

"Do people ever talk about the murders?" Stevie said.

The girl poked out her lower lip a bit in thought. Another girl, dressed in a black bathing suit, with black hair and nails to match, leaned in.

"Oh yeah," she said. "The Box in the Woods thing. That was a serial killer from the seventies called the Woodsman."

Stevie fought back the urge to editorialize.

"They caught the guy," the girl went on, wrongly. "You can go out into the woods and see where it happened, but there's not much there. I went the first year I worked here. It's really weird. You can still see stuff that was there from when they were murdered."

Again, this was not true. Stevie twitched internally.

"You know you want to," Nate whispered.

She elbowed him.

Perhaps sensing that Nate and Stevie were not the chatty kind, the group talked among themselves. There was a public grill, and several of the counselors had brought over hot dogs. Dylan and that group got some and sat back down to eat.

"Hold my camera," Dylan said to one of the girls.

While she did so, he took a hot dog roll and pressed the entire thing into his mouth, squashing it in and making himself gag. Nate watched blankly, too defeated to comment.

Stevie, however, was transfixed.

"Son of a bitch," she said.

This came out a bit louder than intended and got the attention of the group, including Dylan.

"Son of a *bitch*," Stevie said again, jumping to her feet and scrabbling for her phone.

"Not you," she heard Janelle say behind her. "She's . . . um . . ."

Stevie was already marching off toward the parking lot, looking for a clearer phone signal, and waiting for someone on the other end to answer her call. Finally, they did.

"We have to talk," she said. "Now."

15

STEVIE CHOSE THE PLACE FOR THE MEETING—THE UNUSED TREE-house, the one that was meant to be Nate's home for the summer. His bunk sat ready for his arrival behind a thin wooden wall.

Now that she had seen this place, Stevie felt like the treehouse thing was maybe overselling it. It was really a second-level building, accessible via a set of wooden steps, with an open area below for storing excess sporting equipment. Mostly it was a screened-in box with a bunch of empty shelves under the windows, and bench seats that had probably had cushions on them at one point. It was next to a tree, which was likely how it got the name. It was a hot, spidery mess lit by one ineffectual overhead light.

"See," Janelle said to Nate when they entered. "You're not missing out on much."

This had not cheered Nate up.

Stevie sat on the least cobwebby window seat and watched the ground below, waiting for her guest. She finally saw him approach, dressed in flowing orange harem pants and a Box

Box T-shirt. Carson came up the steps two at a time.

"What's going on?" he asked. "Sounds important."

"I know who left the message on our wall," Stevie said. "And the box on your path."

"Oh! Oh, great!" He nodded, but his eyes darted a bit and he tucked his hands into his slouchy harem pant pockets.

"You did," Stevie said.

This much she had already revealed to Nate and Janelle, who looked at Carson with unimpressed faces.

"Me? I . . ."

"I wouldn't recommend whatever you're planning on saying," Janelle said, joining Stevie on the window bench.

"I would." Nate was sprawled on the floor, picking at the splinters. "I like it when Stevie goes feral."

To his credit, Carson said no more. He sat down on the floor and crossed his legs in a full yogic knot.

"Now will you tell us the how?" Janelle said. "That's more what I want to know."

"Sure." Stevie stretched out a bit and her neck made a loud crack. "We knew from the start that the message was put on our wall in advance. We know that because it was dry and because there was paint under my bed. Also, we went all over the cabin to see how someone might get in. The screen windows have metal grates over them, the door was locked from the inside, and the floor is made of concrete. Impossible, right? But there was one way—there's a hole in the screen on the window, only an inch or two big. And tonight, when I saw Dylan stick that entire hot dog roll in his mouth, I realized how someone could use a hole that size to gain access to our cabin."

"Not what I expected to hear you say," Nate said, "but okay."

"You can get something large through a small opening if it's soft," Stevie went on. "The hot dog roll was soft, so Dylan could shove it in his mouth. So what might go through a little hole in a screen? Maybe something like this."

Stevie held up the reusable bag Carson had given her. She made an *okay* gesture with her right hand, and with the left, pulled the bag through the circle made by her fingers.

"Fabric," she said. "And who has a lot of fabric in custom, photorealistic patterns?"

"Oh no," Janelle said, shaking her head. "Oh . . . you have got to be kidding me."

"There's an entire wall of it at the Bounce House," Stevie said. "All you'd need to do is make a wood pattern. It was probably up there on the wall. You painted the message on the wall—kind of high up, so it was more in line with the window, and more in shadow. You let the paint drip, but not too much, because you had to make sure the message fit under the piece of fabric you were going to use to cover it. You wiped away any extra so it wouldn't show. When it was dry, you covered it up with the piece of fabric, attaching it with some tape."

She held up the piece of tape she'd found under the bed. She had gone back and retrieved it before this meeting.

"All you needed to do then was attach some thread or fishing line or something and string it out the window. Sometime in the night, you gave the string a tug and the fabric slid out through the screen. I think it must have brushed against my face as it came down. I thought what I felt was some kind of insect. And that was it. A message mysteriously appears on our wall. Then, of course, you prepared the box of dolls and claimed to find it on your run."

"Yes!" he said, breaking into a huge grin. "Yes! You"—he pointed at Stevie—"are the real deal. That was nuts! That was so good! I knew I made the right decision."

"Was this supposed to be some kind of test?" Nate asked.

"I don't think so," Stevie said. "It was for the show, wasn't it?"

"Sometimes you need to prime the pump," Carson said. "A little drama to get things going."

"And your plan was to freak us out and make us feel like someone was sneaking into our cabin and leaving threatening messages?" Janelle said.

"You were never in any danger!" Carson said.

"How did we know that?"

"But you weren't," he said a bit less enthusiastically.

"So the plan was to fake this message thing and then what?" Stevie said. "Have it be part of the case? Make it seem like someone was trying to stop the podcast?"

"Well, yeah," he said.

"And you didn't think people might be annoyed by that?" Nate asked. "Like, people listening? To know that you faked threats against yourself?"

"Well, the idea was for no one to know . . ."

"When were you going to tell us?" Stevie said.

He reached deep into his messenger bag and pulled out a balled-up bag in a wood pattern.

"Have one. It's the bag from the wood pattern in your cabin. I was going to tell you soon, because I knew you were alarmed. See, I even brought the bags."

He tossed one to Stevie, who let it land on the ground.

"I'm going back," Janelle said, shaking her head. "I have to talk to Vi."

She looked to Nate.

"Oh, I'm staying," Nate said, settling in. "This is absolutely my Think Jam."

Stevie faced off with Carson, who looked altogether too happy for someone she had just busted for leaving creepy messages. He had the glowing contentment of a man who fully believed that he was one with the cosmos, feeling all the feels.

"So we're clear," Stevie said, "I'll still work on this case, but I do it my way, which means never faking stuff."

"No, I've got it, I—"

She held up a hand.

"I'm doing this on my own," she went on. "I'll talk to people."

"And then we'll—"

He just would not stop.

"*I'll*," she said, "tell you if I find anything. But these are real people. Janelle and I are real people. I know you have the money and you own this place, but you don't own this town or their pain. We're supposed to be helping. You're not helping."

If Carson was embarrassed by being dressed down by

a seventeen-year-old girl at his camp, he certainly didn't show it.

"I hear what you're saying," he said.

Nate shook his head in warning.

"Now you're going to answer some questions," Stevie went on. "Were the floors of the bunks always concrete?"

This clearly threw Carson for a loop.

"Always," he said. "In case of flooding. Sometimes the lake spills over the banks."

"Were they redone, or are these the originals?"

"They were redone . . . I think in the sixties?"

"But they were like this in 1978?"

"Yep," he said. "Why? You think there's something encased in the concrete or something?"

"No," she said.

"Then why—"

"No," she said again.

Carson shut up. He unfolded himself from the floor.

"I made the right decision with you," he said. "I was trying to disrupt the narrative, but I promise you, I won't do anything like that again."

"Wow," Nate said when he was gone. "Wow. If you don't want to be a detective, I think you have a future in domination. He's *shorter* now."

Truth be told, Stevie had enjoyed it. She glowed with warm pleasure.

"What was the concrete thing about?"

"Sabrina's diary," Stevie said. "I wanted to know if there was any chance it could have been concealed in the floor. I guess not."

"You know there's basically no chance that thing is still around, right? If they haven't seen it since 1978 and have already looked?"

"I don't know about that," she said. "If she was going out into the woods to buy pot, she wouldn't bring her *diary* with her. It's not like she was going to be sitting out there in the dark writing, 'Dear diary, here I am, buying weed for the first time.'"

"No," he said. "I guess not. What about in a tree? People do that a lot in books—stash something in a hollow tree."

"Possible," Stevie replied. "Seems risky, though. It could be destroyed by weather, or someone might find it. You'd want it to be in a safe, dry place that only you knew about."

"Okay, what about someone obsessed with the case? Souvenir collectors. If someone found that diary, it would be huge."

"True-crime people aren't serial killers—they don't want secret trophies. If someone had that diary, they'd want to tell everyone. That's the whole *point*."

Nate nodded in acceptance of this fact.

"So it seems like the diary is your main thing now. Is this because you feel like the case itself can't be solved?"

"I don't know if the case can be solved," Stevie replied. "I don't know if I'm the one who would be able to do it if it could be. It's probably going to come down to DNA or something.

But looking for the diary is something I can do to help someone who's still around."

"You didn't tell Carson that."

"Carson doesn't need to know," Stevie replied. "Screw Carson."

"Agreed. Also, I think it's a good plan. I don't mean to sound like it's not. It just seems like it also might be hard, but less hard than tracking down a serial killer from 1978."

They fell into silence, listening to the chirp of the crickets or the cicadas or whatever it was that chirped all night in the summer. Some kind of chirping thing.

"People had so little to do back then," Nate said meditatively. "Before the internet, I guess you had to keep a diary or something. How else would you remember what happened?"

Stevie *hmmmm*ed.

"There will be children here tomorrow," Nate said. "Children. With their little child fingers."

"Child fingers?"

"I'm saying we won't be safe anymore. This other counselor better stop being sick really quick."

As Stevie walked into her cabin later, Janelle was wrapping up a call with Vi. Stevie could see their short silver hair on the screen, and their pink-tinted round glasses. Whatever lovey-dovey talk they were engaged in cut off quickly. Stevie said hello, then went over and flopped on her bed. It was not a particularly forgiving sort of bed, and the springs squeaked in protest. There was a pungent chemical smell in the air, and the message on the wall was gone.

"You got it off the wall," she said as Janelle finished the call.

"Yeah, I used some denatured alcohol to soften it, then I scraped it off."

"Denatured alcohol?"

"They use it for camping stoves, so there was some around. The smell will go away soon."

"I don't know if I want it to," Stevie replied. "That's probably the only thing I'll solve all summer."

She waited for Janelle to jump in and say no, of course not. Janelle was always encouraging, but she was also realistic. Her silence confirmed Stevie's worries.

However, there was something that changed her mood immediately. A text from David popped up on her phone:

Got off work a day early. See you tomorrow.

16

STEVIE WOKE UP IN A BRIGHT AND BEAUTIFUL MOOD THAT BEFITTED Barlow Corners. Today, David would be here. Today, she had something she could give to a family member of one of the Box in the Woods victims. Today the kids were coming, and that seemed wonderful too.

Again, Stevie set out in the morning on a bike. The route to town was easy enough, with only two turns to make. Still, most of the country roads had no bike lanes, no sidewalks—you were supposed to ride along the edge of the street and *trust*. She wobbled at times and pumped the brakes anxiously, never really sure if she was about to skid off the side of the road or into traffic. No one else seemed to be having these problems. People on racing bikes whizzed around her, utterly sure of their command of the road.

When she arrived in the town center about half an hour later, she was a shattered husk of her former self, but she had grown in her own personal estimation. She rolled the bike up the sidewalk for the last few blocks of the journey and chained it in front of the library.

The library air was shockingly cool on skin that was slick with sweat. Allison was in the new reading room, organizing some picture books. She had on a cheerful yellow shirtdress with a matching necklace made of big yellow beads. Janelle would have appreciated the lemony color and the precision.

"Hey," Stevie said quietly.

Allison turned.

"I have something for you," Stevie said, reaching into her backpack and producing the typed paper of art supplies. "We found it when we were organizing the art pavilion. It was in a big box of junk, but . . . I know you like to have anything Sabrina made or wrote, so . . ."

Allison stared at the paper, then looked up at her, a strange expression on her face.

"The art pavilion?" she said.

"Yeah. We were cleaning it. Well, Janelle was, and she found this, and I thought . . ."

Allison turned her gaze back to the paper. Stevie couldn't make out what she was thinking, but there was a lot of movement behind her eyes. Stevie was not great with intense emotions and felt the pull of the exit on her heels.

"I should get going," she said.

"Yes . . . ," Allison said distractedly. "Yes."

Stevie was halfway to the library door when Allison hurried up to her and took her gently by the arm.

"Thank you," she said. "That was . . . it was kind. Thank you so much."

"It's no problem," Stevie said. Because really, it wasn't.

"Sabrina was bad at typing," she said. "It was a joke in our family. Sabrina could do everything, but she couldn't type to save her . . ."

Allison reconsidered finishing the sentence, blinked, and reset the conversation.

"How is your research going?"

"Not great," Stevie said. "Most people probably won't talk to us because of Carson."

"They will if I ask," Allison said, her eyes bright. "Who do you want to speak to?"

"Anyone who will talk to me," Stevie replied. "People who were there. Shawn Greenvale, Susan Marks, Paul Penhale . . ."

"Do you have to be back right away?"

"Not really?"

"Come on," Allison said. "Paul's practice is only a few doors away."

The Barlow Corners Veterinary Hospital was actually four doors down, next to the Pilates and barre studio. It was a brightly colored office, intensely cheerful, with many children's drawings of their pets in crayon, almost all with messages thanking Dr. Penhale for caring for them. There was a coffee station and fresh-baked cookies on the side. A man with tidily trimmed gray hair and scrubs covered in cartoon puppies sat behind the desk. Stevie vaguely recognized him from the picnic.

"Hey, Joe," Allison said. "Is Paul in with a patient?"

"He is but should be done in a second."

As he said that, a door opened and a man in maroon scrubs stepped out, carrying a small curly-haired dog in his arms. The dog looked a little loopy and had a bandage on his ear.

"You can take that bandage off before you go to bed this evening," he said, passing the dog to a woman in the waiting room. "But he's going to have to wear the cone for a week, until the stitches heal. And no dog park for a while."

Once patient and owner were checking out at the desk, he came over to greet them.

"Hey, Allison," he said, looking between her and Stevie with some confusion. "What's up?"

"This is Stevie from the event the other night," Allison said. "You remember."

"Hard to forget," he replied, but he nodded a polite greeting to Stevie.

"Stevie's okay," Allison said. "It would mean a lot to me if you would give her an interview about the case."

Paul raised his eyebrows in surprise. "Really?"

"Really," she said. "She's all right."

The owner and the small dog left, and Paul waved his goodbye. Then he turned to the man at the desk, who was typing into a scheduling program with lightning speed.

"Hon, when's my next?"

"You have forty-five minutes," the man replied. "Your ten fifteen spaying appointment asked to bump to this afternoon."

"Looks like I have some time now," Paul said. "I could use

a coffee. That okay with you, Joe?"

"Fine by me," Joe replied. "Gives me a chance to unpack the surgical supplies."

"My husband," Paul explained. "Keeps everything going."

Joe did not deny it. He peered over the desk to regard Stevie.

"So the Box Box guy owns the camp now, huh?" he asked.

Stevie nodded.

"And he also wants to make a podcast about the . . . about what happened? Seems like a broad remit. Still, I have to admit I like those boxes."

Stevie shrugged, because Joe was right. It was a weird combination of interests.

"Joe likes organization," Dr. Penhale explained. "I joked that he wanted us to take our honeymoon at the Container Store."

Joe held up his hands, indicating that he was guilty as charged.

"So you're set here," Allison said. "If you need anything else, you ask me."

With a nod, she exited.

"You seem to have made a big impression on Allison," Paul said. "And if you're all right with Allison, then you're all right with me. Let's walk over to Patty's, get a coffee or a soda or something."

They crossed the street to the Sunshine Bakery. Patty Horne was in the back, decorating a cake. She gave a wave but continued with her work as her assistant rang up the coffees and prepared them. Paul insisted on paying. All the tables were empty, so they took the one by the window. Sunshine Bakery was, true to its name, extremely sunny. Sunlight poured in over the cheerful yellow table, decorated with a red Gerbera daisy in a jar.

"So what can I help you with?" he asked.

"Do you mind if I record this?" Stevie said, getting out her phone. "Not for the podcast. For me. Just to remember."

Paul gave an expansive gesture that indicated she should do as she liked.

"I guess . . . ," Stevie said, and then regretted starting that way. She needed to sound more sure, more confident. But that was easier said than done. She was facing a man who had lost a brother, as Allison had lost a sister, and Patty had lost her friends. Everyone around here had *lost*, and she felt it in her bones.

Paul was waiting. She needed to stop sounding so unsure.

"Your brother," she said. It was not a question, but Paul seemed to understand. "If that's okay," she added.

Paul nodded, his chin dipping toward his chest a bit.

"It's all right," he said. "I've been talking about what happened to my brother—about everything that happened here—since I was seventeen years old. It's been with me for most of my life. My brother died in December of 1977, about seven months before the murders. It was right before Christmas. He was in the junior high band. He played the trumpet. They were doing a special long rehearsal for a holiday concert. I was home. I was watching *Starsky and Hutch* downstairs and doing homework. The phone rang and I heard this . . . scream from upstairs . . ."

He stopped and looked down at his coffee for a moment.

"It was our neighbor, Mrs. Campbell, who called," Paul said. "It happened right around the corner. He would have been home in a minute or two. Someone came around the corner and mowed him down. Mrs. Campbell heard it happen and ran out, she was with him when . . ."

He shook his head.

"He didn't die right away. She stayed with him while the ambulance came. He died en route."

"And people think Todd Cooper was the one who—"

"I don't think," he cut in. "I *know* Todd Cooper was the one who hit him. Everyone knows Todd Cooper was the one who hit him."

His voice rose a bit and Patty looked up from her cake decorating. Paul cleared his throat a little. "Why don't we step outside?" he asked. "It's a nice morning."

The temperature had climbed even in the short period they had been in the bakery, and Stevie felt herself immediately start to sweat.

"This is a small town," he said as soon as they were clear of the door and any passersby. "Everybody really does know everyone. And it's not like there are any secrets about what happened with Todd and my brother. Certainly Patty knows all about it. But it always feels best to maybe keep this conversation—well, I don't know. It's a reflex."

They drifted toward the green and sat down on one of the

benches by the statue.

"The town felt even smaller back then," he said. "Everyone was in and out of everyone else's house or yard. We all knew what everyone else was up to. I knew Todd. We were good friends. Todd drove a brown Jeep with a red stripe. He drove fast, with the music up loud. And he drove high, he drove drunk. Lots of people did back then. Todd did it a lot. I was in the car many of those times. There were near misses that we'd laugh off. That night, it wasn't a near miss. Someone saw him. There was a girl named Dana Silverman, who was in band as well. She was walking home from the same rehearsal. She said she saw his Jeep turn the corner of Mason Road and Prospect Avenue right after the accident, and that it was going fast. She even saw the green fuzzy dice he had hanging from the rearview mirror. The next day, after the accident, Todd didn't drive to school. He turned up in his girlfriend Diane's car. That had never happened before."

"Did anyone ask why?" Stevie asked.

"*I* asked Diane why, lots of people asked her why. She said Todd's dad took the keys because he'd gotten a D on a major test. Like I said, I knew Todd. I rode in that car and I knew all about his life. His dad might have been pissed about a test, but his dad *never* took his keys."

"Didn't the police question him?" Stevie said.

"The police said they did. He said he was at home all night. His parents said the same thing, said they were all sitting in the living room watching TV."

"But they would have looked at the car."

"So you'd think," Paul said, smiling mirthlessly.

"No one *checked the car*?"

"After the accident, the Jeep wasn't in the driveway, where it normally would have been. No one saw that car for a *week*. And then, after a week, the police gave us some report, some form, that said that someone had gone out and looked at the Jeep and that it was fine and showed no signs of damage. It was dated the day after the accident, but no one—*no one*—thinks that's when they actually went over and looked at it. Again, this is a small town. Todd's father was the mayor. He said his son was home all night, so his son was home all night. The Jeep vanishes, the Jeep reappears a week later, and the police say the Jeep is fine. So the Jeep was fine."

"Did anyone keep the bike?" Stevie asked. "They could check for paint."

"I think about this all the time," Paul said, shaking his head. "This was 1978. No one knew to ask about things like that. Years later I went back and asked about the bike, but there's no record of what happened to it. It's gone. I assume they got rid of it. I mean, it was a hit-and-run in a small town. It was sad, but not a lot could be done about it. That was the general attitude."

"So if everyone knew it was Todd, what happened?"

"Well, there were basically three camps in town. There were people who thought Todd did it and supported us. There were some people who thought Todd was innocent—not many, but a few. Those people make me furious, but not as furious as the third group, which I think was the biggest group of all—the people who *knew* Todd did it and chose to do nothing. They *knew* Dana saw him. They *knew* the car was missing for a week. They knew it all, but they thought, *It was just an accident. Why ruin a kid's life over an accident?* They knew the mayor was lying, but they put it down to protecting his kid. Being a good *dad*. Those are the people I could never forgive."

He had to pause for a moment and shift in his seat. Stevie could see the weight he still felt, all these years later.

"I had to go back to school with the guy I knew had run my brother down and gotten away with it," he said. "I had to see him every day. I avoided him, and he avoided me. I was also dealing with the fact that I was a gay, closeted jock in the late 1970s, so I was trying to compensate and seem really . . . whatever straight and manly looked like then. It wasn't an easy time, but we got through it. My parents were amazing people. My dad wanted justice. Fairness. He didn't want revenge. He wasn't that kind of person. He wanted people to do the right thing. He never stopped trying to get someone to look into it. When the local police let him down, he tried the state police. When the state police couldn't help, he went to the local press. He talked to everyone who would listen. He would have kept going, but seven months later, Todd was dead."

He lifted his hands gently as if to say, *And that was that*.

"You were at the camp that night," Stevie said. "The night of the murders."

"I was, like every other teenager in town. Everyone knew that group was going out that night. It was an open secret when Eric was going to get the weed. Back then, it was both illegal and everywhere. I bought off him. Everyone did. Every week he would come around and ask you what you wanted, and you'd give him a few bucks, and he went somewhere and picked up the stash."

"Who would have known where that was?" Stevie asked.

"Everyone knew it was in the woods somewhere—the whole thing was kind of an open secret. The only part Eric really kept quiet was the exact spot it was hidden, to make sure it wasn't stolen. I mean, he took Sabrina out there, and she wasn't really in that group of people for very long. It was in all other respects a totally normal night. There were three lifeguards—Todd, Greg Dempsey, and Shawn Greenvale. Todd was out in the woods, Greg was on house arrest in one of the camp admin offices, so I went over to the lake house to hang out with Shawn. I would never have gone in with Todd there, or Greg, really. Shawn was learning guitar, and he was trying to learn how to play Led Zeppelin's 'Stairway to Heaven,' just like every other kid in the seventies. Susan checked on us. Then I went back to my bunk. I think I read a book or something for a while, then I went to sleep. I remember waking up to someone screaming the next morning. That's really all I know. Obviously, people looked at my family because of what happened to Michael, but we got lucky in one respect—our neighbors were over at our house all the time after Michael died, bringing us food, generally taking care of us and keeping us company. On the night of the murders, our neighbors, Mr. and Mrs. Atkins, were over for dinner and stayed to watch television. My mom took medication every night to help her sleep, and she went to bed around nine thirty. Mrs. Atkins went home, but Mr. Atkins stayed until two in the morning having beers with my dad on the porch and playing cards. At least that left my parents out of it. And I was with Shawn up until the time I went to bed. The other counselor saw me come in. So we were spared that mostly. People still looked at us funny sometimes, but everyone knew we had nothing to do with it."

"What do you think happened?" she asked.

"It was so chaotic," he said. "The police were in *way* over their heads. Everything was botched from the jump. First they said it was something to do with drugs, but no one was going to murder four people over a bag of grass at a summer camp—and then, on top of it all, *leave the grass there*. So then they started talking about the serial killer. That was the big angle, and I guess most people thought that must have been what happened, but that's fallen apart with time as well. So what do I think?"

He looked up and around at his town for a moment.

"There was too much wrong in our town," he said. "I knew it. I'd experienced it. I don't believe in curses. I'm not superstitious or anything like that. I just mean that ours was the kind of town where bad things could happen and everything could remain under the surface. Something about it always felt . . . personal. Local. Something about finding that spot in the woods, being there at the right time, something about the timing of it all."

He crumpled his empty coffee cup.

"Hope that helps," he said. "Honestly, I think too much time has passed. I don't think we'll ever know. Good luck anyway. I hope you get to enjoy camp at least."

He smiled and left Stevie alone with her thoughts, sitting in the shadow of John Barlow and his horse.

As Stevie left town and headed back to the camp, she had a thought. She swerved and looped down one of the side streets.

It maybe was tempting fate to visit the spot where someone had been struck down on a bicycle *on* a bicycle— especially when you were uncertain about your skills on said bicycle. But Stevie had never been one to take the prudent course. She looked up directions to the site on her phone. It was a nondescript corner—a four-way stop lined with low suburban houses. There were no sidewalks here, just lawn all the way up to the street. It was placid and tree-lined, and there was nothing to mark the spot where Michael Penhale had fallen on that December night. But it was easy to see how such an accident could have happened. At night, it would be dark here. There were no streetlights now that she could see, which meant there were probably none then either. A car barreling along, not stopping, or clipping the edge . . .

She leaned on the handlebars, looking carefully at the traffic around her.

As she rode back, she came up on the sharp curve that

turned down the road toward the local high school. This was where Patty said Greg Dempsey had crashed his motorcycle in the week after the accident. It was easy to see how he had done it. The turn was sharp, heavily bordered by a wall of trees and rock. If you didn't make it, you'd go right into it, as he had done. It was a death turn. It certainly seemed like others had made the same mistake, because there were remnants of old memorials—a decrepit cross, half-buried by tall grass, and a teddy bear coming apart from age and exposure.

Stevie looked down the length of the road and saw the comically large Liberty High sign. There was something eerie about being out here alone, even though it was just a roadside on a bright summer's day. A lot of bad things happened in this town in a short time between December 1977 and July 1978. Seven months or so of tragedy. It was grim.

She stuck very close to the grass edge of the road as she cycled back toward the town center, more than once getting off the bike and wheeling it by her side out of nervousness of someone coming along the road and striking her from behind. By the time she got back, Camp Sunny Pines had changed. The children had arrived. They came in cars and buses, in ones and twos. They came with their shiny backpacks and their scooter helmets. They came, screaming their high-pitched screams over the peace of the lake.

Obviously, this was no surprise, but still, the landscape was so totally altered by their presence that Stevie was confused. She had started to know this place, its long stretches of field that always smelled of fresh-cut grass, the little brown buildings, the outdoor pipes, the signs. It had been hers first, then shared with a few people her age, but now? The children were *everywhere*.

It suddenly occurred to her what she had actually signed up for.

She wandered past as parents slowly detached crying children from their legs, or watched as happy children ran off, unaware that their parents were still there.

Janelle and Nate were two of the last counselors left in the dining area. Breakfast was largely closed up and over, but Stevie managed to convince the woman behind the counter to peel back the plastic wrap and let her have some cold pancakes. She didn't even need silverware or a plate. She put them in a napkin and ate them by hand, dry. She snagged a cup of the substance that passed as orange juice and sat down with her friends. As soon as she did so, she felt a presence at her back. Nicole sat down on the bench next to her.

"You in town this morning?"

Stevie sipped some acidic orange juice–like drink and *hmm*ed.

"I know you have special permission from Carson, but the kids are here now."

"I know," Stevie said. Because she did know. She could *see* the children, who were being rounded up by some of the counselors and led off to their bunks in the distance.

"So that means you have a job to do."

"I am," Stevie said. "It took longer to get back from town . . ."

"I'm just saying," Nicole said, then said no more and got up and walked away.

"She likes you," Nate said.

"Don't worry about it," Janelle added. "I have it all covered."

She produced a binder, inside of which were a series of color-coded spreadsheets, each tagged with sticky notes.

"I've got all the crafts set up by age," she said. "Now, let's see . . ."

And that morning and afternoon, Stevie did see. They made samples of everything on Janelle's chart while attending multiple assemblies, where names were learned and rules were read and everyone was welcomed. The kids were, Stevie had to admit, fairly cute. At least, most of them were. The oldest ones were eleven, and they clearly viewed the counselors not quite as equals, but certainly as peers of a sort. Stevie kept glancing at her phone, checking for updates, and the one she was waiting for finally came around four.

I'm here, David wrote.

"See you later," Janelle said, smiling.

Even though Stevie had just been told not to leave, nothing was going to keep her away. She slipped away from one of the sessions, ducking between the cabins and hurrying across the fields, right on to the camp entrance, running over the road that split the camp from the park. She hustled down the paths until she reached the place where she could see the parking lot. There, standing by an old gray Nissan, was David.

David and Stevie had last been together at school every day in December. Fate (and a bunch of murders, and a senator) had separated them. There had been lots of video and endless pics, so they were constantly in each other's lives. But she had not seen him in the flesh since that cold, snowy morning up on the mountain in Vermont when they had come to take him away. She knew every element of his face from every angle a camera screen and her memory had captured, but seeing him here, fully assembled, scrambled her brain for a second. Had he always been that tall, that wiry, with tight coils of muscle? Was the shirt big, or was he thinner? Had those always been his legs? And his hair—dark, loose curls that had grown ragged and free at Ellingham were clipped a bit shorter now. She had known that, had seen the images, but now nothing quite fit.

But her body knew what to do. She ran up to him, jumping, and he caught her clumsily. They fell back against the car door, and she kissed him through his smile.

Yes. It all made sense again. The picture reassembled itself. The feel of her face in the hollow of his neck. The way his arms wrapped around her back and they curved into one another. His breath. His heartbeat. David.

Also, she was on her toes and they were both sliding sideways down the side of the car, and they stumbled apart, laughing.

"Have we met?" he said.

She squeezed him around the middle.

"Want to help me set up?" he said. "It would be good to have a place to sleep before the sun goes down."

Stevie and David removed a bunch of equipment from the back of the car—a tent, a cooler, a camp stove, two folding chairs, and a small folding table. They walked this to an empty area close to the lake edge.

"The sleeping bag is mine," he said. "I use that in some of the shadier places we stay in on the road. The rest of the stuff I rented from a place in town. I even rented a kayak from their boathouse. Now, how does one *tent* . . ."

The tent proved to be more challenging than it first appeared. There was a lot of staking things into the ground, and rolling in the right way, and inserting tubes in pockets and attaching. But somewhere around the two-hour mark, Stevie and David entered the tent, found it to be stable, and immediately tried out the floor.

This was so private. It was unlike anything Stevie had ever experienced, even in their rooms at Ellingham. This was wild, and separate. And they had come together here for a reason. David had come a long way to be with her. Her. That was the *only* reason he was here.

"I need to go soon," she said.

"Do you have to go back?"

She considered for a long minute. The temptation to stay exactly where she was, on this sleeping bag in this tent, was tremendous. On the other hand, Nicole had been unambiguous when it came to things like skipping out for the night.

"I have to go," she said.

"I'll walk you over," he said. "These are murder woods, right?"

"But then you'll be walking back alone. These are murder woods."

"Good point. Stay."

"Stop," she said, pushing him and not wanting him to stop at all. There immediately followed a round of making out, which ended only when Janelle called Stevie and told her that Nicole had been around, and curfew was falling fast.

"Really have to go," Stevie said. "Quick, quick go."

"Then I'll drive you," he said.

It was convenient to have a car here now. Stevie scrambled to make herself presentable again, still pulling on her socks and shoes as they left the tent. David drove her out of the park's parking lot and down the short stretch of road to the opening of the camp. He drove her almost the full way down the driveway, stopping before the entrance sign and the lights. Stevie hopped out into the warm night, waving and watching all the way, and ran to the cabin. When Nicole checked again, Stevie was on her bed, looking at her tablet like she had never been gone.

18

"GOOD MORNING, SUNNY PINES!"

Stevie blinked into her pillow and turned her head to look at Janelle. Janelle was not there. When Stevie gathered up her things and stepped outside to take her shower, she found a long line of children waiting to get into the bathroom. Janelle stood somewhere in the middle.

"This is bad," she said out loud.

The line was so long that Stevie ended up skipping the shower entirely and heading to breakfast with Janelle. Nate was already there, waiting for them. He picked up a tray and stepped into line between them, then followed them to a table.

"How was the first night?" Janelle asked.

"Do you see the kid with the red hair?" he replied. "Blue shirt? His name is Lucas. He is my nemesis."

"You can't have an eight-year-old nemesis," Janelle said, picking the grapes out of her fruit cup.

"Don't tell me how to live my life. He's . . . oh god. He's coming over here."

Lucas, the nemesis, had noticed Nate and was indeed

walking toward them, eating a sausage link with his fingers as he did so. He sat down at the table with them without asking permission and looked at Janelle and Stevie.

"Are you his friends?" he asked.

Lucas was direct.

"Yes," Janelle said sweetly. "We go to school together."

"I've read his book seven times," he said.

"Wow," Janelle replied. "That's a lot!"

Because it was a lot, and this kid was eight years old.

"Yeah," Lucas replied. "I'm still waiting for the next one. He says he's not done."

Nate's head shrank a bit into his shoulders, like a slowly descending elevator.

"Can you get him to finish it?" Lucas asked.

"I don't think so," Janelle replied. "But he will."

"I have ideas," Lucas went on.

"I wrote it," Nate said as Lucas wandered back to his bunk's table. "I don't *need* ideas."

"You kind of do," Janelle said under her breath.

"I'm in hell."

"He's eight," Janelle pointed out again. "And he read your book. That's nice."

Nate physically recoiled.

"You'll have more time soon," Janelle went on. "It's just another day or so until the other counselor gets here."

If Stevie thought that the morning had been an abrupt swing into action, she had no idea what the day had in store. The minute that the trays were cleared from the picnic tables, the entire camp moved over to the green, where they assembled in a ring around the flagpole, said the Pledge of Allegiance, and listened to some announcements. Then all the groups split off and activities began.

It was a good thing that Janelle was the way she was. The art pavilion was ready. In fact, it was likely that in the entire history of the camp, the art pavilion had never been as ready as it was on that morning. Janelle had waited her whole life for this moment, and now it was upon her. These children had no idea what they were in for. They would craft like they had never crafted in their lives.

For a few hours, there was no case, there was no David. There were pipe cleaners and markers and rounded scissors. Stevie had glue stuck on her fingertips and paint on her arms and had helped make half a dozen flapping owls out of paper plates, several beaded necklaces, some kind of thing with paint and feet. During the short periods that the pavilion was free of kids, Janelle was sweeping around, an ecstatic glow on her face, as she was combining her loves of crafting, organizing, and cleaning into one geode of pleasure. Lunch came and went, then the entire afternoon. Soon there was dinner, during which Nate hid behind one of the dining pavilion pillars before vanishing entirely, and then the first day was over.

"I'm going to get set up for tomorrow and talk to Vi," Janelle said. "Meet you back in the cabin."

Stevie called David on the way back.

"Finally," he said. "I wondered where you were."

"There are so many . . ." She looked around nervously. ". . . little kids."

"At a summer camp? Holy shit, we need to tell someone about this."

"Also," Stevie said, "I have to make sure the head of camp doesn't notice I'm gone. It may be harder now that kids are here. Kids see things, right?"

"How about I come there? I can kayak over. I was out paddling around on that side of the lake earlier, and there's a stream deep enough to ride over on. It'll only take a few minutes."

This was a good plan. It took a long time to go *around* the lake, but going *over* the lake was quick and easy, and there were plenty of places to dock the kayak or whatever it was you did with them. Stevie had a vague sense that maybe this was not allowed, but a vague sense is not a clear, definite sense.

A purple twilight fell over the lake as Stevie sat alone, on the far side of the lake house. She could hear kids singing in the distance, and fireflies floated and twinkled all around her. There was a magical quality to the night already, when David came gliding along the dark waters in a yellow plastic kayak, beaching it (maybe that was the verb) next to her on the rocky sand.

"Pretty good entrance," he said. "Right?"

Stevie could see at once that he had make an extra effort that night. His hair was tousled, but in a very artful way. He wore a fitted black T-shirt that she had never seen before, and she was immediately certain that he'd bought it just because it fit him in exactly the right ways. He was wearing long swim trunks and flip-flops, but even these seemed to be part of an ensemble. He bent down and whispered low in her ear, "Do you live around here?"

Stevie actually shivered. Her body went loose, like the screws all fell out at once. She grabbed his hand and took him around behind the bunks, weaving out of the way of any lights or people, until they reached her cabin. For one extremely fleeting second, she thought about Sabrina and the others slipping into the woods way back when, the thrill of getting away with something at this dark, warm place alongside the lake. She felt herself understand something about them, and the understanding was deep and profound, and also gone a few seconds later. They had reached the cabin and shut the door. In the next minute, they were on the camp bed. The next thing she knew, there was a firm pounding on the door, and her eyes ached from the light when she opened them. She sprang up, straightening out her clothes. There was nowhere to hide David; the cabin had no closets. So she had no choice but to open the door and take whatever was coming.

Nicole stood on the step, looking grim. She glanced inside and sighed deeply.

"Who are you?" she asked David, who was sitting on the edge of the bed and maybe looking a little too amused.

"I'm . . ." He looked at Stevie, as if she held the secret to his true identity, the one he had never been able to share with the world. ". . . David?"

"David who? How did you get here?"

"Kayak?"

"You need to go, now."

Nicole waited for him to get up and straighten his shirt.

"I'll walk you back to your kayak," she said. "You shouldn't be out on the lake after dark. Do you have a flashlight?"

"I, um . . ."

"Stevie, give him a flashlight."

Stevie did so, and David took it with a nervous smile. The two of them were about to leave, when Nicole drew her head back and looked above the door.

"Is that a camera?"

"I'm recording birds," Stevie said.

She had no idea why she said that. It's just what came out.

"I'll be back in a few minutes. We need to talk."

She was back a short time later, alone. Stevie had tidied the cabin in her absence, as if the situation might improve if her shower caddy was in better order.

"I want to be very clear about something," Nicole said. "I know you are here as Carson's guest, but if I catch you bringing people into the camp at any time unauthorized, you will be gone, Carson or no Carson. This is a camp. For children. Which means we have a duty of care. I'm responsible for every single person on these grounds. No strangers around the kids. No people kayaking at night on the lake. That lake can be dangerous. This is the one and only time I am going to say this."

This was all delivered in such a tone of serious, grinding

finality that Stevie was humiliated to her bone marrow.

"Yep," she said. "Got it. Yep."

As Nicole left, Janelle came in. Stevie could tell that Janelle had heard everything that had gone down, and she looked at Stevie wide-eyed as she shut the door.

"Fun night?" she asked.

"Kind of got busted with David."

"I know," she said, sounding maybe a little irritated. "I came back before. You didn't even hear me. I shut the door and backed out. I saw Nicole coming, but she was ahead of me and I couldn't get to the door in time. I texted you, but . . ."

Stevie looked over and saw that there were seven texts from Janelle waiting to be read. "Sorry."

"Can you . . . ask next time? Or tell me? Except, I don't think there will be a next time, because she just handed you your ass. But you know what I mean. If it were me and Vi, I'd tell you."

"Sorry," Stevie said again, and she was.

"It's okay." Janelle went to her bureau and started going through her various creams and washes to get ready for the night. Her tone indicated that it wasn't entirely okay yet, but it would be. After a few minutes, she turned to Stevie.

"Vietnam is *far*," Janelle said. "We don't all have people to sneak into our cabins at night."

Stevie nodded sympathetically.

"Any chance you have two thousand dollars I can borrow for a plane ticket?" Janelle asked.

"I've got a punch card for a free coffee that's almost full."
Janelle let out a long sigh.

"Only a little while until we're back at school," Stevie said.

"Now I know how Nate feels," Janelle replied. "Nothing is longer than a little while."

The next morning at breakfast, Stevie averted her eyes as they passed Nicole on the way in. Nate was already there when they arrived, avoiding his bunk's table and skulking in the corner with a tray of pancakes and bacon.

"I thought you'd never get here," he said, sitting down with them.

"Don't you have to be over there?" Janelle asked.

Lucas peered up when he saw Nate. Nate slouched over his tray.

"All night," he said. "All. Night. He talked about my book. Mostly, what he thought was wrong with it. And where is the second one? He knows more about that book than I do. He is a *sentient internet comment*."

"He is *eight years old*," Janelle pointed out again.

"You don't understand," Nate said, shaking his head. "Where is this other counselor? Why isn't he better? It was supposed to be, like, one day."

"Nicole said a few days," Janelle said, belying her understanding of the night before.

"I did not sign up for this."

Stevie ate bacon and watched her friends squabble. She had missed them so much when they were all apart.

"Your friend is here," Nate said. "Captain Big Box. Box Bag. Bag Boss."

Stevie turned to look in the direction Nate was facing. Sure enough, Carson was speed-walking through the patch of grass bordering the dining pavilion, weaving his way through the clumps of children, heading toward their table. He looked like he was on a mission, his brow furrowed.

"Oh god," Stevie said. "What does he want? Nicole's going to yell at me again for bringing weirdos to the camp, even if that one does own it."

Nate looked like he wanted an explanation about that, immediately, but Carson was upon them. He squatted down at the end of their table.

"I need to talk to you," he said to Stevie in a low, breathless voice.

Stevie looked at her rapidly cooling pancakes. "Could I finish . . ."

He shook his head. "No time."

"Podcasts sleep for no one," Nate said.

Stevie sawed into the pancake stack in a desperate attempt to get them into her mouth.

"Listen," he said, "Allison Abbott is dead."

19

Stevie froze, a forkful of cold pancake inches from her mouth.

"What?" she asked.

"Arrowhead Point," Carson said. "She fell during her morning run."

Stevie felt everything slowly spin away from her. She'd just seen Allison, just gone on that morning run with her, seen that spot on Arrowhead Point, where all of Lake Wonder Falls spread out below in a glorious display.

"We have to go *now*," Carson said.

"To do what?" Nate asked.

Stevie did not need an explanation. She had to go, to try to see, to understand. She set her fork and knife down automatically and grabbed her phone and bag. They were halfway across the dining area when Nicole stopped them.

"What's up?" she said to Carson. "What are you doing?"

"I need Stevie."

"She's got a job here."

"Not today," he said.

He and Stevie continued on before Nicole could make any reply and were soon in the Tesla. A minute later, they were tearing (or at least going at a moderate speed in a more or less responsible manner in a nearly silent electric car) out of camp. They drove out of the main entrance and turned toward the public side of the lake. Up ahead, Stevie could see a police car blocking the entrance road by the ranger check-in cabin.

"How did you find out?" she asked numbly.

"I was out doing walking meditation this morning," he said. "Two police cars and an ambulance went by, going toward the lake. So I ran in that direction. I tried to go in, but one of the cops stopped me on the path. I ran home and got a drone to have a look and a listen. I got some footage, but I couldn't get that close . . ."

Stevie turned in disgust, but found she had nothing to say. The shock was still too strong and her head was fuzzy.

"They're closing off the main entrances," Carson said, continuing past the police cars. "But we can get in through the woods."

Her phone buzzed. A text from David appeared:

Come over when you can.

David was here for five days. All their time for the summer. What was going to happen now? She couldn't think about it. Her head was swirling. She texted back.

Is there anything weird going on there this morning?

No, he replied. Why?

That made some sense. The lake was big, and Arrowhead

Point was at the far end. David was more near the middle, by Point 23.

Carson slid the Tesla to a stop on the side of the road.

"Here," he said, handing her a tiny microphone. "Better audio for your phone. You go in through here and see if you can record any witnesses. I'm going to try to sneak in closer near Arrowhead Point and get video footage."

Stevie didn't actually care about what Carson was doing. She needed to get into the woods and see and hear for herself what had happened to Allison. She took the microphone and hopped out of the car, sprinting across the quiet country lane. Once she was actually in the woods, her phone lost all sense of where she was located. It put her position as either in the road or in the middle of the lake. So she picked her way through the trees until she could see the glint of the water, and then she found one of the paths that wound around the lake. She walked in the direction of Arrowhead Point, trying to keep out of sight of any police or emergency personnel that might be around. But she saw no one except a woman walking her dog, who seemed to have no idea that anything was going on. Strange how someone could die in these woods and everything would be normal and peaceful. These woods ate people up and were quiet about it.

Stevie felt cold despite the heat. She pressed on, in a haze, finding her way on the slatted-wood bridges over the hollows and the silent wood chips, always keeping the lake on her left-hand side, watching it out of one eye, scanning for activity.

Finally, she heard the sound of people talking up ahead.

240

She left the path and wove through the trees until she could see a small group of older women gathered on a bit of sandy beach, speaking in a huddle. From here, she could see the rise of Arrowhead Point, and maybe some people walking around on top, but not much else. She slipped out of the trees, making a bit of noise so she didn't just pop out of nowhere and scare these strangers. After fitting the microphone into the jack of her phone and tucking it as far into her pocket as she could, she tried to act like she was out taking a casual walk.

"Did something happen?" she said, approaching them and squinting up at the point.

"Woman fell," said one of the swimmers. "From up there." She nodded toward Arrowhead Point.

"She just . . . fell?"

"We heard a scream and she kind of tumbled off . . ."

"Like she tripped," said another swimmer.

"Yeah, she must have tripped."

This was why you weren't supposed to let witnesses talk to one another before you spoke to them—when people all see something together and discuss it, details will start to merge. All that seemed to be known was that Allison had screamed and fallen, but the story had already become that she had tripped.

"Barbara—she's Barbara—she went back to the dock because her shorts were close to the edge and she could get her phone, and I went up to wait for the police. Our friends swam over to try to help, but . . ."

"It was too late," Barbara said.

"She fell onto those rocks. No one would survive that."

"Was there anyone else up there?" Stevie said.

"You mean, did someone push her?" Barbara said. "Oh god. No. There was no one. We would have seen. We could see her clearly. There was no one up there but her. She was screaming. She must have tripped."

"She must have tripped," the woman who was not Barbara repeated sadly.

Stevie decided not to press Barbara and not-Barbara any further. They were upset, and they had conveyed what they had witnessed—a woman screaming and tumbling off a rocky point.

Not *a* woman. Allison Abbott. The librarian, the archivist of her sister's life. The runner. The person who had been through so much, who loved her sister so fiercely.

Stevie felt nauseous and turned back into the woods, walking the way she had come, taking big gulps of soft pine-scented air, trying to let the curtain of greens and browns and pinpoint sunlight soothe her.

Screaming. Tumbling. Her brain, fueled by thousands of hours of absorbing true and fictional crime, painted the scene in vivid detail.

Then the rush came—the flush of anxiety and panic, the one that made the trees loom and the ground sinister. The one that twisted the morning into something that mocked her and separated her from all that was familiar.

"No," she said out loud, stopping. She closed her eyes and practiced her breathing, in slowly, holding, releasing even slower. Breathe. Exhale. She let the world wobble and fall away for a moment.

When she opened her eyes again, all had not been fixed in its entirety, but things were a bit more stable. And she was going somewhere that would help. She tramped on, passing several camping areas, until she finally saw some tents she recognized, and beyond them, the red one she was looking for. She jogged up to it, then wasn't sure what to do for a moment. You can't knock on a tent.

"Hey," she said, her voice coming out rushed. "Hey?"

There was a stirring within.

"Stevie?" said a sleepy voice.

A shuffling. Then the zipper opened itself from the inside and a tousled-haired David in a T-shirt and shorts peered out. He smiled, but this faded when he saw her face.

"What's wrong?"

Stevie sat down in one of the portable camping chairs outside the tent and stared at the ground for a moment.

"Allison Abbott is dead."

"Allison . . . Abbott?" he said, ducking to get out of the tent. "Who is Allison Abbott?"

"Sabrina's sister. The librarian. She fell off the point at the top of the lake. Arrowhead Point."

"Oh shit," he said, rubbing at his jaw, taking this in. He didn't know Allison or Arrowhead Point, but he knew Stevie, and he knew pain and confusion. He looked around for a moment, then opened a cooler and pulled out a can of coffee.

"You want this?" he said, offering her the can.

Stevie took it. He dragged over another folding chair and sat close to her.

"You okay?" he asked. He was asking that a lot now.

"I don't understand," she said.

"Neither do I, but I have no idea what's going on."

She had explained some of the case to him, but not every detail of what she had done here. The cool parts, of course, like busting Carson and things like that, but not what it felt like to be in Allison's house, surrounded by Sabrina's things. Not the feeling of being able to give Allison something her sister had made, however minor.

David studied her face for a moment.

"Someone's died," he said. "Someone connected to a murder that happened here. We've been here before."

He meant back at Ellingham, when someone had died at a place that was so famous for murder. She took a sip of the coffee, which was bitter and strong. She didn't love the taste, but it had a clarifying effect, so she gulped it down. "Your kayak," she said. "Can it fit two people?"

"Just one. They have canoes, though. They can fit up to three."

"Then we need to get one."

David didn't bother changing out of his sleeping clothes. He found a pair of shoes, and they walked to the little boat rental place a bit farther in, closer to Sunny Pines, and took possession of a canoe. When they helped lift it down and push it along the sand, it seemed much larger than Stevie thought it would be. And as they got it into the water, it was far wobblier than she'd hoped. But she was focused and got herself into the bench seat and worked out how to paddle. After a few minutes of confused splashing and going in circles, they were drifting out onto the placid waters of Lake Wonder Falls and headed toward Arrowhead Point. The police were moving people away from the shoreline under the peak, and they had hung a tarp over the area where Allison had landed so that nobody could view the body. But nothing stopped them from drifting closer on the water. A few people were doing the same—watching from canoes or rafts or floating tubes. Not that there was much to see. The tarp screened off most of the action. A few police officers were on the edge of the point, examining it. Stevie watched this activity for some time in silence, as David paddled a bit to keep them as stationary as possible. One of the police officers crawled along the point, then got up and walked back to the path. Presumably they would look for any sign of what had caused Allison to fall.

"I don't get it," Stevie finally said.

"I'm not sure what there is to get."

"You don't understand what I saw at her house," Stevie replied. "Allison was *precise*. She made *Janelle* look disorganized. Everything exactly in the right place. Schedules followed to the minute. It was part of her coping mechanism to deal with her sister's death. She ran that path at the exact same time every day. I went with her. She knew every bump on the ground. I stood on the point with her. She warned me about how it tapered."

"It's still a steep edge. People can fall off steep edges."

"No," she said firmly. "It wasn't an accident."

"You never think it's an accident."

It was true that there had been several "accidents" at Ellingham Academy that Stevie didn't think were accidents. The thing was—she'd been right about those.

She was right now.

Stevie watched a blue dragonfly buzz the surface of the pond. The water was still, and though covered in a thin green algae haze, it managed to reflect the sky in patches and was somehow more beautiful for what marred it. If she didn't see the police working on the rocks, she would never have believed that anything could happen here.

Carson called several times, and Stevie pushed them all to voicemail. She leaned back in the canoe and tried to understand how, somewhere between the puffy clouds above and their reflections below, Allison Abbott had ceased to exist.

20

THE REST OF THE DAY THAT ALLISON DIED SLIPPED PAST IN A STRANGE haze. Stevie went through the motions at the art pavilion, her brain churning. By dinner, she was tired from her circular thinking. She sat, her untouched food in front of her, repeating the story to Nate and Janelle for what had to have been the fifteenth time.

"From everything you're saying, it really sounds like she fell," Janelle said. "You know, most car accidents happen on roads people know the best. People go into autopilot and feel like they don't have to pay as much attention. She could have been preoccupied."

"No," Stevie said again. "Something's not right."

"Did anything seem off about her when you gave her the list?" Janelle asked.

"No. She was happy to get it."

She could tell from their expressions that, like David, they knew Stevie was quick to say that something was not an accident. They also knew better than to voice this in the state Stevie was in. She walked back to their cabin, feeling lightheaded and sleepy. She called David.

"Hey," she said.

"You sound weird."

"Just tired," she said.

"The kayak thing didn't work out so well. Do you want to walk over and I'll meet you by the path?"

Stevie rubbed her face with her hand. She had so little time with David—every day counted—but she was leaden with exhaustion. Something about Allison's death had knocked her sideways.

"I think I need to sleep," she said.

She heard him sigh.

"Get some rest," he said. "I'll see you tomorrow?"

"Tomorrow," she said, going up the steps to her cabin.

Once she got inside, she flopped onto her bed, not even bothering to take off her shoes. It was only seven in the evening—still light out—but Stevie was shutting down. She closed her eyes, letting the cabin and the camp and the confusion of the day slip away. Just as she was nodding off, her phone rang. It was an unknown local number.

"Is this Stephanie Bell?" said a woman's voice.

"Yes?"

"My name is Susan Marks," she said. "I used to run the camp when it was Wonder Falls."

Stevie knew the name and sat up.

"Allison . . ." The woman sounded pained. "Allison Abbott gave me your name and said I should contact you. As you knew her, I thought I should let you know . . ."

"I know," Stevie said softly.

Susan was silent in acknowledgment.

"She asked me to talk to you about what happened here, before. . . . I was hesitant, but I want to honor her wishes. If you'd like to speak to me."

"Definitely," Stevie said. "Yes. Could I . . . come to town? In the morning?"

"Fine. Come by any time after eight."

After giving Stevie her address, Susan Marks hung up. Stevie texted this update to David, then slipped into a deep, unbroken sleep.

"So who is it we're going to see?" David asked as they pulled out of the camp the next morning.

David had come in the old gray Nissan to take Stevie into town, thus sparing her from the treacherous and sweaty bike ride. Stevie had made a show of going over to the art pavilion, but left as soon as Nicole had done the morning rounds. The day was almost unbearably humid. The air-conditioning in the car didn't work, so they had the windows open. The morning was bright, but the sun shone through a haze of cloud. Some kind of wild summer weather was afoot.

The twelve hours of sleep Stevie had gotten seemed to have revived her. Her body had decided to shut down completely and reboot, and now she was alert, maybe even a little hyper. Sometimes anxiety did that—it could slow you down or speed you up.

"Susan Marks," she said. "She was the head of the camp in 1978."

"What am I supposed to be doing during this interrogation? When do I get to pound my fist on the desk? Or am I the one who offers the coffee? You tell me who I'm supposed to be."

"I'm not interrogating anyone," she said.

It was kind of weird being in a car with David. No one had a car at Ellingham. They had been in all kinds of places and spaces together there. They'd lived in a small dorm house together, cozy little Minerva, with its fireplace and old sofas. They'd been in each other's rooms, eaten meals together, seen each other from dawn to dusk. They'd occupied closets together, slept in a ballroom, and crept side by side through tunnels and hidden spaces underground.

So a car should not have been a big deal. And yet, she found herself staring at his profile as he drove, one hand on the wheel, the other casually dangling partway out the window. The air knocked his wavy hair back from his forehead. He'd gotten a bit of a tan on the road, an uneven one.

Here was the thing about romantic feelings—the sensation was incredible, like a warm flood through every highway and byway of her body. Every good chemical she could produce turned up, like some kind of bountiful harvest. But the feelings and the chemicals blocked out everything else. They dulled logic and sense and focus. They made everything else seem kind of irrelevant and time started to move jerkily—too fast, then too slow. And they came on with no advance warning, like now, watching him drive. Everything went loose, and all the orderly thoughts in her brain were now just a bag of parts. She wanted to lean over, to kiss him on the soft hollow of his cheek, to pull over and forget going to see Susan. Susan could wait. They could go into the woods. . . .

"You're staring at me," he said, not turning his gaze. "Are you about to bite my face or something?"

"Yes," she said.

"Thought so."

She took a long gulp of thick air and told herself to get it together. David was smiling a knowing smile, like he knew precisely what was going on in her head.

They drove past Liberty High, with its giant blue billboard.

"They should get a bigger sign," David said. "That one is too subtle."

"I can barely see it," Stevie said.

"Small towns really love their high schools. They seem to scream about them. Why do you think that is?"

"People love to scream."

"That's probably it," he said, turning to her with a wolfish grin. "I know I do."

Focus, she told herself. They were almost there.

Susan Marks lived in the center of town, on one of the side streets off the main road. They parked by the library and the green. Barlow Corners was quiet but not completely still. There were a few people going in and out of the shops. There were people in the Sunshine Bakery with coffee. Stevie followed the map on her phone, which guided them through the painfully quaint lanes that trailed back behind the main drag. The roads here were one lane only, with tidy little Victorian houses groaning under the weight of flower baskets, decorative flags, and wicker porch furniture. Susan's was the last one on this particular lane. She had fewer flags, but many more flowers and shrubs.

A woman with sharply cut gray hair was on her knees in a flower bed in front of the house. As Stevie and David turned down her path, she rose and dusted off her knees. Susan Marks was in her midseventies, and despite a little stiffness as she stood, she had the look of someone who did an hour of yoga a day to warm up for the second hour of yoga she did each day.

"Stevie," she said. She had the firm, commanding tone of someone who was used to doing roll call. "And you are?"

"Her assistant," David said. "The one that asks the stupid questions."

"Watson, huh?"

"That's me," David replied, smiling.

"It's going to be a hot one today, so I wanted to finish up some of this weeding early. Come on in."

She marched inside, and Stevie and David followed. The inside of the house was almost as plant heavy as the outside, with ferns and greenery of all sorts in dozens of pots. Two orange cats sat on a perch in a sunny window, lazily entwined around each other. There was a framed collage of photos of

Susan and another woman. Stevie paused a moment to look at them.

"My wife," Susan said, noting where Stevie was looking. "Magda. She passed away eight years ago."

"Oh, I'm . . ."

"It's all right," Susan said. "I didn't say it to make you feel bad. She was the nurse at the camp. That's where we met. There are good memories of the camp too. She was also an artist. All of these are hers."

Susan indicated the shelves and surfaces full of pottery. Stevie didn't know much about whether pottery was good or bad, but these seemed nice enough to her, and the colors were vibrant.

They were led to the kitchen, which was decorated in a surprising pink color. Pink everything—walls, mixer, towels, floor mats.

"Magda liked a pink kitchen," Susan explained. "Sit down."

They did as they were told, and Susan put mugs of coffee in front of them.

"I'm sorry about Allison," Stevie said.

"So am I," Susan replied. "It's a damn shame. Horrific. So many terrible things have happened here. She had been through so much and did so well. I used to stop at the same spot on my morning runs. A lot of people do. It's got the best view. It's a bad place to fall from. . . ."

"She seemed really careful to me," Stevie said.

"Yes . . ." Susan's gaze drifted a bit. "She was. Very careful. Not like her to make a mistake like that. People do, of course. Her head must have been somewhere else."

Susan sighed deeply and seemed to collect herself somewhere in the bottom of her coffee cup.

"So," she said, "why is it you—or that person at the event the other night—think you can solve this case when no one else has?"

"I don't know if I can," Stevie said. "It's more that we're trying to tell the story. . . ."

"People know the story," Susan replied. "People have been coming here for years, making their shows, writing their books, making money off a tragedy. How are you different?"

"She's pretty good," David said, nodding at Stevie. "Never count her out. She succeeds where others fail. And she's not about money."

Stevie felt herself flush. This conversation had gotten off to a very weird start and was perhaps slipping out of her control. Susan regarded David with interest.

"And does she pay you to say that?" she joked dryly.

"Me? Oh yeah. I'm *really* cheap."

Susan smirked and nodded. "I looked you up," she said to Stevie. "And I know you were okay with Allison, so I suppose there's no harm in going over things again. Where do you want me to start?"

Susan Marks was all business, so Stevie would be the same. She confirmed that it was all right to record, which got a terse nod but a slightly disapproving look.

"I guess . . ." She reminded herself to stop saying things like that. She had to sound more like she knew what she was doing. "How did you end up at Camp Wonder Falls?"

"Back in the seventies, I was the head of health and physical education at Liberty High," Susan said. "I taught during the school year, and then there was an opening to run the camp in the summer and I took it. It suited me—I like to keep busy, and the camp had so many sports and activities to manage. That summer was my fifth one in the job."

"So you knew all the . . . everyone involved . . . well?"

"Oh, I knew them all," Susan replied. "Todd, Diane, Eric, Sabrina . . . they were all my students, all grew up in town. This town is a bit like a family, but even families . . ."

She let that statement hang for a moment.

"You didn't like all of them," Stevie said, trying to read Susan's expression.

"No. I didn't like all of them. I never like to say kids are rotten, but . . . Todd Cooper, he was a rotten kid. Charming. Polite to your face, always. But he was the son of the mayor, who was himself—pardon my French—a real son of a bitch."

"Do you think Todd had anything to do with Michael Penhale's death?" Stevie asked.

"Oh, I absolutely think so," she said, her voice getting louder and her expression more animated. "I don't think anyone doubts that. He was guilty as sin, and everyone knew it. That was the shame of our town. It was a disgrace, and that no-good sheriff we had did nothing, just like he did nothing when the murders happened. Then there was Diane

255

McClure. You know, I liked Diane. She was a good kid, deep down. Her parents owned the Dairy Duchess, the ice cream place across the way. But she was a hard nut. Tough. Good athlete. I tried more than once to get her to join the track team, but she never would. I think Diane liked a good time and bad boys. Todd was a bad boy. I was unhappy to see those two together, but it wasn't a surprise."

"What about Sabrina?" Stevie said. "No one seems to understand why she was there."

"Sabrina was everything people say she was. She was bright as hell. Hardworking. Nice kid. Really nice kid. She would have left town, done something special with her life. Her parents put a lot of pressure on her to be perfect, and that concerned me sometimes. She was hard on herself. I think she was probably trying to cut loose a little that summer, after graduation. She was starting to hang around with Eric Wilde. . . ." She trailed off. "Eric Wilde," she said, smiling. "I knew him since he was a little boy. His father taught at the school, and his mom was the librarian in town. He was smart, funny. He was also mischievous, but not in a malicious way. It didn't exactly surprise me to find out he was the one supplying the pot to the camp. There's less of a stigma about that now—it's legal here—but at the time, it was a bigger deal. When we found him on that path, it was . . ."

She sighed deeply and reached down to pet the orange cat who had come over and stretched up on his hind legs for a head scratch.

"Talking about it gets easier with time, but the feeling

never goes away completely. Which is good, I suppose. It means it matters. It *should* matter. I was in charge. I ran that camp. I was responsible for them. No one ever blamed me, which I think was really generous. I don't know where I stand on blaming myself. I ran a tight ship, for the time. You have to understand, never in a million years did we think anything like this could happen. Maybe it was a more innocent time. I'm not sure. There's more monitoring now. Kids don't play unsupervised. Everyone has a phone. Back then, even little kids went out to play on their own, sometimes all day. Kids rode their bikes all around town. I was considered a hardass for doing spot bed checks and having a lot of rules. So people in town were very good to me after it happened. No one thought I'd failed when those kids went out to the woods. Because that's what kids did back then. We expected them to, to a degree. More coffee?"

Without waiting for a reply, she took the mugs and went to the counter to refill them.

"The night of the murders was very normal," she went on as she put the mugs into her coffee machine. "It was a few days after the Fourth of July. Dinner was served between five and six, and then from six to eight the kids were allowed to play outside, with the counselors supervising them. At eight, everyone returned to their bunks for the night. One counselor always had to be present, but the other could have some free time. I'd walk around the camp at night, generally checking on things. Our biggest concern was the lake, that a camper or a counselor might try to swim at night and drown. That's why we had the lifeguards stay in the lake house, and one of them was always up and around at night. So that night I stopped by the lake house and Paul and Shawn were in there. They were playing guitar, trying to learn that song that was all the rage—'Stairway to Heaven.' God, they played that song endlessly. I continued around the camp doing a few spot checks on bunks, then I returned to my cabin to go over notes for the day and set up for the next. I would often be awoken during the night for some reason or other, a sick camper or kids getting upset about a snake or something, but nobody came that night. It was quiet."

She put fresh cups of coffee in front of Stevie and David, who now had the orange cat on his lap, sniffing his face.

"And the next day?" Stevie said.

"I'd just made the wake-up announcement," Susan said, her gaze drifting as she remembered. "I was going over the schedule, and I heard a scream. It was one of those noises—you don't hear them often in life, thankfully—where you know something terrible has happened. I went to find the source of it. As I walked, I called Magda on the walkie. She'd heard it too and was also heading in that direction. We both got to the path that led to the theater and the archery range. It was Brandy Clark who'd screamed. I'll never forget her face; she'd gone completely gray. She pointed, and we went up the path and saw Eric. How detailed do you want me to get?"

She fixed Stevie with a firm look. David raised his eyebrows a bit.

"As detailed as you want," Stevie said. "It's okay."

"Well, this isn't about being salacious. I give details because people should know this was *brutal*. Those kids died terribly. Eric had big, curly blond hair. I could see that hair of his as we walked toward him. I remember—because we didn't know what it was precisely that we were looking at— but Magda and I slowed a bit, then we ran. He was facedown. Cold to the touch. He had a wound on the back of his head— dark, bloody, coagulated. Then we saw the stab wounds."

She took a moment as the cat climbed into her lap and immediately coiled up and began purring loudly.

"So that was around seven forty-five in the morning. We had a serious situation on our hands. At that point, of course, we had no idea the extent of it. We knew Eric had been killed, and we had to get all the kids and counselors in order and make sure everyone was safe, and then get them away from the area. Patty Horne came running up and asked about the others—that's when we found out there were more missing kids. When I heard the names—Todd and Diane, that made sense to me. But the third was Sabrina Abbott, and that didn't. I suppose Patty would have been with them, but she was in trouble and had to stay in the infirmary. We'd caught her and her boyfriend up to some—romantic business. Kids could have seen them. Magda had terrible insomnia. It came in very handy. Whenever we had a staff member who broke the rules, we would have them sleep on one of the infirmary cots and Magda would keep an eye on them. Because there were two of them, I made Greg spend the nights at home. That punishment also worked well because it put a burden on the other counselors. People were less likely to break the rules if it made things hard for all their friends as well. There was social pressure not to do that. Anyway, once we found out there were three more missing, the police went out in the woods to search. You know the rest about what they found."

She inhaled through her nose, as if it was all happening again in front of her.

"Obviously, camp didn't continue that year. We had to make a few hundred calls, get everyone home. I don't think I slept much that week. As I said, I didn't have a great deal of faith in our local sheriff. As soon as they saw there was pot there, he assumed that it was a drug-related case. Then the FBI came in some time that week, I think, when the talk of the Woodsman started. I mean, it was complete chaos. Everyone was terrified that the woods were full of murderous drug dealers or serial killers."

Susan wrinkled her nose in a way that indicated she had not shared those feelings.

"It didn't end there," she went on. "Patty's boyfriend, Greg, the one I said she'd been caught with? You know he died that week as well. All the kids had gathered on the playing field behind the school the night the town had a gathering. I was driving over in that direction. I remember Patty was standing at the end of the school driveway, crying and waving a flashlight around, really upset and beside herself. I was about to pull in and stop to check on her, and there was a kind of lightning flash up ahead as Greg crashed. I didn't know what it was at the time. That's how that week was, horror upon horror."

"What do you think happened?" Stevie said.

"You don't know what to think when four teenagers are stabbed to death in the woods. It makes no sense, so you assume it must be someone sick, some stranger, something like that. My gut always told me it had nothing to do with drugs or serial killers, but the truth is, I have absolutely no idea what happened in the woods that night. It was so barbaric, so confusing."

"So," Stevie said, "if not drugs or a serial killer . . ."

"I don't know," Susan said again, and her tone was final. She was done. Stevie glanced over at David, who drained his coffee in one gulp.

"One last thing," Stevie said. "Sabrina's diary . . ."

"Oh yes. Allison has been . . . Allison wanted that diary for years. She asked me about it many times. I packed up Sabrina's things for the family, but it wasn't there."

"Could someone have taken it?"

"Of course," Susan said, as if this was a stupid question, which it kind of was. Anyone can take anything.

"I mean," Stevie said, "it sounds like Sabrina hid it to keep campers from reading it."

"I had hundreds of hysterical kids and parents to take care of," Susan said. "It took a few days—some people had gone on vacation, things like that. I got every single one of those kids packed up and home. Then I spent two full days packing up everything those four brought to camp. I made sure their parents got every last thing, neat and packed with care. Well, almost every last thing. Anything like cigarettes, drug related—I put those things in separate boxes."

"Didn't the police go through their things first?"

"No," Susan said, smirking. "Never bothered to go through their stuff in their cabins. I asked them several times if they wanted to search the bunks, but they had no interest."

"Do you still have the boxes?" Stevie asked.

"No. Eventually, maybe fifteen years later, the police asked for them. The whole investigation was a mess. But to answer your question, no. I cleaned out every inch of Sabrina's cabin. The diary was not there. I told Allison that, and I'm telling you that."

She picked up the cat, who was circling her ankles.

"Good luck," she said. "It would be nice if someone *did* solve this case. I'd like to see whatever bastard did this get everything they deserve. We all would."

21

"LEARN ANYTHING?" DAVID ASKED AS THEY HEADED BACK TO THE CAR.

Stevie stuffed her hands into the pockets of her shorts and concentrated on the cracks in the sidewalk.

"Don't know," Stevie said. "I mean, on the surface it was all stuff that's in all the articles. But there was something—I don't know what. Something was weird."

"Weird like she was involved?"

"No," she said, turning toward him. "I mean, I don't know, but I don't *think* so? Something's sticking out. There's something about it that . . ."

Sometimes Stevie could see thoughts in her head—like little blocks, objects that arranged themselves, stuck themselves together. The words that Susan had said were moving around in a more or less orderly fashion, but one thing was trying to wriggle free. What was it . . . ?

"On another note," David said, "you know, in September . . ."

"Huh?"

"September."

"What about September?" she said. All the thoughts vanished into the corners of her mind, like mice scurrying away when a person turned on the light and came into the room. She frowned in annoyance.

"What?" he said. "Why are you making that face?"

"What about September? What are you talking about?"

"I'm saying that in September, it'll be, you know, school."

Stevie waited for clarification on this scintillating fact. She had been so close to placing her thought. Why did he have to start talking about school? School was far in the distance.

"Well," he said, noting her irritation and responding with his infuriating smile, "you'll be back on the mountaintop, and . . ."

Stevie turned her focus back to the street they were walking down. Sleepy, sunny Barlow Corners. Everything here was so snug in this town center. There was the library, sitting proudly on the green, with its stupid statue. There was the Sunshine Bakery and the Dairy Duchess. . . . There was the cute little store full of household novelties and gifts, like funny socks and mugs with inspirational sayings. . . . There was Dr. Penhale's veterinary office . . . the drugstore . . . the dentist's office, and Shawn Greenvale stepping out of the door. . . .

Shawn Greenvale.

". . . and you'll be busy, I don't know, maybe murdering someone in the woods, and . . ."

David was still going on about school. Stevie grabbed his arm and tugged it.

"Up there," she said. "That guy. The one in the blue shirt walking toward the truck. That's Shawn Greenvale."

"Shawn . . ."

"Sabrina Abbott's ex-boyfriend," Stevie said, already quickening her pace. Shawn had been on her list. Here was her moment. She race-walked along, trying not to draw attention to herself while making sure that Shawn did not get away before she caught up to him. She had to run the last half block.

"Excuse me!" She was out of breath way too quickly. Susan Marks, former phys ed teacher, would not have been impressed with her lung capacity. "Shawn?"

The man looked up at the blond, sweating girl dressed in all black who hurried up to him and was now pressing her palms into the hood of his truck and the lanky boy who followed behind her.

"My name is Stevie Bell and . . ."

"I know who you are." His tone wasn't warm or inviting.

"I was wondering if I could talk to you."

"About what?" he asked.

"About what happened here. In 1978. I just spoke to Susan Marks and . . ."

He reached into his car and took the silver sun blocker off the windshield, folded it, and threw it into the back seat.

"No," he said.

"I . . ."

"No," he said again.

Stevie bit her top lip, silencing herself. Shawn began to get into the truck. He was going to go away, and her chance would be gone. She had to try. She maneuvered herself a bit closer to the opening of the door, so it would be harder to shut it without swiping her.

"I don't want to bother you," she said quickly.

"Then don't," Shawn said shortly. "Could you move back, please?"

Stevie stepped away. He closed the truck door and drove off. Stevie rubbed at her face, annoyed with herself. She should have waited, taken her time, gotten a proper introduction—not just run down the street yelling his name.

"I think he likes you," David said. "It's because you play coy."

She groaned and pressed the heels of her hands into her eyes.

"Was he important?" David asked.

She nodded. He reached over and took her wrists, gently peeling her hands from her face.

"Live and learn," he said. "It's fine."

It wasn't, but there was nothing she could do about it now. Whatever she had been thinking about Susan was long gone, and Shawn was now up the road. She was back in the moment, with David.

"What were you saying about school?" she said.

A strange half smile spread across David's lips.

"Nothing," he said. "Just making conversation."

When David dropped Stevie back at camp, the day was well underway, and it was punishingly hot. By the time she walked from the parking lot to the art pavilion, she was drenched in sweat. Janelle was holding court over a group of nine-year-olds who were filling bottles with colored sand under her watchful gaze. Stevie made her way around the room, trying to figure out how to assist, but there wasn't much to explain about putting sand in bottles. So she planted herself at an empty table and pulled out her phone to listen to the recording she had made of the conversation with Susan. She began to jot the important points down.

- nothing special about night before
- Paul and Shawn in lake house playing Stairway to Heaven
- a scream
- ran, met Magda McMurphy (Magda and Susan married)
- gathered everyone in dining pavilion
- found three more missing
- Patty Horne knew location
- campers sent home
- went to football field on the night of the vigil, saw Patty Horne crying, saw light of the crash up the road
- doesn't feel that it was a drug deal or the Woodsman but can't explain why

Once she had gone over the recording, she stared at the list, unsure what to do next. She picked at a torn cuticle. "Stairway to Heaven." She'd heard of the song, but she had no idea how it went. She sometimes tried to listen to things that would evoke the time or place of the thing she wanted to understand. Sometimes, at Ellingham, she listened to thirties music to try to get into the mindset of what it was like back when Albert and Iris had first moved to the mountain. Maybe the music would help her now. She found Led Zeppelin online, then found the song and hit play.

It started off as a plinky-plonky guitar song with a flute, gradually morphing into something more hard rocking. It had cryptic lyrics about magic staircases and laughing forests. This seemed like music for people who thought they might be wizards.

What were the seventies even about? Was it all smoking and listening to this kind of stuff and riding around in huge cars without wearing seat belts? *This* was the song everyone liked?

The song ground on:

And as we wind on down the road
Our shadows taller than our soul
There walks a lady we all know

But there was something, something, something in what Susan had said. The music summoned it out of hiding and

Stevie saw its shadow flit across her thoughts. What the hell *was* it? Stevie ran down her list of notes again, reading them under her breath, letting them sink into her subconscious. Paul, Shawn, Magda, Patty, Patty . . .

Only one person's name came up twice: Patty Horne. But Patty had the most ironclad of all alibis—someone literally had seen her all night long. Plus, she had absolutely no reason to kill her friends. Todd, Eric, and Diane were her people, like Nate and Vi and Janelle were Stevie's people. But what about Greg Dempsey, who died later that week in a bright flash of light and a wall of rock and trees?

Another dead bike rider in Barlow Corners.

An idea took shape.

As Patty had said, if they hadn't been busted in a makeup nookie session, they most likely would have been victims as well. Or perhaps the killer (or killers) wouldn't have been able to attack a group of that size. Four people—that would have been hard enough. But six? What if you had wanted to kill someone in that group? And you knew that instead of six people, there would only have been four out there that night because Patty and Greg were under lock and key. Maybe you saw an opportunity.

But again, why? Why Sabrina, Diane, Todd, and Eric?

She flicked through the photos again, landing on Todd's. She put her earbuds in and listened to the part of the recording where Susan talked about Todd:

"I never like to say kids are rotten, but . . . Todd Cooper, he was a

rotten kid. Charming. Polite to your face, always. . . . He was guilty as sin, and everyone knew it. That was the shame of our town. . . ."

Todd Cooper had killed Michael Penhale, and everyone in town knew it. Out of the four of them, he was the only one who really made any sense as a target. The Penhale family was in the clear, and Paul Penhale had been seen in the lake house with Shawn. Susan had confirmed it. Even if Shawn and Paul wanted to team up to murder people they thought had wronged them, there seemed little chance that the woman she'd just met would have had any part in that.

But that didn't mean that the Penhales were the only people in town who might want Todd Cooper to get what he had coming to him and wouldn't be heartbroken to take out a few others along the way. Almost everyone noted that Todd was a dangerous driver.

Maybe Michael Penhale hadn't been the first? Maybe someone else, someone walking along the side of the road—a hitchhiker? A drifter? Someone from the public camp? And maybe the others had all been there when it happened. Maybe that's why they all had to die. . . .

She didn't know. It all went around and around in her head. She saw, but she did not *observe*.

She looked around the art pavilion. No one needed her. She pulled out the Nutshell Studies book and flipped through until something spoke to her. The scenes all had simple names: Dark Bathroom, Attic, Striped Bedroom. . . . That was part of the genius of Frances: she did not glamorize.

She did not go to the most high-profile crimes or scenes. She tended to show ordinary places, often inhabited by people without much money. These were people whose deaths might be overlooked or dismissed. She demanded that the investigator look and care. Look at the neatly folded towels with the single, tiny paring knife on top. Observe the worn clothing. (In fact, she often wore clothing over and over herself to wear it out enough, then cut it down to make the outfits for her studies, such was her dedication.) Examine the meat left out of the icebox, the position of the pillow, the contents of the garbage pail. Feel the textures, note the positions.

If Stevie could observe, she could make sense of it all. The word written on the inside of the hunting blind. The red cord that wasn't the right type. The wounds on Sabrina's hands. Eric Wilde's position on the path. A missing diary. A boy knocked off his bicycle and killed. A brown Jeep that everyone in town knew. A seasoned runner falling from a spot she visited every day. Not all these things mattered—the point of the studies was to see that *some* of them did. She just had to figure out which ones. . . .

"Hey."

Stevie looked up and pulled out her earbuds. Standing in front of her, inches away from her face, was Lucas. A new group of kids had come in and she hadn't even noticed. Nate came in with the group, but hung back, far away from Lucas.

"What's that?" He leaned in to look at her book. "Is that guy hanging?"

Stevie tried to close the book, but Lucas had his hand on the page.

"Why is that guy hanging? What is this?"

"Research," she said.

"For what?"

Stevie looked around for Janelle to help her, but Janelle was busy demonstrating proper sand-in-bottle technique to some kids. Some would have called this "doing her job," but to Stevie, this was abandonment.

"Have you read *The Moonbright Cycles*?" Lucas asked.

Stevie had read Nate's book right before they started Ellingham. Her tastes ran toward true crime, and fictional crime, and fictional crime based on true crime, so an eight-hundred-page book about monsters that lived in caves and dragons and swords was not really in her wheelhouse. She'd thought it was fine. But mostly she cared because she loved Nate, and it seemed like a lot of work to write a book. She wouldn't have been able to do it.

"Uh . . . uh-huh?"

"Don't you think Moonbright should have stayed in Solarium? It was stupid to leave. He could have fought Marlak there."

Nothing this child was saying corresponded to real words or ideas in her head.

"He doesn't like suggestions," Lucas said.

"That's okay. He doesn't like writing either."

A strange look passed over Lucas's face.

"He will," he said, before drifting off to the opposite

corner of the pavilion to fill his sand bottle. When he was gone, Nate approached Stevie and sat down.

"I think Lucas is going to *Misery* your ass," Stevie said. "Sorry about your ankles."

"I swear to god that kid has been watching me in my sleep," Nate said, wrapping his arms around himself. He noted the book that Stevie had in front of her. "That's terrifying," he said, pulling it toward him and opening it up. He flipped through it, asking no questions about why Stevie was examining miniature scenes of horrible deaths.

"I've got to figure out something to do," she said. "About Allison."

"What's there to *do*, though?"

"This case, this place—it's too much, and at the same time, it feels like it all fits together. Like when you do a puzzle and you first open the box and it's just a pile of random pieces, then as you go, they get easier to snap together. I *feel* it, but I'm not there yet. I feel how Allison's death fits in. I *feel* that it wasn't an accident. I feel like I've even seen how it happened, like I already know, but it's in some part of my brain I can't get to? Do you know what I mean?"

Nate nodded.

"Like when I write. I kind of know what it is I want to do, and I can't write for so long because it feels out of reach and it drives me crazy, but when I see it I can . . ."

She tuned out for a moment, focusing on something happening over his shoulder. He turned to see what she was looking at. Nicole was striding toward them.

"Shit," Stevie said. "I didn't even do anything wrong this time."

She put the Nutshell Studies book on her lap under the table. Nicole came over, but she wasn't looking at Stevie.

"Fisher," she said. "Josh Whitley, the other counselor, has arrived. You can move your things over to the treehouse now."

Nate's eyes grew wide.

"I can help you," Stevie said. "Janelle's got this."

Nate was a new man as they went back over to his cabin to get his things. Stevie was amazed when she entered. The kids had stuff everywhere, and even though the place was well-vented, there was a strange funk in the air. She stepped over a pair of small, used underpants that were in the middle of the floor as she followed Nate back to his sleeping area. Nate had never unpacked. He'd been ready to flee at all times. Dylan, however, had spread his things far and wide. He had a ring light for selfies, plus loads of equipment. He had about nine pairs of sunglasses spread out over his bureau, several shady-looking dietary supplements, and many items that suggested a life of surfing, skateboarding, and *influencing*.

"Here," Nate said, passing Stevie his computer bag.

There was a buzzing in Stevie's pocket. She pulled out her phone to see a text from David.

The police are gone. They've opened the trail back up on the point.

That was all Stevie needed to hear.

22

WHILE STEVIE WANTED TO WASTE NO TIME IN GETTING OVER TO EXAM-ine Arrowhead Point (and also to examine David—those feelings from the morning had not abated), she made a brief stop at her cabin. A shower would take too long, but she could manage a change of clothes. She was dismayed to discover that she had already worn all her T-shirts, due to the frequent changes of clothes. The only remaining one was the squeaky-white Camp Sunny Pines shirt she had been issued on arrival. She shrugged it on. The shirt was made of a thick, stiff cotton and was almost rectangular; it was like she was wearing a milk carton. Whatever sexy was—and Stevie had never claimed to hold this knowledge—she was sure this was the opposite. She considered borrowing Janelle's lipstick, which she knew Janelle would be okay with, but decided against it. If Stevie put on lipstick, it would be so out of character that it would signal that something was up. It might seem like a cry for help. David might call 911. So she hurried out the door in her massive, rectangular shirt, bare-lipped.

She stopped at the bathroom cabin to fill her water bottle

at the sink and caught a glimpse of herself in the mirror. She was developing a patchy, uneven sunburn on her face—more on the left than on the right. The heavy, wet air made her short blond locks stick to her head.

"I'm a pretty, pretty princess," she mumbled.

David was waiting for Stevie when she got over to the campsite. It seemed that he had been swimming—he was still wet, his hair flattened to his head. (This suited him. Maybe wet, flat hair was not so bad.) He wore only his swimsuit, and he was stretched out in one of the camping chairs, looking maybe better than Stevie had ever seen him. It was during moments like these that she realized what all those hard-boiled detectives meant when they were seemingly knocked into some kind of drunken oblivion when a woman in a veiled hat walked into their office. Human hormones were powerful drugs.

There was time, of course, to maybe visit the inside of David's tent for a while, and she was feeling optimistic when he went in that direction, but he reached in and grabbed a shirt.

"I let you know as soon as I saw them drive away," he said. "I was watching out for you."

Which was really good and focused of him, and only a little disappointing in terms of the moment.

"Good," she said, nodding. "Good, yeah . . ."

They began the walk around the lake, which again was riddled with opportunities to stop for a little light making out, but David was strangely quiet and seemed pensive. He did reach over and take her hand for a good part of the walk, which was very sweet, and also kind of weird. Something was up.

"Are you all right?" she asked.

"Yeah," he said, looking at her with his slow smile. "Fine."

By the time they reached Arrowhead Point, she had turned her mind back to the matter at hand a bit. It was sobering to be here, at this beautiful spot that Allison had showed her.

"Wow," David said, standing beside her. "It's a good view."

He made his way to the edge more quickly than Stevie liked.

"You could fall here really easily," he said. "If she was distracted or something."

Stevie began taking slow, measured steps forward toward the edge. Where would Allison have stopped? At the safest spot with the best view, most likely. *Don't just look at it—see it.* What did she see? A dark jag of rock, a bit of a slope, but it was gentle. Stevie squatted down and opened her water bottle, letting a trickle of water flow out and down the point. It made a slow, meandering path. It picked up a bit of speed at a point about halfway in, where the ledge had a small dip and really started to tip down. Stevie got down on her stomach and pressed herself along, like a snake, until she could peek over the edge. It was a straight drop onto the rocks below, then a bit of path and some trees, and about ten feet out to the lake edge. There was no sign of the body or what had happened there, but she shivered nonetheless.

It was a bad way to die.

She scooted back, only standing when she felt grass against her ankles. She joined David, who was sitting on the ground.

"So what are you thinking?" David asked.

Stevie brushed at a dark muddy stain that had gotten on the front of her white shirt.

"I don't know," she said. "I know that depression isn't something you can always see and you can't always tell if someone is in crisis, but I don't think she went over the edge on purpose. The people below described her tumbling over the edge, screaming."

"Then she tripped. It would be super easy to do. You're running. You're tired. You're distracted and looking around, and you trip and go over the edge."

It made sense. It was not just possible—it was likely. It certainly fit the description of what the witnesses had seen.

There was a low rumble of thunder in the distance, and though there were still hours of daylight left, the sky grew dark.

"It's going to storm tonight," he said, resting on his back and looking up at the sky.

She rested next to him, tucking her head into his shoulder. He rolled toward her, and his lips were on hers.

If it was bad form to make out in the spot that Allison Abbott had fallen from, Stevie tried not to dwell on it. There was a rush to the moment, as if something pent-up was being expressed, and David rolled on top of her, and then she on

278

him. They were more or less on the public path, but they were also alone with the woods and the sky. Soon they both had pine needles in their hair and were breathless. Then, as suddenly as the kissing began, it stopped. He smiled again, a questioning smile, and balanced himself up on his elbows.

"So," David said. "Fall. School."

He was back to whatever conversation he had started that morning when they left Susan's house.

"Fall," she repeated. "School."

"You're going back to Ellingham. I am a man without a plan at the moment."

"I thought you were going to keep working with the group you work with now," she said.

"That was my plan, yeah . . . but something's come up. I've been offered something."

She sat up as well.

"There's someone who's known me since I was little," he said, looking at the ground between them. "He doesn't like my dad—not a lot of people who know him do. He got in touch because he suspected that I had something to do with my dad's fall from grace, and he knows that I've been cut off. He offered to help me out."

"With money?"

"Kind of. More like with a future. He guessed, correctly, that it can be hard to be related to my dad and be in America sometimes. He has connections in England. He's offered to make some calls and get me into a program at a university in England and would help cover the costs."

Stevie blinked. Maybe it was the heat, or the rush of events, but her brain was not making a picture of the words coming out of David's mouth.

"England?" she said.

"England," he repeated. A nervous flicker flashed across his features.

"For school?"

"For school."

"So what did you say?" she asked.

"I said I would think it over. I have to get back to them soon, though. Definitely by this week."

Something Stevie had learned about herself in the months that she had been in some kind of relationship with David was this: she didn't take emotionally taxing conversations well. It didn't take much for her to spiral. She went from feeling completely connected to him and swimming in the warm waters of happy hormones, to a cold, frightened feeling. She had just gotten David back, and now he was going again, farther than before.

"So you're saying this now?" she asked. "After a woman I met fell off a cliff?"

"That wasn't my plan," he said, a little archly. "I've been trying to tell you since I got here. It's never the right time with you. I'm going to have to go soon, so . . ."

"So you're dropping this news and leaving?"

"Stevie," he said, a flinty edge coming into his voice, "I came out here as soon as I could. I'm trying to—"

"I know what you're trying to do," she said, even though

she had absolutely no idea what he was trying to do, or even what that meant. That's the thing about speaking—you can talk and talk and have no idea at all what the words leaving your mouth mean, or where they came from.

"This is an opportunity," he said. "I need to talk about it, think about it."

"What's there to think about?" she said. "It would be terrible if you had to pay for school like a normal person."

He pushed himself up to his hands and stretched his arms long behind him.

"Yeah," he said. "Like a *normal person*."

The air between them chilled.

Stevie didn't want to be saying what she was saying. She only sort of meant it. It wasn't his fault that someone had offered to pay for his school, or that he could take it or leave it. At the same time, it wasn't exactly fair that, once again, David had the world handed to him on a silver platter. People like David didn't have to make their own luck. It was fair to bet that no one was going to offer Stevie a free ride to school in England, and she'd solved a *murder*.

It also meant he might be going far away, and just when they were happy. Was there some kind of law that said things couldn't go well between them?

"I can't deal with this right now," she said, pushing herself up from the ground.

Shut up, Stevie, shut up, stop talking like you're in a reality show....

"I'm sorry things can't always follow your schedule," he

snapped back, starting to match her tone.

She was walking away, and she didn't even know why. She was crying. She walked faster, then she jogged, then she stopped jogging because she still was no good at running. Overhead, the sky continued to darken quickly, turning a kind of green color.

At some point, as she was reaching the road that divided the park with Sunny Pines, she decided to turn back. But that was also the moment the sky decided to open up, and in short order, it began to hail. Stevie had to run with all her might to get back under cover at the entrance of the camp, then dodge from building to building to reach her cabin.

It rained all that afternoon and night, more persistently than it had at any other point during their time at the camp. Things shifted entirely to indoor mode, which was clammy and close. Aside from dinner, all the other activities were off, and the campers retreated to any covered space to stare into their tablets and phones until they went cross-eyed.

Then, sometime in the evening, there was an almighty crack as a bolt of lightning fell close by. The kids screamed as one, at first out of fear, and then because screaming was awesome. In the next minute, the power was out, and it stayed that way all night. There were some generators, but not in the cabins. Stevie had not thought to charge her devices, and so everything she owned ran out of juice within the first hour, cutting off any communication with David on the other side of the lake.

That night, it rained with a kind of biblical ferocity,

pounding the cabin roof and flicking in through the screened windows, misting Stevie's face and sheets. She occasionally woke to mighty flashes of lightning and cracks of thunder that definitely landed somewhere not too far away. Janelle slept through it, her earbuds snugly in place. Many people might have enjoyed the sound and found it peaceful, maybe even Stevie under the right conditions.

These were not the right conditions.

She stood at the window a long time, then she went out onto the little porch of the cabin and watched the rain fall in the dark. She considered walking over to the campsite, but she had enough self-preservation to know that a walk through the dark murder woods in this kind of storm was not a good idea. So she paced the few feet of the porch so as not to wake Janelle. Sometime before dawn, her body wearied and she went inside and lay on top of the sheets. The next thing she knew, the awful, familiar crackle blasted her away.

"Good morning, Sunny Pines! Happy Fourth of July!"

From the bed, Stevie could see the sky through the screen window. It was big and blue, as if to say, "What? I didn't do anything last night. What are you even talking about?" Janelle's bed was empty—she had already greeted the day and gone off for a shower. Stevie had had the forethought to plug everything in before she finally went to sleep, and her phone and tablet had taken long, refreshing drinks of electricity during the night and were prepared for duty. She immediately checked for texts from David. There were none.

She wasted no time. The white T-shirt from yesterday

had a long, angry black slash on the front, but she pulled it on anyway. There was no time to wait for Janelle to tell her where she was going, or even to text. She had to move, now, toward David. She half ran through the camp, across the path, and over to the public side of the lake.

Stevie had heard of this thing called forest bathing, where you went out into the woods or the wild and simply breathed it all in, made contact with nature. It was supposed to be good for you. This was the kind of thing she would have doubted before, but this morning, the woods did have a calming effect. That deep smell of leaves and soil after a rain, the cooling effect of morning shade—it soothed her and made her think more clearly. So they fought. They'd fought before. Arguments had punctuated their entire relationship. It would be okay. They would talk it out. They would kiss it out. It would be one of those makeup scenes she always heard about. It would be fine, except for one small problem:

When she reached the place his tent had been, she found that he was gone.

23

Spiders had it made. This one, for instance. All day now, she (Stevie was sure she was a she even though she was a daddy longlegs) had been chilling in this corner under the window bench, watching over a loose weave of webbing, waiting for a snack to show up. It looked like a good life under there, shooting your own house out of your butt, food flying over to you, everybody basically leaving you alone.

"You have to stop that," Nate said.

"Stop what?"

Stevie's voice was flattened by her position on the floor, her face tilted toward the wall.

"Whatever it is you're doing. You look like a *Blair Witch* remake."

She had been here for almost an hour. Maybe more. Maybe even a lot more. Who even knew? She was on Spider Time now.

When she'd left David's campsite, she walked around the lake for a while, her thoughts unmoored. She must have arrived back at camp sometime after lunch, then come right up here to the treehouse, where Nate had been on his laptop, alone and content. Then she got down on the floor and started thinking about the spiders. That had been her day so far.

Nate poked her with the toe of his sneaker.

"This is a David thing," he said. "Obviously."

She did not reply.

"Romance seems fun," he added.

"Don't."

"I'm not. I don't know what happened. I don't even want to know. But I know you can't do whatever the hell this is. Don't you have things to do?"

"Janelle's got it. She doesn't need me."

"I don't mean Janelle." He crossed around and sat on the bare window seat and looked down at her.

"I screwed everything up. I ruined everything."

Nate banged his head against the screen behind him, then jerked forward when it proved to be looser than he imagined.

"Stevie." He sounded annoyed enough that she pulled her chin off the floor, then gradually pulled herself up. She was dizzy from the extended period of time she'd spent staring at nothing. She looked down at herself, at the white T-shirt that had been so pristine the day before. The shirt was still as rectangular, but it was no longer clean or stiff; it had melted into a bag of damp wrinkles, slashed all over with grime. The marks from Arrowhead Point were really pronounced, almost black. She tried to rub them away, but they didn't budge. Whatever was on it wasn't dirt—it was something more inky and permanent. The shirt was ruined.

This seemed like a bad omen, a dark mark. A message. Her focus was shot. David was gone. The summer split apart like a wet paper bag.

"*Stevie.*"

Stevie blinked and looked up.

"I got some weird shit on my shirt," she explained.

"Why don't we get out of here?" he said. "I have nothing to do up here now, which is great. You've abandoned your post. Let's get out of here and go to town."

"For what?"

"For something to *do*. There's a diner, right? Let's go there."

She was about to refuse, but when Nate looked annoyed, it truly startled her. His pale brows furrowed into a point.

"Fine," she said.

She pushed off the floor. As she did so, she snuck a glance at her texts.

Nothing. Not that that surprised her. Her phone had been sitting by her head the whole time and had never made a peep.

She and Nate got bikes out of the rack, took their locks and keys, and headed down the path, out of Sunny Pines and back onto the now-familiar stretch of tree-lined road. This activity shook off the top layer of her malaise, which was unfortunate, because that layer had been keeping the other, more painful layers in soft focus. David had probably just driven off down this road. Or maybe he would drive by now. She should stop and call him. Or not. Maybe when she got to town. Call him before he got too far away, onto the highway, out of Massachusetts, out of her life, forever.

England. He was going to *England*?

Why was her life over when she was only seventeen? She'd peaked. It was done.

Also, screw him. Screw him for sneaking up on her with this information when she was trying to figure out what had happened to Allison Abbott. He could have told her about this on any one of their phone calls. He'd had so many chances.

Also, also? Free college? Poor little rich boy. She had no idea how her family was going to afford college. She would have to get so many loans that she would be in debt until she died. *Oh, so you're sad about your dad? Here's free everything.*

She pumped the bike harder, working all her feelings out on the road, riding more on the driving lane than the side. Go ahead and hit her from behind. She *dared* them. Nate was struggling to keep up with her, occasionally yelling something about the fact that she was "riding in the middle of the fucking road" or whatever. The pedaling stopped the thinking, and the road belonged to her now. Let them try to take it.

They arrived in Barlow Corners in record time, Nate red-faced and looking regretful that he had ever had this idea in the first place. Stevie, though, was mildly renewed. At least, she was hungry. It was a start. They locked their bikes by the library, near Sabrina's reading room.

"Jesus," Nate said as they crossed the street to the Dairy Duchess. "Never again. Next time I leave you there."

It was only when they crossed the street and Stevie saw the red, white, and blue bunting that was on some of the storefronts that she remembered that it was the Fourth of July. There would be fireworks tonight. She checked her phone and found, to her surprise, that it was almost six o'clock. If she had guessed before, she would have thought it was maybe two, three at the latest. Somehow, she had lost almost an *entire day* in misery. No wonder Nate had finally peeled her off the floor.

The Dairy Duchess was an old-fashioned diner, the kind you saw on TV, that never seemed to exist in real life. There was a long counter with red stools, and Formica tables. It was also air-conditioned, which was a sweet, freezing relief. The place was basically empty when Nate and Stevie came in, so they took the prime booth by the window, looking out on the street and the town green across the way. The top of John Barlow's hat peered above the menu that was tucked behind the ketchup bottles.

They both decided on some milk shakes and burgers, because Nate and Stevie had similar views on nutrition. To Stevie's surprise, Nate got out his laptop and immediately starting typing.

"What are you doing?" she asked.

"Nothing."

"Are you *writing*?"

"I'm just . . . I'm doing something."

"You're writing, aren't you?"

"Solve," he said. "*Solve*."

"I can't *solve*."

"Okay, then sit there. At least you're not on the floor anymore. I've done my job."

This was a bit of a betrayal.

She opened her backpack and put her things on the table. Her tablet. Her phone. A notebook. Everything she knew about this case—aside from whatever was floating around in her head—was here. All the tools she needed. Now there was time and space to think.

She looked at the items.

She looked at the ketchup.

She looked at the menu and John Barlow's hat.

She looked at the library.

She felt herself beginning to *see*.

Allison Abbot was dead. Allison Abbott had been murdered, and almost certainly because of something to do with this case. She hadn't just fallen off that cliff. It didn't matter how she, Stevie, felt. Allison Abbott was not alive anymore, and someone had to do something. She had promised Allison she would get the diary—and then Allison died.

Which meant, logically, that someone thought that Allison was close to getting that diary.

It followed that there was something in that diary

that was worth killing for. Which meant it was Sabrina Abbott—perfect, wonderful, hardworking Sabrina—who was somehow at the center of this.

The burgers and milk shakes came, and Stevie started in on them while letting her focus rest on the reading room across the street. She softened her gaze, letting the contours of the building blur. Sabrina. Reading. Writing. Checking out books right up until the time she died.

Her brain began to settle. Stevie reached for the tablet, trying to maintain the mental state, and flicked back to the pictures of the room of mementos in Allison's house—all those tidily arranged things. Books, clothes, knickknacks, photographs, record albums. A teenage life, frozen in time in 1978. She looked at the picture of the interlibrary loan slips for the books Sabrina had requested right before she died: *A Woman in Berlin* and *The Rise and Fall of the Third Reich*. Serious reading for a serious person, someone preparing for her future at Columbia University. She thought about Sabrina's 1977 diary, with the list of subjects and amount of time studied. Sabrina was a detailed reporter of events.

The shadow of an idea danced through the halls of her mind again. And another, and another. Dancing shadows on the wall. Ghosts. Answers—intangible answers, taunting her.

"Shit," she said.

"What?"

She tapped her palms on the table in disgust.

"I've *seen* it," she said. "Bits of it. Little flashes. Like that time I saw a moose behind some trees. I've seen *something*. Or heard it. And I can't work out what it is."

"Sounds like writing," he said. "It's the worst."

He took a long sip of his milk shake as Stevie set her forehead down on the table. Perhaps sensing that she wasn't coming back up anytime soon, he kept talking.

"People ask stuff like 'What's your process?' I don't know what my process is. I sit down and type stuff about monsters. Or I think about it. Or I type-think."

The shadows flashed back up on the wall, the edges clearer. More of a shape.

She lifted her head.

"What did you say?" she asked.

"What? When? Which thing?"

"Writing. Typing. Thinking. What?"

"What?"

"Stop saying *what*," she said. "What do you mean? You type and think?"

"Yeah," he said. "I kind of think with my fingers? That sounds bad. You know what I mean."

"You type stuff," she said. "You type. Shit, shit, shit. . . . Give me your computer."

"Are you going to finish my book?" he said, pushing it over to her. "Because this is good news for me."

Instead of typing, or even looking at the screen, Stevie instead stared at the keyboard, lightly running her finger from the L key all the way over to the return, then back again.

Then she grabbed her tablet and frantically swiped back and back until she found what she wanted.

"Oh my god," she said. "I have to go."

"What?"

"Stop saying *what*! I have to go."

"Stop saying you have to go," Nate shot back, grabbing the bike lock key. "Go where?"

"Allison's house," she replied, waving her hand for the check.

"No. You can't do that. Allison is dead."

"So she won't care," she said. "Give me back the bike key. I know where Sabrina hid her diary. It's not lost."

"Stevie, *explain*."

Stevie wriggled in frustration, but pulled up a photo.

"Here," she said, passing him her tablet. "That's a pic of the list of supplies ordered for the camp art pavilion in 1978 and how much it cost."

```
Ceramics: ring boxes, earring stands, cats,
dogs, cookie jars; trash cann, turtle,
teddy bear, roller skate ($ 28)
```

"Typewriters sucked," she said. "They didn't have backspace keys. Look at this weird semicolon after 'cookie jars.' Stupid typo, right? And this was the seventies, so if you hit the wrong key, you couldn't fix it easily. Now look at your keyboard. The semicolon and colon key are the same. You get a semicolon if you forget to hit the shift. If you hit the shift, it's a colon, which makes more sense. A colon would mean . . ."

"It was a list."

"Exactly. That means they ordered cookie jars in the following shapes—trash can, turtle, teddy bear, roller skates. Who typed this list? Sabrina. Who has to make projects as part of her job? Sabrina. Who loves turtles? Sabrina. Remember the big turtle in the reading room at the library?" She tapped on the glass of the window in the direction of the reading room. "Sabrina said the kids went through her things, so she made something to hide things in. She made a *turtle cookie jar*. And she wouldn't have had that with her on the night she died. It was back in the bunk. And now . . ."

She flipped back through the photos again, finding the images of the room in Allison's house. She turned the tablet back toward Nate triumphantly.

"Right there," she said, pointing at the large turtle figure on one of the shelves. "What does that look like to you?"

"A turtle," he said. "Possibly a turtle cookie jar."

"Give me the bike key."

"I'm coming with you," he said.

"You hate coming with me on stuff like this."

"I know," he said. "And I know you. This is what you do. It's your *move*."

"I have to do it. It's part of the job."

"You love that shit, though."

Stevie did not reply to this because she did, in fact, love that shit.

"You know I love you too, right?" she said.

"Tell it to my grieving family when you get me killed," he replied, reaching for his wallet. "Let's pay and go before I change my mind."

24

THE DAY WAS FADING FAST. BY THE TIME THEY DRIFTED INTO ALLISON'S driveway, there was little light left, and she and Nate were sweating and heaving.

"When . . . we . . . get in . . . there," Nate said between breaths, "I . . . am drinking . . . whatever . . . is in . . . the fridge. Don't care. Maybe it's . . . stealing. Don't care."

Stevie nodded heavily.

"We should probably hide the bikes," she said.

"Why? There's no one around."

"In case anyone comes by. Because it's still . . ."

She decided to omit the words *breaking and entering*. Nate regarded his friend with a look that walked the line between weariness and terror. They rolled the bikes into the trees and set them on their sides, then walked the rest of the way up the dark lane and into Allison's driveway.

"She could have a doorcam or something," Nate said in a low voice.

"Well, she's not monitoring it now," Stevie replied.

Even though there was no one around, it seemed like a

bad idea to go through the front door. There was a side one, which was a bit more private. Stevie guided Nate in that direction as she dug around in her bag and pulled out the nitrile gloves.

"Snap 'em on," she said, handing a pair to Nate. "Feels good."

She got out her wallet. She had a debit card, which she needed. She had a credit card, which was largely a joke; still—better to preserve it. Her Ellingham ID was sturdy, and she would be getting a new one anyway in the fall. She pulled this one out and wiggled it into the crack in the doorway.

"It's really that easy to open a door, huh?" Nate said.

"You've seen me do it before."

"Yeah, but I wanted to think that's because the Ellingham locks are old and shit. I wanted to believe houses are more secure."

"The theater of security," Stevie said. "Believe what you want."

The lock popped open gently, and Stevie opened the door, and then the two of them stepped into the darkened house. Stevie had crept through private spaces before, even ones recently vacated by people who had met unfortunate ends. She hadn't done this *a lot*, but that she had done it at all was notable. Ellingham Academy had afforded her many bespoke experiences.

The last time Stevie had entered this house, she had come in through the kitchen. This doorway led into a lower level of the house, a furnished basement that Allison had turned into a home gym. From here, they headed up the steps, emerging in the hallway with the many framed photographs. Outside, the first pops of fireworks sounded in the distance.

"Happy Independence Day," Nate said.

The Sabrina room, as Stevie was now calling it in her head, was behind the closed door at the end of the hall. She considered turning on the overhead light but opted instead to use her flashlight out of an abundance of caution. She shone it around, trying to find the large turtle. It wasn't where it had been. Nate, meanwhile, was looking along the shelves.

"What *is* this?" he said. "Hairbrushes? Old pencils? This is—"

"The work of a grieving sister," Stevie cut in.

". . . from a horror novel."

Stevie did a full three-sixty, scanning every surface.

"The turtle is gone," she said. She considered for a moment, then it hit her. Allison's reaction had been profound when Stevie had shown her the list of art supplies—she'd been so touched that she immediately took Stevie over to Paul Penhale's veterinary office.

"She figured it out," Stevie said. "She moved the turtle. We have to find it."

They began upstairs, since they were already there. The bathroom was easily eliminated. Allison's bedroom was perhaps the most awkward place to go, but Stevie pushed down any discomfort. Surfaces first—the turtle wasn't on any of the bedside stands or bureaus. She had a quick look in the closet, where everything was tidily hung or shelved. No turtle. Nate looked under the bed and otherwise peered unhappily around the room. They gave the linen closet a cursory go-through. Nothing.

They headed back downstairs as the fireworks were starting in earnest outside. They could see trails of light past the tree line outside. Nate was sent to check the living room, while Stevie headed back into the kitchen. She found what she had come for soon enough—the turtle was pushed back into the corner of the countertop space, where a cookie jar should go.

"Gotcha," she said, lifting it up and sitting with it on the floor behind the kitchen island. "Nate! In here!"

Nate joined her in the kitchen and sank down next to her on the floor.

"Keep a light on it," she said, setting down her phone to pry the jar open.

It did not open.

"Cookie jars have rubberized sealing rings," she said. "You have to . . ."

She grabbed the edge of the turtle's shell and pulled harder. Nothing. She pulled once more. She felt something give ever so slightly. Once more and she got another wiggle.

"Maybe it's rotted or something," Nate said.

Stevie sat back and considered the turtle for a long moment. It was cheerfully painted in bright greens and yellows and had a small, satisfied smile. It was a nice turtle, made by someone who cared for it. Which was why the next part was unfortunate but necessary.

"Sorry, Sabrina," she said.

She stood up, glanced along the countertop, opened a drawer or two, and found a marble rolling pin. She brought it down on the turtle's back, hard.

"Or you could do that," Nate said.

The shell broke into three large pieces. She removed them, revealing a decayed rubber ring and a hollow space for cookies. But instead of cookies, there was a small, soft-backed red book with the year *1978* written on the front in gold script.

"The truth in a shell," Stevie said quietly.

The diary had curved into the shape of the jar with time and it was stuck when Stevie tried to get it out without damaging it, so she had to break the turtle's head and one of his legs off for wiggle room to get it out. Once you start to break precious ceramic turtles, you might as well keep going.

Aside from bending it, the airless jar had kept the diary in good condition. It was dust-free, dry but not brittle. Stevie opened the cover with care. The first page made it clear what they had found.

PROPERTY OF SABRINA ABBOTT

"I'm never questioning you again," Nate said.

Stevie turned the curved page to the first entry.

JANUARY 3, 1978
Welcome, 1978. Nice to meet you. Time to crack open this fresh new diary I got for Christmas. I like

that this one has a plain red cover this time. I liked
the Snoopy one from last year because I will always
love Snoopy and nothing can stop that, but this one
is more of what I've got in mind for the future.

"We've got it," Nate said. "We should take it and go. We'll
read it back at camp."
She read on a few more sentences.

We went back to school today after the holiday
break. There was talk about delaying the opening
because of Michael Penhale, but apparently it was
too complicated so we went back at the normal
time. I can't believe it's been two weeks now since
Michael died. I went in with a few student council
people.

"Stevie . . ."
"Yeah," she said, shutting the book and putting it in her
backpack. "Yeah . . ."
He put his hand over her mouth. She widened her eyes in
confusion, then she realized why he had done it. There was
the unmistakable sound of someone opening the front door.
People in mystery and suspense novels were always talking about how their heart was in their throat. Stevie now
understood precisely what that meant—she was experiencing
something that felt exactly like that, a big, throbbing knot
wedged right in there, making it feel like she might barf or

breathe blood or choke. Nate had, for some reason, pancaked himself on the ground, like he was pretending to be a kitchen rug. Then, realizing this was not the move to make, he got up on all fours. Stevie put out her hands in a *don't move* position and listened to see what she could understand from the noises.

The door opened. There were footsteps as someone entered. It sounded like it was one person who paused by the door, like they were listening back, which she did not like at all. The person walked through the living room, down the uncarpeted hallway, and then stopped somewhere beyond the passage into the kitchen. There was a pause that was hatefully long, then the footsteps moved back toward the steps, creaking up them.

Stevie swallowed, checked to make sure she was still breathing, examined Nate for signs of life, and then tilted her head toward the kitchen door. She got up, moving first to her knees, then up to her feet, tiptoeing over to it. It had a deadbolt, plus a twisty thing above the knob. She turned both of these gingerly. That went well, but as she pulled the door open, the door made a strange rattling noise. The footsteps overhead stopped moving.

There was no time to be precious now, no time to pretend they weren't there. She grabbed for Nate and yanked him through the door, only barely concealing the sound of their leaving. Outside, night had fallen, and fireflies twinkled around the warm garden behind the house. If they ran straight out, whoever it was would be able to see them from the windows. She gestured for Nate to follow her, creeping close to the house. They went around to the front, which faced the trees and the driveway.

"Go!" she whispered to him.

The two of them tore off, running as fast and as quietly as they could down the gravel driveway. The moon was unfortunately high and bright and there were fireworks going off overhead, so there was no cover as they hurried away, but they were soon through the opening in the trees and down into the wooded part of the drive, away from the view of the house. Once they reached where it met the street, she turned back.

"Wait," she said, catching his arm. "Wait, wait, wait . . ."

Stevie turned around and was taking a few steps back up the drive toward the house.

"Stevie."

"Look," she said. She remained there until he came up beside her to see what she was indicating.

"What?" he hissed. "There's nothing."

"Right. There's nothing. There's no car."

Nate had nothing to say for a moment.

"What does that mean?" he finally replied.

"It means someone came here on foot."

"But what does that mean?" he said again.

"Something," she said. "Probably bad. Come on."

They hurried back down the lane. Nate went ahead a bit and ducked into the trees. He emerged a moment later and stood there until Stevie reached him.

"The bikes are gone," he said simply. "Must be the wrong spot, but . . . we put them by this sign right here. . . ."

On some level, once she had noticed there was no car in the driveway, Stevie had expected this. When things go bad, they tend to go bad all over.

"Come on," she said, pulling him into the trees. "We're going to walk back, but we're going to stay off the road. We'll go around the lake."

She pulled out her phone as they walked and thumbed open a map. It was slow to load. The signal was poor. It finally opened the map, but it was of no use.

"It thinks we're in the middle of the lake," she said, shoving the phone in her pocket. "We'll have to get to the lake somehow and follow it around. It's got to be this way."

"So we're going to wander around the murder forest in the dark when there's someone at the house we broke into."

"Unless you have another plan," she said.

"Just making sure I was up to speed."

She reached for her keys. One of her keychains was a small pill container. She unscrewed this as they walked and shook out the tiny pill it held. She always had one Ativan on her, in case of a panic attack. Being lost in the murder woods was a pretty good occasion to take it. At home, it would make her sleepy. Here, in the woods, it would keep her under control in case her brain decided to spin out. She swallowed it dry, which wasn't too hard as it was a small pill. She was putting the keys back in her bag when she noticed a small glint of light behind them. In one movement, she pushed Nate behind a tree. He nodded, indicating that he wasn't going to speak.

A crunch of a step. *Crunch, crunch.*

Nothing. The person stopped moving.

There were two choices here. One, they could accept that whoever it was who had been at the house had followed them into the woods for completely sensible reasons. They had come to the house to do something, suspected someone was inside, looked around, seen two figures going into the woods, and followed. So they could simply step out from behind the tree and see whoever it was and fess up.

But this person had come with no car and had taken their bikes. This left option two.

"We need to run," she whispered in his ear.

They ran straight out onto the cedar-chip path that rimmed the lake. This was good in terms of informing them of where they were, and bad in terms of being seen. But at this point, that didn't really matter anymore. They could run faster on the path and they would know where they were going. She could hear the person following them and glanced behind once to try to catch a glimpse, but the person was out of sight. Stevie ran like she did in dreams—furiously, almost flying through the dark. Nate was just in front of her, ripping along.

She felt the bullet go past before she heard it, which was odd. It was this little whizzing thing, like a dragonfly. It landed in a tree nearby, sending out a spray of splinters.

"Holy shit," Nate yelled, spinning around. *"Shit."*

They both instinctively left the path, cutting between the trees, dodging and weaving in the dark. The ground was a tangle of roots and pits, giving way in unexpected places. Stevie was dimly aware of the branches that slapped and tore at her skin, of the way her ankles twisted from under her as she hit a snag or a hole. There was no telling where they were now—the woods had consumed them. Maybe they were heading toward camp; maybe they were running in circles. Trees all look the same in the dark. Up ahead, though, there was a peephole of a clearing through which she could see the fireworks crackling in the sky in happy red, white, and blue. She used the sparks as a guide point, making her way toward them, ducking behind the trees. From the tension in her legs and knees she could tell they were moving higher, which at least indicated a different, new direction.

Whizz. Another object cracked nearby; Stevie felt its explosive force. She could tell Nate was yelling and swearing, but she couldn't hear him anymore, not over the blood in her ears and the crescendo of fireworks. The ground got rockier, easier to move on . . .

And then, the tree cover was gone. The forest opened up and the sky was all theirs. She realized that the opening she had been using to guide them was, in fact, Point 23. She backed off and tried to continue on through the wooded area, but the ground was impenetrable from here on out, cascading down in a perilous slope. She'd lost track of where their pursuer was as well.

"We have to," Nate said, breathless, pulling at her arm.

"What?"

"We're cornered. Jump out when you go. As far as you can. Feet together."

She could see the lake below, silent and dark, like a black mirror, reflecting the moon and the fireworks. She had been in bad positions before—down in tunnels at Ellingham, trapped in the snow. This was different. This required action—a calculated leap into the unknown. She was too terrified to be merely afraid.

"Out as far as you can," he said again. "Go in straight, feet down and together. Back up and run for it. Now!"

She didn't know how. Her feet wouldn't move. She willed them to go, but they wouldn't.

A shot made contact with the tree she was next to.

Time moved very slowly over the next few seconds. Nate was yelling for her to go, go go. She pressed herself back, crouching toward the ground. Nate did the same, then he pushed her on the back. She felt the ground for what may have been the last time, and then launched herself forward.

The edge of the rock was there to welcome her, and as she jumped out and made contact with the sky, she wanted to close her eyes but found she was unable to. She was tumbling. The mirror was coming up fast, and then . . .

25

For a moment, there was nothing. She was nowhere. There was no Stevie. She was totally and utterly free from space and time, with the air a soft whistling noise in her ear. Something hard made contact with her left side. But that was nothing compared to what came a second later. It was like smashing through glass. Cold water shot into her mouth and nose. Everything was burning from pain and air hunger. She didn't know where to go. She didn't know what was the surface and what was the bottom. The dark water consumed her every sense.

She was going to die.

That was interesting. No effort was required on her part. Just some bubbles in the dark and a fall to some unknown depth. She was aware enough to know that her backpack was still on her back and was weighing her down. She wriggled, through the confusion and burning, trying to get it off. It came off easily on one side. She didn't understand how the other side of her body worked in the water, but eventually she turned in the right way and it gave. It buoyed her a bit, but she still couldn't figure out which way to go. The panic swept over her, blanketing her in a rush. The world fragmented into black and white dots as she slid toward unconsciousness. In the next moment, the world next to her exploded—some weird mayhem of turbulence and violence and she was going to the bottom of the lake and her lungs were . . .

Something was on her arm, something pulling her. She broke the surface, gagging and coughing. She couldn't make herself breathe. There was water in her. Nate slammed her as hard as he could on the back and water came pouring out of her mouth and nose, thick with mucus. She retched as it tried to figure out how to take in air, how to clear itself. There was water in her ears, so his words were muffled, and she couldn't see from all the tears in her eyes.

She was too weak to tread water, but they weren't too far from the rocks at the bottom of the point. Together, they managed to pull each other toward them.

"The diary-y!" she screamed between shivering breaths. "It's gon-n-n-e."

"It do-o-es-n-n't matt-tt-ter. Forget it-t-t-t-t. Stevie. *Stee-e-e-vv-ie.*"

Stevie gripped the rock with her right hand, but it was tiring out. She went to switch to the left, but when she did so, a shock of pain shot through her arm. She almost slipped down the rock, but Nate grabbed her shirt and pulled her back.

"I think-k-k my arm-m-m . . . ," she said, but that was all she could manage before the pain blotted out the sentence.

The water was black and still, with a tiny cartoon moon

bobbing on the surface. She tried to look up to see if anyone was visible above them, but it was all rock and darkness.

"Do-o you think they're g-g-g-one?" Nate sputtered.

She shook her head, unsure if she meant no or that she didn't know.

"Hey!" came a yell from the other side of the lake. "Hey! Are you okay?"

David's voice. Was she hallucinating? Had any of this happened? The shots, the fall . . . did she die in the water?

"No-o!" Nate screamed back.

"Nate? Hang on! Hang on!"

"Well-ll, yeah-h-h," Nate said, his shivering growing worse.

Not a hallucination. That was David.

Stevie watched David and his kayak come closer through the water. Whether it took him five minutes or five hours, she had no idea. Everything was cold, and her hold on the rock was ever weakening. She wanted to try to belly-crawl on top of it to get out of the water, but she didn't have that kind of strength.

As David glided up to them, Stevie was surprised to find that the first emotion to bubble back to the surface with the rest of her body was annoyance.

"What-t-t the hel-l-l-l a-r-r-re you doing-g here?"

"Getting your ass out of the lake," he shot back. "What the hell are *you* doing here?"

"Oh-h my Go-d-d," Nate said. "Shut-t up-p."

That tiny burst of emotion drained whatever reserve of

energy Stevie had. Her body was numb and exhaustion took over. She began to slip from the rock.

"Whoa . . . whoa . . ." David swung his legs over the side of the kayak and slipped into the water, catching her in a clumsy hold. She was dead weight and he struggled to get a grip on her and keep the other hand on the kayak.

"Okay," he said, seeming to sense the gravity of the situation, "how do we do this? Nate, do you think you can get over here and grab the kayak?"

"I think-k so," Nate said, reaching for the kayak. He fumbled once or twice but finally got a firm enough grip on one of the ropes on the side and hauled his body over it.

"Arm-m," Stevie mumbled. "Doesn't-t-t work-k."

"Okay," David said, trying to sound calm, and failing. "It's okay. I've got you."

He reached up into the kayak and pulled out a life vest, which he put over her functioning arm. Nate was holding the back of the kayak, so David helped guide Stevie into a resting position slumped over the front.

"Okay," he said. "It's a short distance to the beach area there. Nate, hold on."

David climbed up on the rock and got himself into the kayak, pushing back with the paddle and narrowly missing Nate's head. With choppy strokes, made to avoid striking either of the people attached to the front and back of the kayak, David began to paddle. The closest stretch of dirt beach was about thirty yards away—not a great distance, but impossible in Stevie's current state. Stevie felt herself growing sleepy at points. She wanted to close her eyes, but her inner voice and David's outer voice kept telling her to wake up, hold on. She needed both arms through the life vest. She tried to move her left arm again, and a white-hot pain shot behind her eyes, causing the world to scramble into black-and-white dots. No left arm. Instead, she put further demands on her right. Her right arm was going to give the performance of its life. She commanded it to ignore cold, ignore fatigue. It was the strongest, best arm in the world.

She could feel something under her—her feet were dragging on the ground.

"Almost," David said. "Here . . . here . . ."

Nate released his grip, which caused the kayak to turn a bit. He staggered onto the beach. By this point, Stevie's right arm was numb from overwork and she felt herself slide, but she held on until the ground hit her knees. David got out of the kayak, half falling, and got her up under his arm and moved her to the shore. The kayak, its job finished, decided to embrace the moment and float away.

David leaned over Stevie and Nate on the cold, rocky sand.

"You guys," he said. "Are you okay? What the actual fuck . . ."

Stevie looked up at him. His face blocked out the moon and the fireworks.

"I think my-y-y arm's broken-n-n," she said.

And then, mercifully, she passed out.

* * *

The next few hours were hazy. Someone from the campground had summoned a ranger, who found them on the beach. Stevie partially noted the conversation that went on, the questions about whether she could walk. She must have failed that test, because someone put her on a backboard and secured something around her neck. There was a strange journey through the woods, bumping along on a board held by two people who had appeared out of the ether. Then she was in an ambulance with Nate.

"The diary . . . ," she said.

"Forget the diary," he replied, shivering in his metallic blanket.

Everything hurt—a dull, allover ache that penetrated the depths of her bones. She kept trying to close her eyes, only to have a paramedic wake her and shine a light in them. Why wouldn't anyone let her sleep? Maybe if she slept, she could read Sabrina's diary in her dreams. . . .

The thing she was resting on suddenly popped up and she was wheeled into a bitterly cold and obscenely bright emergency room. She watched the ceiling tiles go by as she was wheeled along, watched the fluorescent lights, the signs over doorways. She was taken to a curtained compartment, where a nurse asked her questions like what her name was. People kept appearing, not looking urgent or alarmed, but refusing to let her be. They wanted to see her pupils, listen to her chest, move her arm . . .

313

That got a little scream.

She kept trying to close her eyes and recall Sabrina's writing, hold the diary in her mind. But then she got something better. A face. That face, with the wide brown eyes and dark brown hair. Sabrina. She couldn't quite see her, but she sensed her nearby, whispering something she couldn't make out.

"Hold it right there, Stevie. You're doing great."

She opened her eyes to find that she was not speaking to Sabrina, but to a member of the hospital staff who was inserting her head into a massive machine. It was a brief stay, then she was removed.

God, this place was freezing. She shivered uncontrollably.

"I'll have the nurse get you a blanket," the person said.

Back out in the hall, a nurse came along with the promised blanket and tucked it around her.

"Is that too tight?" he said. "Do you want it loose?"

"Moose?"

"Loose."

"I saw a moose once," Stevie replied.

The nurse frowned, but she settled Stevie in and wheeled her to her next destination, which was the X-ray department. From there, she went to a small room where her left arm was put in a cast. Finally, her journey through the hospital complete, she was returned to the emergency room. For a few minutes, she was alone, then the curtain scraped back and Nate appeared, shuffling in in a voluminous pair of purple yoga pants and a Box Box fleece.

"Hey, stupid," he said. "Let's never do this again."

He came closer, standing by the edge of her bed.

"You're okay," he said. "They think it's mostly shock. They weren't sure if you hit your head, so they've been watching you. You had a CAT scan. Do you remember?"

"Vaguely."

"They think we were messing around and jumped off Point 23," he said. "They think we're two assholes. I didn't explain that we jumped because someone shot at us. I thought about it—because someone shot at us. But we had broken into a house, so . . ."

Stevie nodded wearily.

"I told them to call Carson. Which is why I'm dressed like this. Since he owns the camp, he has access to all the parental consent forms our families had to sign and copies of our insurance information, stuff like that. And he's irresponsible enough not to call our parents, so we might get out of this night in one piece."

Stevie felt her eyes well up.

"I'm sorry," she said.

"It's fine," he said, looking down. "Whoever follows you to a second location deserves what they get. We called Janelle. She was so determined to get here that I thought she was going to walk, but I convinced her to wait until morning. They're probably going to admit you, to keep an eye on you. I can go home. David's going to stay until they take you upstairs."

"You know I love you, right?" she asked.

"You better."

It looked like he was going to take her good hand and squeeze it, but then at the last moment, he tapped the back of it in an abbreviated gesture of affection.

David had not gotten a change of clothes. Nobody had thought of him. His shirt was still clammy and damp, and his hair was drier, but not dry. As a gesture, he had been given a sheet to wind around himself, which was odd and also somehow fitting.

She remembered the first time they had kissed—he was sitting on the floor of her room in Minerva House. He was leaning up against the wall in a pair of ancient Yale sweatpants he had taken from his dad. She was explaining the problems with witness testimony using office supplies as props. It had been, in many ways, the defining moment of their relationship before this one, with Stevie in a hospital bed after breaking into a house, and him wound in a sheet, wandering the emergency room.

This was *them*.

He came up to the side of her bed and leaned down, his elbows on the rail, looking at her. He shifted his gaze from left to right, and from the way he was looking, she knew there had to be something about her face that wasn't great. She decided not to worry about it.

"What else do you want to do tonight?" he asked quietly. "Wanna steal a car?"

She was too tired to joke. She considered smiling, but whatever it was that was wrong with her face was too sore for that.

"Yeah," he said. "Maybe tomorrow night."

She continued looking up at him, his head haloed by the greenish fluorescent lights.

"Nate didn't want to say why you guys jumped off a cliff in the middle of the night," he said. "I know you both well enough to guess there was probably a good reason. Or a reason."

"You left," she said, her voice hoarse. "You were gone, before. Your tent . . ."

"Flooded. Completely. I had to move site."

"I texted . . ."

"My tent flooded," he said again. "My phone was on the ground. It stopped working until it dried out."

"I thought you just left," she said.

"I wasn't going to *leave*," he replied.

The nurse snapped back the curtain and made her way behind David.

"Time to go upstairs," she said, arranging and tucking the various wires and bits connected to Stevie's bed.

"I'll be back in the morning," he said. "Call me if you need me. It works now."

She was wheeled to the far side of an empty double room. Once the nurse settled her in, putting all the wires and rails and bits and pieces in place, Stevie was left to rest with the door to her room open. She tried to close her eyes, but there was a flicking light. It was a reflection of something in the hall, bouncing off the whiteboard by the door with her nurse's name on it. There was a beeping sound that went with it, but it was out of sync.

Flash. Pause. Beep. Flash. Pause. Beep.

Stevie tried not to think about it, to close her eyes and sleep, but even with her eyes closed, the light seeped in under her eyelids.

Flash. Pause. Beep. Flash. Pause. Longer pause. Beep.

This was intolerable. But her head didn't hurt anymore, and neither did her arm. That's right—they said something about giving her medicine for the pain.

Still, even through the haze, it was amazing how distracting a flashing light could be. Maybe she would make the light her friend. The light was saying, *Go to sleep, Stevie. Night night, Stevie.*

No it wasn't. No flashing light says that. The point of a flashing light is to say, *Look at me! Look at me! Something is happening!*

What was happening? Nothing. She was in this bed, tired and sleepless, a cast molded neatly to her arm.

Flash. Pause. Beep. Flash. Pause. Pause. Beep. Flash.

Look at me! Look at me!

Stevie felt something click in her brain.

The cast was snug. The cast was a part of her. The cast—

Look at me!

Stevie fumbled around in the bed, scrambling in the half dark with her right hand until she found the clicker she sort of remembered the nurse putting by her hand. She pressed it once, then again. A figure appeared in the doorway after several minutes.

"You okay?" said the nurse.

"Pen?"

"What?"

"Please can I have a pen?" she said. "Please. It's important."

The nurse let out a barely audible sigh but produced a Sharpie and handed it to her.

"Thank you," Stevie croaked. Her throat was rough from coughing out that water.

When the nurse was gone, she pulled off the cap with her teeth, realizing after she did it that maybe it wasn't a great idea to stick hospital pens in her mouth. No matter. She had the Sharpie now. It was dark, but she could about make out the words she was writing on the cast:

light. flash. form.

Now she could sleep.

26

STEVIE WOKE IN A STRANGE, NARROW BED, DRESSED IN THE THIN HOS-pital gown.

She sat up slowly, using her unbroken arm to push herself up. She was surprised when this hurt her hand and looked to find her palms covered in scratches and cuts. The fall off the point had not been elegant or clean. She padded her way over to the bathroom in the grippy sock-slippers someone had put on her feet the night before. The bathroom mirror revealed the extent of the damage—her hair was sticking up at all angles, there were dark circles under her eyes along with a long scrape down the right side of her face. Her arm was green with bruises, which were accentuated by the green fiberglass cast that now adorned it.

These were all things that suggested she should return to the bed behind her. But then she looked down at the three words she had written on the cast the night before. She splashed water on her face (a mistake, this hurt), then shuffled over to the landline phone on the wheeled bedside table. She blinked, trying to recall the number she needed, then dialed.

"I need you," she said when the person picked up. "And I need clothes."

David turned up within the hour. Stevie had spent that hour wandering the halls, trying to find her nurse, and then bugging that nurse about when she would be allowed to go. The nurse asked her politely to return to bed, explaining that the doctor would be up in the early afternoon, and that she would likely be allowed to go then. But early afternoon was too far away.

So when David walked through the door with the bag of clothes, Stevie immediately pushed herself out of bed, took it, and disappeared into the bathroom.

"How are you feeling?" David asked through the door.

"Everything hurts," she said. "Fine."

He had come with a pair of sweatpants and a stretched-out T-shirt. She fumbled, trying to work out how to shimmy out of her hospital gown. She pulled on the ties, loosening it, and it fell off the one side of her body, but it got stuck on the side with the sling. She managed to get this off and shake the gown to the bathroom floor. They had taken all her clothes last night, cut them off her body (which felt excessive, but it turned out they had to do that if they thought you broke your neck or spine or something). She was wearing giant stretchy underpants and nothing else.

"So you're being discharged?" David asked.

Stevie was too busy trying to figure out how to get the sweatpants on to answer. She dropped them onto the floor next to the gown and stepped into them, then dragged them up with her right hand, hoisting each side. She looped the shirt around her neck and got the right arm through, but the left was going to be difficult.

"Help," she said, tapping the door open with her foot and presenting her back to him. He was her boyfriend, but this was a messy situation, and also a public one. She wanted to get the shirt on. He moved around, trying to work out the physics of the situation, was big enough not to make any side-boob comments, and guided the sleeve over her cast.

"Okay," she said. "Time to go."

"Go? Don't they have to . . ."

She shook her head.

"Time to go," she said more quietly.

"Is that a good idea? Forget that—I mean, is that a medically sound idea?"

"I'm fine," she said, padding out into the room in her non-slip slippers and looking for wherever they had put her shoes and whatever else of hers was still intact. She found both the shoes and the remains of her clothes in a plastic bag marked PATIENT BELONGINGS in a chair by the window. She scooped it up and examined the contents. Her camp T-shirt had been cut open and there was condensation from the trapped moisture inside the bag. She tucked it under her good arm and went to the door to look out. Her nurse was not in the hall. If they hurried, they had a clear shot at getting to the turn to the elevator bank. Without waiting another moment, she slipped out of the room, David following behind.

"Are you sure?" he asked as they reached the elevator.

"Seriously," she said. "I have a broken arm. I'm fine."

The elevator arrived and she stepped inside, so he followed. No one paid them any attention as they wandered out the front door of the hospital to the old Nissan. David opened the door for her, and Stevie lowered herself into the passenger seat, choosing to ignore the aches through her body. She leaned back, closing her eyes for a moment against the sun. David got into the driver's side. She could feel him looking at her, but he had the good sense to start the engine and not ask her again if she was sure.

"Some good news for you," he said. "The head of the camp was freaked out when you two went off on bikes to town and never came back. Carson and Nate came up with some kind of cover story where you were riding in town, and a car pulled out fast in front of you, and you both swerved and fell."

"It's good to have an irresponsible adult on our side. It's the only way to get anything done."

"Camp?" he said. "Carson's house?"

"Camp," she said. "Not the Sunny Pines side. Your side."

"You want to tell me why you walked out of the hospital without waiting an hour or two for the doctor? I'll bet there's a reason."

"Someone shot at us last night," she said, opening her eyes and looking out the window. The bright light stunned her for a moment, but she acclimated.

"Someone . . ."

"Shot at us," she said.

"Who?"

Stevie's mind was going too fast to explain. All the threads, the wires, the tangled mess of stuff—it was connecting in her head in a way that she could not articulate.

"I'll know soon," she said.

When they reached the camping area, Stevie staggered out of the car and immediately walked to the wooded path that looped the lake. "We have to walk around," she said.

"Where are we going?"

"Over there," she said, indicating Point 23.

They began the long tramp around the lake, Stevie's body aching the entire way. The force at which she had hit the water had strained all her muscles, and her lungs and throat still burned. Her sneakers were still waterlogged and squelched with every step. Every once in a while, Stevie would dip off the path to get a clear view of the water.

"I'm looking for my backpack," she said. "I had to take it off in the water. Either it sank or someone recovered it."

"Does it matter? It's just a backpack."

"I had Sabrina Abbott's diary," she said. "I found it. I didn't have a chance to read it, but I found it."

"You found it? Where?"

"Inside a turtle at Allison's house. I would have read it already, but someone tried to kill us."

"So you were right about Allison."

"Looks that way," she replied.

The backpack was nowhere to be seen.

They had reached the space where the woods peeled back and the point jutted out in front of them, in all its terrible glory. Stevie's head began to swim as she approached it. She backed up several paces and got on her hands and knees, picking through the undergrowth and tree roots with her good hand.

"You think you can find a bullet?" he asked.

"Maybe . . ."

David got down on the ground as well, examining the earth. Stevie paused in her efforts for a moment to turn and have a look at him combing the dirt with his fingers. He was a good one. A weird one. A difficult one. But he always came through.

"Someone at the camp may have a metal detector," he said. "I could go back and ask."

Stevie returned to her examination of the forest floor. She felt the ground, digging in with her fingers.

"You sounded mad when I found you guys last night," David said.

"I think I was."

"We both have problems. Serious ones."

Stevie suddenly flattened herself on the ground on her back. She stretched out, looking at the blue sky above.

"Did you find one?" David asked.

"Nope."

"You okay?"

"Yep."

"Tired?"

"Yep. But there are a few things I have to do today."

"Like tell the police someone shot at you? Don't worry, I already know the answer to that one. I say these things for my own amusement."

"I need to have a Think Jam," she replied. "And I need Janelle to make a craft. Ask me why."

"Are you a hundred percent sure you didn't crack your head?"

"Thank you for asking," she said, looking over at him and smiling. "I'll tell you why—because it's what Frances Glessner Lee would do. It's time to show Barlow Corners a nutshell."

27

IN MANY OF THE MURDER MYSTERIES STEVIE LOVED, THE DETECTIVE would gather the suspects in a room, then explain who didn't do it before getting to who did. She never really understood why suspects would want to go to something like that, except maybe because these books took place in the past, and there wasn't that much to do then. Today, she got it. People would come because everyone wants to know the answer—especially in a place like a small town, where everyone knows everyone, and murder had cast a shadow for decades.

A murder reveal is worth skipping Netflix for.

In this case, it barely took any effort. All Stevie had to do was go on Nextdoor and put up a post in the Barlow Corners community page. It read: FIND OUT WHAT HAPPENED IN 1978. TONIGHT, 8:30 p.m. She listed the address of Carson's barn. For good measure, she had Carson go to town and let it be known in the right places that something was going down. The machinery of Barlow Corners did the rest. At eight thirty that night, the unreal orange walls of the Bounce House seemed to thrum as a small crowd of Barlow Corners residents came in and took their places on the sea of bean-bags. It was a good turnout, more than she needed. The key people had come: Paul Penhale, Susan Marks, Patty Horne, Shawn Greenvale, and Sergeant Graves. (The latter had gotten the courtesy of a phone call.)

Stevie had spent most of the day working on a borrowed laptop, revising Carson's slideshow. It was loaded up and ready to go. There was only one more piece she needed, and she waited, pacing in the corner of the room. Finally, David came through the barn door and stepped up to her.

"It's done," he said. "They're bringing it in through the back door."

"Okay," she said, mostly to herself. "It's time."

Carson and some of his crew had set up their cameras and equipment around the barn. Stevie nodded to him, and he dimmed the lights.

Stevie stepped up in front of the group. There were about thirty people. Plenty for her purposes, and not enough to be terrifying. Nerve-wracking, though, for sure.

Nate and Janelle came in quietly and slid along the wall to sit closer to the front. Stevie swallowed hard and began speaking.

"Thank you for coming," she said. "As you know, we came here to make a podcast about the Box in the Woods case, in the hopes of telling the story and trying to help with closure. But what I want to talk to you about tonight is the story a town tells about itself."

She hit the clicker, and the picture of the Bicentennial

dedication of the John Barlow statue appeared on the screen, in all its seventies polyester glory.

"Here are two moments of Barlow Corners' fame in one picture," she said. "In 1976, the town built a statue to the town founder, a Revolutionary War hero named John Barlow. His big act of heroism, as it turns out, was stealing some British horses and delaying a battle for a few hours. And he owned enslaved persons. Not very heroic. But people build myths, right? Tell the story enough times and it becomes true. John Barlow must be a hero—he has a statue. And then, this picture is taken, because doesn't this look like the perfect all-American town, building a statue of a Revolutionary War hero? Another story to put on top of the first story. But something was wrong in Barlow Corners."

She scanned the room.

"People got away with things here," she went on. "And then there was a new, terrible story to add, almost like an urban legend or a slasher movie. Four camp counselors went into the woods to do drugs . . . and none came out alive. At first the police thought it was about drugs, because why wouldn't it be? But that makes no sense. It was a small amount of pot, and it was left at the scene. The scene looked like the killings of the Woodsman, but the scene was also wrong in critical ways, and the DNA found on Eric's shirt didn't match the Woodsman's profile. Most people discount those theories now. But who could it be? There was suspicion in town, because there were people who might have had good reason to want Todd Cooper dead. Todd Cooper had run down an innocent boy with this car—Michael Penhale—and no one did anything about it. He got away with it because he was the son of the mayor. But he was guilty, and pretty much everyone knew it. No one would blame the Penhale family for wanting revenge. . . ."

The color drained from Paul's face, and his husband, Joe, looked like he was about to leap out of his seat. Stevie crossed the front of the room quickly, to stand by Susan Marks.

"Something bothered me about the conversation I had with you," she said. "I couldn't figure out what it was until now."

Susan looked at Stevie, with a glint of interest in her eye.

"There's a thing that people sometimes do when they make up a lie," Stevie said. "They make up details, specific ones. Paul told me that he and Shawn were in the lake house that night learning 'Stairway to Heaven' on guitar. That made sense. But then you told me the same thing. You were really vague about everything else. You said you did some random checks and went to bed. But you made sure to tell me about the guitar and the song. When I left your house, I ran into Shawn on the street."

Stevie looked to Shawn, who folded his arms across his chest.

"He didn't want to talk to me," Stevie said. "But then he *really* didn't want to talk to me when I said I'd spoken to you. All three of you really seemed to want everyone to know that Paul and Shawn were in the lake house playing 'Stairway to Heaven'—like it was the *most important thing* that happened that night. There's really only one reason you'd all be so specific and all tell that same story over and over in the same way. It's because it wasn't true."

Shawn put his head down and glowered a bit. Paul put his hands to his eyes and wiped away a tear, as his husband patted his arm. Susan continued to look at Stevie with a growing wariness.

"Paul," Stevie said, "you weren't in the lake house."

Everyone in the barn fell utterly silent, so Paul's reply seemed to boom out.

"No," he said quietly. "I wasn't. It's not their fault. They were helping me."

"I know," Stevie said. "Only Shawn was in there that night, watching over the lake. He probably was playing the guitar and learning 'Stairway to Heaven.' Susan, you did check in there to make sure there was a lifeguard on duty, but I doubt you noticed what song it was. I don't think you were a big Led Zeppelin fan."

Susan gave a soft snort.

"Paul," Stevie continued, "you were somewhere else, but you weren't murdering anyone."

"No," he said, folding his hands on his lap. "No, I wasn't. It's been so long. It's so ridiculous we've had to keep this up. I wasn't doing anything wrong."

"No," Stevie said, "you were meeting a boy."

Paul nodded. "He was from another town. He drove over to meet me in the woods. Then the murders happened and I had to prove where I was. I couldn't be gay. I would have been run out of town. I wouldn't have been allowed to work at a camp, for sure, because they would have believed that a gay guy couldn't work with kids, because . . ."

"Because it was 1978," Stevie said. "The same reason you had to keep quiet, even though you'd met your wife and were falling in love." This was to Susan, whose lip wobbled a little. She gave Stevie a nod.

"So what happened?" Stevie asked gently.

Susan looked at Shawn, who sighed and nodded.

"The morning after," Susan said, "I spoke to each counselor, one-on-one, to find out exactly what was going on that night. When I got to Paul—he couldn't really answer. He said something vague about taking a walk. I knew right away what that meant. I knew he was gay. I knew who most of my gay kids were, and I always tried to look out for them. I was gay and closeted too, but I was an adult. He was just a kid, and he'd already been through so much that year. I knew what would happen to him if he had to tell the police he was meeting a boy. He could have lied, made up a girl, but then they might have asked who she was. Then I remembered that Shawn had been all alone in the lake house. Paul and Shawn were friends, and they were both good kids. I realized that both Shawn and Paul might have trouble with this situation—Shawn because of Sabrina, and Paul because of Todd. So I got the idea for them to say they were together. To protect them, you understand. So I brought Shawn in . . ."

"He was amazing," Paul said. "I had to come out, right there, and he was incredible about it. You were incredible."

"It was no big deal," Shawn said. "You know that."

"So I had Shawn go over in detail what he had been doing," Susan went on, "and then I made them work out the story right then and practice it. They were in the lake house, playing guitar. I made them specify the song, so that all the details would match. And I would tell the same story too. You have to understand, this wasn't a story we thought we'd have to keep up. I figured the police would speak to everyone, and then they'd find out who did it, and that would be that. I knew those two boys had nothing to do with it and they needed protection."

"But then it was never solved," Paul said. "I wanted to tell the truth, but that would have caused problems for Shawn and Susan. The more famous the case got, the more we had to stick to it, because changing the story would have been a huge deal. So we had to keep telling the same story over and over."

He let out a long sigh.

"I'm glad," he said. "God, I'm so glad. Thank you. Thank you both."

The crowd in the Bounce House began to stir, sensing that things had come to a close.

"That's not the big reveal," Stevie said, holding up her good arm. "It's part of it, but it's not the whole thing. See, this is still about the story that the town tells about what happened that week in 1978, the four murder victims . . ."

Stevie looked up at the trapeze hanging from the ceiling. Time to swing for the sky—or at least, swing for the windows.

". . . except, that's wrong. There weren't four victims. And when you understand that, the whole story starts to make sense."

A long silence followed.

"What?" Susan finally said.

She seemed to express the feeling of the assembled. Stevie had been hoping someone might say something like that, otherwise her pause was just weird.

"It wasn't four victims," Stevie reiterated. "It was *six*. One before the box in the woods, and one after. Those four counselors weren't killed by some serial killer or because of a little pot. They were killed because one of them had seen something they weren't supposed to see. This person knew something terrible had happened in Barlow Corners and tried to do something about it."

"Sabrina," Shawn said. "I have no idea what you're talking about, but that person has to be Sabrina."

"Sabrina," Stevie repeated, nodding. "She was smart, she was persistent. And . . . *she wrote it all down in her diary*."

"Wait," Shawn said. "Are you saying . . . you have Sabrina's diary? The one Allison was always looking for?"

The inside of Stevie's cast began to itch furiously.

"I'm saying that I . . . we . . . found the diary," Stevie said. "Someone didn't want us to. Someone went after us, shot at us, and chased us right off the edge of Point 23 to try to get it from us. Because they knew Sabrina was the only witness."

Stevie looked over at her friends. Nate begged her with his eyes to stop.

Stevie was not going to stop.

She turned her focus on one person in the room—someone she needed to maintain eye contact with.

"This person was right to worry about Sabrina," Stevie continued. "And Allison. And me. They tried to shut us all up. But it didn't work."

Out of the corner of her eye, Stevie saw Nate sag. Janelle kept looking at Stevie, her eyes worried but curious. David, agent of chaos that he was, looked ready to ride with whatever lie was about to come out of Stevie's mouth.

It was now or never.

Stevie slid her uninjured hand into her cast sling and withdrew the diary.

"Who wants to hear what Sabrina Abbott has to say?" she asked.

28

OVER THE COURSE OF THE AFTERNOON, STEVIE HAD GOTTEN VERY familiar with the contents of this little book. She had marked pages with sticky notes—dozens of them. Now it was time to read:

JANUARY 3, 1978

Welcome, 1978. Nice to meet you. Time to crack open this fresh new diary I got for Christmas. I like that this one has a plain red cover this time. I liked the Snoopy one from last year because I will always love Snoopy and nothing can stop that, but this one is more of what I've got in mind for the future.

We went back to school today after the holiday break. There was talk about delaying the opening because of Michael Penhale, but apparently it was too complicated so we went back at the normal time. I can't believe it's been two weeks now since Michael died. In school today it was all anyone was talking about. Even if you couldn't hear people talking, it was everywhere. You knew if people were keeping their voices down, that was why. I saw Todd Cooper about twenty times. He was walking around like nothing was wrong, like half the town doesn't think he killed Michael.

My parents said the police checked into it and found he was at home when Michael died. They think someone from out of town who didn't know the road did it. Dana probably did see a brown Jeep, but there are loads of brown Jeeps.

And I guess I think that too?

Piano: 45 minutes
History: 35 minutes
German: 20 minutes
Admission essays: 3 hours

JANUARY 7, 1978

Maybe I'm strange, but I was really happy when school opened back up. The holidays are nice, and I usually love them, but Shawn was around all the time. I used to like that, but it's starting to wear on me. I guess it's because I have to get my college applications out this week and I'm not done with all my essays. I've written them out in my notebook and I'm almost done with the edits. Then I have to type all four of them up, which will take a full night. (I really need to learn how to type. I can play piano, why can't I type? Goal for 1978: learn to type.) Anyway, even if he comes over to work, I can feel his presence in the room. I want to be on my own to finish this up.

Maybe part of it is that he asks me a lot of questions about whether I *really* want to apply to Columbia, is that *really* my top choice. Don't I want to apply to Cornell instead? Or SUNY? He doesn't understand that what I want is something entirely different, entirely new. I want to live where there is culture, and art, and life. All kinds of life.

Piano: 25 minutes
Calc: 45 minutes
German: 35 minutes
Physics: 30 minutes
History: 25 minutes
Admission essays: 2 hours 15 minutes

January 9, 1978

I stayed at school late today to use the typing lab to type up my applications. I thought that would give me some privacy and let me finish. Shawn found me. I didn't even tell him I was staying. Doesn't he do anything else except float around the halls like a ghost looking for me?

He said he wanted to drive me home, which is something I guess. Maybe my parents sent him over so I wouldn't take my bike. After what happened with Michael, everyone is a little freaked out by the thought of riding a bike after dark.

But still, someone could ask me.

Calc: 20 minutes

German: 50 minutes

Admission essays and application forms: 3 hours

APRIL 5, 1978

It's three in the morning. I can't do this anymore. Have to go to sleep.

I managed to get home from school by four, so I thought I could get done early. I practiced piano for an hour, and then Shawn came over. My parents told him to stay for dinner, even though I didn't really want that. I have things to do. He hung out to "study" with me in the rec room, even though he didn't want to study and I actually did. I sat on the beanbag and he was sulking on the sofa, pretending to read *The Catcher in the Rye*. I finally told him to go around eight, because I could feel him looking at me and I couldn't concentrate. He complained. My mom brought down some Pepsi, so he dragged that out. It took him an *hour* to drink it, like it was a magical bottomless glass. Finally, he left just after nine, and I got down to my physics project.

When I was done, I put my headphones on and listened to Fleetwood Mac in the dark, sitting on the floor. This album, *Rumours,* is supposed to be about how everyone in the band was breaking up with each other even as they had to work together. Stevie and Lindsey are clearly fighting. You can hear it. It started to rain while I was sitting there, and Stevie was singing "When the rain washes you clean, you'll know." And in that moment, I did know.

I don't want to go out with Shawn anymore. I want to break up. Yes. Even as I write this, I realize it's true. The rain is washing me clean, and I do know.

Oh my god, I'm going to break up with him.

I feel good. Like, good in a way that I haven't felt in a while.

Now they're singing "You can go your own way." Are they singing to *me*?

Thank you, Lindsey. Thank you, Stevie.

This is the last time I count the hours I spent on subjects, because after this, my hours will be mine:

Piano: 1 hour
Calc: 25 minutes
German: 45 minutes
English: 45 minutes (reading)
History: 1 hour (reading)
Physics: 3 hours
Shawn: done.

April 6, 1978

I've decided to do it this weekend. Somewhere neutral. Somewhere I can get out of. I'm thinking the Dairy Duchess.

April 8, 1978

What a goddamned nightmare.

April 9, 1978

I couldn't write about it yesterday. It was too much.

I met him at Dairy Duchess. I thought it would take me forever to get to it, so I jumped ahead. I said, "I think we should break up."

He stared at me. It was obvious he had *no idea* this was about to happen. I think maybe he thought I was kidding at first? I started to say it again. He said, "No." Not mean. Not angry. Just confused? I started to panic, because he looked so baffled and sad.

I don't want to go into detail about what happened for the next hour. There was a lot of crying. From him. I just sat there. He was begging me. In public.

I left him there and biked home.

Then I had to tell my family what I'd done. They freaked out in a way I did not expect. My parents didn't exactly yell at me, but they definitely gave me the third degree about it, like was I sure? Was I acting in haste? I swear to god they asked me more about this than where I was applying to college. I mentioned this, very calmly, and my mom said, "You can go to college anywhere, but you only marry one person."

Which doesn't even make sense.

I said I'm not like them. I don't want to marry someone from high school and be here forever. And they gave some lip service, saying they knew that, but Shawn is so wonderful, blah, blah, blah and prom etc.

In the middle of this, Allison came in from roller-skating up and down the street and asked what was going on. When she found out she started *bawling*. Like someone had *died*. I get it. She's twelve, and Shawn has been around since she was nine. He's like an older brother. But what am I going to do? Get married to him because my little sister loves him?

Anyway, the house was a mess for about two hours. Even Cookie started barking and wouldn't stop. I went to my room and listened to records with my headphones on. I played *Rumours*. I listened to the song "Never Going Back Again" five times. That song goes right into "Don't Stop." I feel like they're guiding me. "Don't stop thinking about tomorrow, don't stop, it'll soon be here."

It had better be.

It's okay here at home now. I think my parents realized that I was serious about what I wanted and they trust me. Allison knocked on the door and asked if I wanted to go to Sizzler for dinner. We're good now. She gets it. She's the best.

April 12, 1978

Oh my god. I got into Columbia. I got a scholarship.

Don't stop thinking about tomorrow.

Don't stop, it'll soon be here.

April 14, 1978

Interesting thing at lunch today.

Shawn and I don't have the same lunch period. He has fourth. But for no reason I can make out, he appeared at fifth lunch today. It's the first time since the other night that I felt really and completely flustered when I saw him. I turned toward the lunch line, and I felt him come up behind me. He said, "Can we talk?"

I told him I wanted to eat lunch. Mostly, at that point, I felt like I was going to barf. No one wants a sloppy joe under these conditions.

He asked again, and I started gripping the tray rail, and then something happened. Diane McClure, who was a few people ahead of me, stepped back and joined me in line.

She said, "She said she wants to eat lunch."

Shawn stammered something, but Diane was not having it. So Shawn backed away. I swear to god I almost started crying in thankfulness.

Diane was waiting tables the day when I broke up with Shawn at the Duchess. She saw it all go down, so she must have figured out what was going on there in line. She said to me, "Why don't you come sit with us?"

Diane hangs out a lot with Eric, Patty, Greg, and Todd. I don't know if I want to get involved with them? Eric is okay, and I know Todd, but I don't really want to hang out with them. Patty and Greg are always sucking face, everywhere, at all times.

But any port in a storm. They were at one of the picnic tables outside, and actually? It was okay?

Diane said I can have lunch with them every day if I want, and maybe I will?

May 2, 1978

Back with my new lunch group today.

I don't know how I feel about being around Todd Cooper. I never really figured out where I came down on what happened with Michael. I think that before I was more inclined to believe that the police were right, that Todd had nothing to do with the accident. But now that I spend more time with him, I see that he is a jackass. Not deliberately scary or hurtful, but someone who could hurt someone by accident so easily. He doesn't seem to notice that other people are real? Does that make sense? Like he could hit someone with his car and know that he did it, and somehow justify to himself completely that it wasn't his fault. That's how he seems to me. I mean, I still don't know and it seems terrible and impossible but. . . ?

Diane is totally dedicated to him. I believe she would lie for him.

Eric is . . .

Yeah, Eric is different. Eric is okay? Maybe Eric is more than okay?

May 31, 1978

Finals are over. It's done. High school is done.

June 6, 1978

It's so weird having nothing to do. I don't know if I've ever had nothing to do. Camp orientation and training starts next Friday, so I have a week and a half to do whatever I want. What do people do with free time?

I was cleaning my room, because I had no idea what else to do, when Diane called.

She said that they were going to hang out at

Patty's house. They have a big pool. Did I want to come? I said sure. So she and Todd came to pick me up.

I knew the Hornes had a nice house, but I've never been in it. It's up on the end of Sparrow Road. It's huge. Behind the house is a pool patio that stretches almost to the wood line. Mr. Horne has a beer fridge that he doesn't mind if we use, and he even came out to make hot dogs on the grill.

Is this fun? Am I having fun?

I think I might be?

June 8, 1978

Two things happened today. I don't know what to do.

After lunch, Greg turned up at the door and asked me if I wanted a ride to Patty's. I said sure. When we got to Sparrow Road, he didn't park in the driveway—he parked at the end of the street and we walked up. I asked why. He said that Patty told him to use the pool, even if she wasn't there to let him in. But it annoys her dad, so she told him to park down the street and come in through the back gate. That way the neighbors don't say anything to Mr. Horne about people going in and out of the house when neither of them are home.

I asked him where Patty was, and he said she was out shopping. He said that Eric and Diane would be coming by soon. Diane was doing a shift at the Duchess and Eric was doing "milkman stuff." (I've come to understand that when Eric buys grass and makes deliveries, he calls that being "the milkman." A few months ago, I would have been more freaked out about that. I've grown.)

Anyway, we swam, hung out. Greg is Patty's boyfriend, so it was fine that we were there. But then there was a noise from inside the house.

He said, "Shit, shit! Grab your stuff!"

He was laughing, but I could tell he was serious. I grabbed my bag and towel and followed him into the cabana.

This is when things got really, really strange.

Mr. Horne and a man came out of the house and sat by the pool, not far from where we were in the cabana, and started talking. The man's name was Wendel something. He was saying that he hadn't seen Mr. Horne since Harvard. Mr. Horne started joking, asking how the man had found him. The man said that he had been at his dentist's office and was leafing through the Bicentennial edition of *Life* magazine in the waiting room when he saw the picture with Mr. Horne and all of us in it.

Mr. Horne started speaking in German. The man asked why, and Mr. Horne said because whenever he talked about the war, he preferred German in case neighbors could hear, because of the nature of what they did. The man seemed to understand that.

My German isn't perfect—I'm good enough to basically follow things, but some of it was too advanced/idiomatic. I'm writing down what I remember. I didn't get all of it.

Something like:

Man: After Berlin, I never heard from you again. I thought the Russians killed you.

Mr. Horne: They almost did.

Man: How long were you in prison there?

Mr. Horne: Eight months.

Man: You've done well for yourself.

Mr. Horne: I've done all right.

Then they talked about the house for a while, and about some military things I didn't understand. Also, Greg was trying to distract me and I had to tell him to stop. I caught up a bit later, and I picked up that his last name was Ralph or something like that.

Man: Who was it you were following? Von Hessen? (Something like that.)

Mr. Horne: Yes.

Man: I don't think they ever found him, did they?

Mr. Horne: I thought they found his body eventually.

Man: No. They never found him.

Mr. Horne: You keep up with this.

Man: Yes.

Mr. Horne: Once I was out, I didn't want to look back.

Man: That surprises me.

Mr. Horne: Why?

Man: You were always so . . . well, it was long ago.

Then Patty came home and interrupted them. Mr. Horne asked the man to come back in the evening around seven, and he'd grill some steaks. The man said he would. Mr. Horne asked where he was staying, and the man said the Holiday House Motel.

We were still stuck inside the stupid cabana. It was getting really hot. I don't know what was wrong with me—I guess I was hot, nervous, kind of giddy. We could hear Mr. Horne telling Patty that she would be allowed to go to the Stones concert in New York, and she started screaming. Greg got close to me and we were listening, and before I knew what was happening, we were making out. I don't even know how it started, and it wasn't all him. I did it too.

Then I panicked. I was totally freaked out. He calmed me down and said it was fine, that he and Patty both made out with other people. This seemed . . . not in keeping with their constant sucking-face policy, but okay? I asked why we were hiding if it was all okay, and he said that while it was fine, at her house it might be awkward.

We managed to get out of the cabana at some point, and over the fence, and home. I'd temporarily forgotten about the weird conversation I'd heard, but sitting here tonight, it keeps playing in my head.

What the hell even happened today?

June 9, 1978

Okay. Even writing this down makes me feel weird.

I went to Patty's again today for the normal pool party. I was nervous, for a lot of reasons. In terms of Greg and Patty, everything was totally normal. Same as ever. He whispered to me that he'd told her, and it was all cool. But he said maybe don't mention it, because that would make it weird. This felt strange to me, but I wasn't totally paying attention.

The pool furniture was rearranged. Not completely, but several of the chairs, which have always been in the same spots, had been moved. And there was change at the bottom of the pool—a few pennies, three nickels, a dime, and a quarter. It was for sure not there yesterday. It wasn't in the shallow end, either. It was in the deep end, and kind of in the middle of the pool.

I was staring at it, and Mr. Horne noticed. He asked me what I was looking at, and I blurted out something about the change. Patty started going on about how I'm the smartest person at Liberty, etc. Which was stupid, because you don't have to be smart to notice change at the bottom of a pool.

Mr. Horne stared at me for a moment and said, "I'm going to have to watch out for you."

Then he said to everyone, "So, who can get that change out for me? There's a beer in it for you!"

At which point, everyone but me dove in headfirst to get the change. Then I looked up at Mr. Horne, who was smiling. By this point, everyone was splashing and flailing and dunking each other and trying to beat everyone else to the bottom to get the change.

Mr. Horne said, "It's a tie! Beers for all!"

He brought beers from the garage fridge and everyone took one. I took one as well, even though I don't like beer. Then he started up the grill and made hot dogs. After that it felt like a normal pool party, with the smell of the grill and the hot dogs.

But something was wrong. I have no idea what.

June 10, 1978

I called Eric today and we met up to ride our bikes for a while. I must have seemed troubled, because we pulled over by the school and he asked me what was up. I came out and told him about what happened with me and Greg, and that Greg said it was fine and that he had told Patty, and that I knew they made out with other people, but things still felt strange. I didn't tell him about the other stuff, because what the hell could I say about that? I don't even know what's so weird about it or why it bothers me.

He laughed, but not in a mean way.

"That's going to be news to Patty," he said. "I love Greg like a brother, but he is a dirtbag."

I got kind of freaked out, but he immediately calmed me down.

"It's not your fault," he said. "If Greg told you that, then you didn't think you were doing anything wrong. It's okay. Greg is a jerk. He likes getting away with stuff."

He ended up making me laugh really hard. Eric is funny.

Eric would make a really good counselor—not camp counselor, a psychologist or something like that.

He offered me a joint. I was embarrassed, but I said I don't smoke them. He put it away. I know I'm pretty much the only person at Liberty who has never smoked grass (okay, one of three that I know of). I know it's not a big deal to smoke it either, because like I said, everyone else does and they are all fine. I don't smoke because I'm an uptight weenie.

I actually said to Eric, "I'm an uptight weenie."

He fell backward laughing. Shawn never laughs like that. It's nice to hang out with someone who laughs.

June 12, 1978

Woke up early today. I was dreaming of that conversation I overheard between Mr. Horne and the man who came over to his house. I can't stop thinking about it. That conversation was odd.

So, since I have time and nothing else to do, I'm going to go over to the Holiday House Motel. I might as well bike over there and get ice cream at the Duchess on the way back. I might as well shut my subconscious up.

Update: 4 p.m.

That did not go how I thought it would. I don't know what to make of what's happened. I'm kind of shaking and I'm sitting here at the foot of my bed.

I went to the motel and said that a friend of my dad's had been staying there a few days ago and left something at our house, and I was kind of worried because he didn't come back for it. I sort of mumbled the name Ralph, and the woman behind the counter picked up on it right away. She said a man had been staying there, and he never actually checked out. He left his key in his room.

I have no idea where I came up with this, but I said that if I could get a copy of the bill I could take it to my dad and he could help take care of it. She hesitated for a moment, but then she went into the file cabinet and pulled it out. The man's name isn't Ralph—it's Wendel Rolf. I couldn't make out his whole address, but I saw that he's from Albany, New York. The bill was for $64, which was for two nights.

So the man never checked out of the hotel?

What do I think happened? That Mr. Horne drowned him in the pool? And while he was doing so, the change fell out of the man's pockets and landed at the bottom?

Like it's an Alfred Hitchcock movie or something.

June 13, 1978

This has to end. I have to put this out of my mind. Let me break it down, make sense of it. What is it that I think I heard and saw?

I'm reading back the conversation I wrote down from the other day:

Wendel Rolf: After Berlin, I never heard from you again. I thought the Russians killed you.

And then:

WR: Who was it you were following? Von Hessen? (Or whatever the name was.)

Mr. Horne: Yes.

WR: I don't think they ever found him, did they?

Mr. Horne: I thought they found his body eventually.

WR: No. They never found him.

Mr. Horne: You keep up with this.

WR: Yes.

What does that add up to?

I can only think of one thing.

A man came to Mr. Horne's house. They seemed to know each other from the war. There was tension between them. Something was wrong. Then the next day, the furniture was moved around. There was change in the pool. Mr. Horne acted strange. And the man never went back to his motel.

You read all kinds of stories about Nazis who escaped. People go looking for them. They take on new identities in different countries.

What the hell is going on?

JUNE 14, 1978

I went to the library today to do the reading circle for the kids. When I was done, I went through the entire history section looking for books about Nazis and the fall of Berlin. We didn't have anything too detailed.

I found the names of some books that might have more information. I put in interlibrary loan requests for them. It will take a little while for them to get here.

When I got home, I called directory assistance and got Wendel Rolf's number. I called it. I called it four times, actually. No one answered.

My essay about what I did on my summer vacation is going to be weird.

June 15, 1978

Called the number again this morning. No answer.

What am I doing? What am I *doing*?

Update: 11 p.m.

There is an obvious answer to all of this: the man is on vacation. He's *not at home.*

I need to get a grip. I go to camp tomorrow for orientation.

June 16, 1978

I cannot believe this. Shawn got a job here at the camp.

June 18, 1978

Well, it's been a shitty two days, but things are starting to improve. Shawn actually keeps his distance, so things aren't too bad.

Also, I love the kids. They are adorable. But they

go through my stuff. I've had to start hiding this diary in the camp library, because pretty much no one goes there but me. Just lonely old nerdy me. Still, need a better place.

JUNE 27, 1978

Been too busy to write much, and the kids are always in my face. I made something in the arts tent to hold this diary, so at least that's taken care of.

Had a dream last night about the man at the Hornes' house, Wendel Rolf, and I kept thinking about it all day. It got in my head and wouldn't get out. I need to let that go. Maybe I can get therapy in New York. They have that there.

I guess while I'm here I can talk to Eric about it? We kind of hang out all the time. We haven't kissed yet, but that is coming soon. I can feel it.

JUNE 28, 1978

I told Eric everything.

He was saying that I put a lot of pressure on myself. I feel bad about Greg and Patty, and it's stressing me out that Shawn is here at camp. I'm starting Columbia in the fall, so I'm moving to New York City soon. All of this is—a lot. So maybe I've put this thing together in my head because I'm overwhelmed.

Oh, and the kissing thing? Yep.

July 1, 1978

Something about me: I can always find something to worry about. The newest one? The thing with Greg. I feel like if I'm not honest about it, the guilt will keep grinding away at me. At the same time, I don't want to hurt Patty. But she should know, right? I'd want to know.

July 2, 1978

It's midnight. I just got back into the bunk and into bed. I'm covered in mosquito bites.

After campfire and once the kids were all in bed, I went over to Patty's bunk and knocked on the wall and asked her to come out. I told her that Greg said it was okay to use the pool at her house, and that while we were there, her dad came back for lunch with a friend of his. I didn't tell her about the weird conversation. That didn't matter. I told her we made out. I said he told me they were okay with seeing other people.

She didn't seem mad at me, but she was really upset. Really upset. So upset that she threw up from crying. Jesus.

Anyway. That was terrible.

July 3, 1978

Patty was so upset she went home for the day, back to town. I feel like shit, but at least I told the truth.

July 4, 1978

Happy Independence Day?

Patty Horne was back today, and she and Greg were sitting together at the big campfire, and I turned when we were watching the fireworks and they were making out. So I guess she's forgiven him?

Eric said, "Don't worry about it. Her dad probably bought her another horse or something to cheer her up."

Honestly, it was so weird. She was so upset that she had to leave? And now things are *fine*?

I was sitting with Eric, and he had his arm around me. Shawn was staring at us.

I need to get out of Barlow Corners. This place is too small.

July 5, 1978

My library books came in today. Mrs. Wilde called over to the camp to let me know. I feel embarrassed now that I had books about Nazis sent to our library, but since I ordered them, I rode my bike over to town while the kids were in group free time and Katie was watching them. I was on my way out holding them and I ran into Mr. Horne. He was on his way into the library. I didn't have them in a bag—I was going to put them in my bike basket. He could see the titles.

He said, "That's some serious summer reading."

I said, "It's for Columbia. They make us do some

reading over the summer before we come. Some literature, some history."

He said wow or something like that, and he was being really normal, but my heart was going *fast*. And there was . . . I don't know? Something in his expression?

I don't know why I did this. I said, "Did you have to do that for Harvard too?"

He said he couldn't remember. Maybe. It was too long ago.

Then he said, "How did you know I went to Harvard?"

I said, "Patty told me."

The trouble was, I hesitated because it took me a second to think of it, because my brain froze. He looked at me for a long second and smiled. Then he said goodbye and good to see you, have fun at camp, and went on doing what he was doing.

This whole thing is making me so paranoid, and the books weren't going to help with that. So I went back to the library and told Mrs. Wilde that they weren't what I needed after all and returned them. I rode back to camp really fast.

Mr. Horne is not a Nazi.

I should try to relax a bit, take a week or so and try to really *enjoy* myself. Really *enjoy* myself. I've done all this hard work. Why can't I have fun like everyone else?

I'm going out to the woods with them tomorrow to hang out. I know what that means. He picks up the grass out there. But they also have fun.

I'm doing it. I need to break some rules for once, or I feel like I'm going to pop. This is my summer to live.

Do you hear me, Sabrina Abbott? This is your summer to LIVE!

So that's what I'm going to do.

29

"THAT'S THE LAST ENTRY," STEVIE SAID, GENTLY CLOSING THE BOOK.

For almost an hour, she had read from the diary. Her throat was dry and her voice was starting to crack a bit. Janelle had seen this and come over with a can of sparkling water. Stevie didn't like sparkling water, but she guzzled it and then had to turn her head and try to conceal the massive belch this caused. She was not successful.

Poirot never burped after he identified the murderer.

Patty Horne had turned the color of five-day-old turkey. She was utterly still, her head cocked slightly to the left, and something almost like a queasy smile spread across her mouth. The rest of the assembled were silent.

Stevie glanced over at Shawn Greenvale, who sat with his chin tucked to his chest. None of that could have been easy for him to hear, no matter how long ago it had happened. But he bore it, like he had stayed strong for Paul. They may have broken up, but clearly Sabrina had been with Shawn because he was a fundamentally good guy. It just hadn't worked out.

"So," Stevie said, feeling another froggy burp rising in her throat and pushing it down painfully, "let's start with this question: Who is Wendel Rolf, and what happened to him after he arrived at your house that day? I needed some help getting the answer. . . ."

She reached over to the laptop and switched the windows. An image projected onto the screen—a person with large glasses and straight, long hair.

"Hi," Stevie said. "Tell everyone what you found out."

"Hey," Germaine said. "I'm Germaine Batt from *The Batt Report*."

Germaine was a classmate of Stevie's from Ellingham who ran her own online news channel. She and Stevie had an unusual, somewhat mercenary relationship, and this favor was going to have to be repaid. It was worth it.

"Okay." Germaine had no problem dispensing with all other formalities and diving in. "I started with Harvard, because that came up in the conversation you showed me. I got in touch with some people there this afternoon and they pulled some yearbooks for me. Wendel Rolf graduated in the class of 1940, along with Arnold Horne. I found enlistment records for both of them on a genealogy website. Wendel Rolf was honorably discharged in 1946, and Arnold Horne in 1947. So far, so normal. But then, everything about Wendel Rolf just—goes away. I had to go through local paper archives and Facebook all day, but I found a relative of his. I pretended I was part of a Harvard alumni research thing, so they talked to me. Wendel Rolf went away for a weekend fishing trip in 1978. He never came back. He was declared dead in 1983. No one knows if he had an accident or not—but it sounds like his family thought he may have taken his own life and wanted to spare them somehow and make sure they got the life insurance money. You can find out a lot if you say you're from Harvard."

"So," Stevie said, "Wendel Rolf sees his old classmate and army buddy Arnold Horne's picture in a magazine. It's definitely him. His name is in the caption. He decides to pay his friend a visit. It seems pretty clear that he realizes right away that something is off—that this isn't Arnold Horne. In the conversation Sabrina overheard, he mentions another man—a von Hessen."

"He was a lot easier to find," Germaine said. "Otto von Hessen was a high-ranking Nazi intelligence officer working out of Berlin. Lots of stuff out there about him. He was last seen in April of 1945, right before Berlin fell. Then he vanished. Want me to put up the pictures?"

Stevie nodded, and Germaine shared her screen, putting Arnold Horne's Harvard photo next to an official photo of von Hessen.

The resemblance was unmistakable.

"Arnold Horne went to Harvard and was a spy in World War II," Stevie said. "He was in Berlin. We know from the conversation that he had a connection to von Hessen. When Berlin was falling and the Nazis needed to make their escape, what better way than to take the identity of an American intelligence officer? They aren't identical, but the resemblance was good enough if you didn't look too closely. The real Arnold Horne went to Germany, but it was Otto von Hessen who came back and started a quiet new life in America and tried to keep himself under the radar. He moved to a small town where nothing ever happened, ran the local bank, and didn't like getting his picture taken. And for years, it worked out. But then, Barlow Corners built a statue, a local photographer took a good picture, and that picture went into a national magazine. Wendel Rolf saw his old friend's photo, paid him a visit, and realized something was wrong—that he wasn't visiting Arnold Horne at all. Wendel Rolf was never seen again. He's victim number one. This is where the story begins. It's also probably where the story would have ended if Sabrina Abbott hadn't been in the cabana with Greg, if she wasn't so observant and determined. Now . . ."

Stevie nodded to Germaine and closed that window, then turned to Patty.

". . . you enter the story. It's graduation, summer 1978. You told me yourself that you were kind of aimless. You had no plan for what you were going to do when the summer was over. Greg, your friends, hanging out—that was your whole world. On the day that Greg and Sabrina were in the cabana and your father met Wendel Rolf, you had no idea what was going on. None of those three people wanted you to know what had happened at your house that afternoon. That night, Wendel Rolf comes back, and your father kills him. The next day, Sabrina returns to the house and sees things have been moved around. She was already curious about what she'd heard. You still have no clue, and neither does your dad. But then, Sabrina's conscience gets to her and she tells you she was in the cabana with Greg. You leave camp and tell your dad, and your dad knows that it's all coming apart. Your friends—the ones he despises—are going to destroy your lives. I'm guessing a lot of things went down in your house that night. I think your dad told you the truth, or some version of it, because you knew your friends had to die, and you had to help your dad kill them. Something had to be done, fast, and he couldn't exactly sneak into the camp and take care of it. It had to happen somewhere else, where there were no people around. And you knew exactly the spot—the weekly drug delivery out in the woods. Sabrina would be there. Eric, Todd, and Diane—they were unlucky. And who knows what they'd been told? They all had to die."

Stevie put the slide with the photos of the four victims back up on the screen, so that Patty would have to look at them.

"You had to be protected. So the next day you returned to camp, and suddenly everything was fine with Greg—so fine that you were busted getting busy with him and put on house arrest. This ensured you had an ironclad alibi. Some details of the Woodsman murders had been in the paper. This was perfect. There was no internet then—if Arnold wanted to get the details, he would have needed to get a copy of the newspaper articles. So it's not that surprising that Sabrina ran into him on July 5, when she was on her way out of the library and he was going in. That encounter sealed her fate."

Stevie waved a stray bug that had gotten inside the

Bounce House away from her face. She had been talking for a long time and her body was starting to ache. She wanted to flop down in a beanbag and rest for a while, but the story was not finished. It was time to open the box in the woods, time to ruin the surprise.

"On the night of the Box in the Woods murders," she continued, "your father went into the woods. He went to the spot you told him to go to. He'd been a Nazi intelligence officer. He'd faked his identity for thirty-three years. Cornering four stoned teenagers in the woods was probably not a big deal. The evidence suggests what happened there. Todd and Diane were probably off by themselves in a sleeping bag. They had no defensive wounds, so they likely never saw him coming. They were killed where they were and taken away in the sleeping bag. Sabrina and Eric were each attacked in a different way. Sabrina fought—there were wounds on her hands. Eric had been struck on the head but managed to run away. That must have been a scare, because if Eric got away, the whole thing would be over. But your father caught him and killed him at the border of the camp. The scene was made to look like one of the Woodsman's crimes, and the job was done. Except . . ."

Stevie brought up a photo of Greg.

". . . Sabrina wasn't the only one in that cabana. Greg was there too. This wasn't a problem that could be partially solved. They *all* had to go. What did you say when your father told you your boyfriend had to die? Were you sad, or were you glad to get him back for cheating?"

Patty put her head down, and Stevie knew she had hit the bull's-eye with this one.

"I was in the hospital last night, after you chased us through the woods with a gun. You ran Nate and me off Point 23, which is why my arm's in this. . . ."

She held up her cast.

"I was kind of out of it last night. I kept trying to sleep, but there was this reflection of a flashing light that kept me up. It was really distracting. It got me thinking again about something you told me, Susan. What did you tell me you saw that night at the football field when all the students gathered?"

"The memorial night?" Susan asked.

Stevie nodded.

"I saw Patty crying at the end of the school driveway, and then I saw the crash up ahead."

"No," Stevie said. "That's not exactly what you saw."

"Well, no. I saw a flash of light as he crashed. He crashed around the bend."

"Why would you see a flash of light when Greg crashed?"

"His headlight, I guess? As the bike spun around? I don't know, actually."

"How bright was it?"

"Very bright," Susan said thoughtfully. "Enough that it's most of what I remember. I suppose that would have been too bright for a headlight. Maybe it was something else."

Stevie turned to Janelle.

"Can you bring it out now?" she asked.

Janelle nodded and tugged on Nate's arm. They went into one of the side rooms and emerged a minute later with a large platform covered in cardboard and crafting materials. A box represented the high school. There was a curving road of fabric, glued down to the pasteboard. Some lumps of modeling clay represented the rocks at the turn of the road, and there were trees made of pipe cleaners and some kind of fluffy, moss-like substance. The Liberty High sign had been re-created with cardboard.

"I didn't have a lot of time to make it look great," Janelle said. "But the proportions are right. And here . . ."

She handed Stevie a few saltshakers, each filled with a different color of craft sand.

"Okay," Stevie said, placing a saltshaker full of pink sand at the end of the driveway. "Here's Patty Horne. And here . . ." She set a shaker full of green sand on the road next to Patty. ". . . this is you. Is this about where you were when you saw the light?"

"Yes," Susan said. "I was about to turn into the driveway."

"And what was Patty doing?"

"She was crying," Susan said.

"But what else was she doing? What did you tell me?"

Susan paused for a moment, cocking her head in thought, puzzled by the question.

"Crying," she said. "Screaming. Really upset. Waving a flashlight around."

Stevie pointed at her, indicating this was the thing she had been waiting for.

"Waving a flashlight around," she said.

"But that's not the light I'm talking about," Susan said quickly. "I saw something in the distance."

"Oh, I know you did," Stevie said, reminding herself not to smile.

She pulled out her phone. She held it next to the pink salt-shaker.

"We need to turn down the lights for a minute," Stevie said.

Carson hit the dimmer on the lights, and the barn fell into shadow. Stevie switched on her phone flashlight. She had already put a little masking tape around the light to narrow the beam. She angled it very slightly, flashing it around on the dark blue Liberty High sign. The little dot of light bounced around.

"Patty flashes her light here," Stevie said. "Janelle, now."

At the far end of the road, Janelle had rested her phone on the little clay rocks and pipe cleaner trees. She switched on her phone flashlight, which was not taped and brighter and broader than Stevie's light. Stevie turned away immediately, as she had planned, and saw many people turn or shield their eyes.

"This is what you saw," Stevie said. "Turn the lights back on."

The lights came back up, and several people were still blinking.

"That's a pretty good reconstruction," Susan said. "But why would you have to demonstrate that?"

"Because what you saw was a *signal* and a *response*. Patty was shining her light on the sign, which is clearly visible from the far end of the road. That meant that Greg had left the parking lot and was traveling in the only direction he could travel—it's a one-way road. Down at the other end of the street, her father was waiting with a high-powered flashlight. As Greg approached, he flashed it on. The light was bright enough that you saw it all the way up the road. Greg, being closer, would have been blinded by something that bright. A little drunk or high, unable to see, he loses control at the turn. The crash was a guarantee. Simple. Clean. Effective. Just an accident."

"You wouldn't even have to stand there to do it," Janelle pointed out. "You could put something reflective there and shine the light from an angle so you were well out of the way. It's so *basic*."

"It really is," Stevie said. "So basic that it looks like nothing at all. It's something someone who studied spy craft would be really good at coming up with. Lights. Mirrors. Signals. Untraceable stuff. Simple, smart, and effective. I think you learned that from your dad, and when you had to kill Allison, you did it in the kind of way he would have done it. Allison always wanted her sister's diary. The police didn't have it. It was never found at the camp. As we learned, it was bad news for you if anyone found it. But if no one had turned it up since 1978, it wasn't likely that it was ever going to be found. You'd always been safe. But then, a few days ago, I gave Allison a paper we found in the art supply tent, and Allison realized that while working the crafts with the counselors, Sabrina ordered a ceramic cookie jar in the shape of a turtle to paint. She made it to hide her diary. She also made the lid nice and tight so that the campers wouldn't be able to get into it. Allison realized that the ceramic turtle she had in her house was a jar, not a figurine. She must have been so excited. She went home and tried to pry it open, but the lid was stuck. She had to figure out how to get it open without damaging it. Allison would never have damaged something of Sabrina's. Did she call you, her friend, to tell you she thought she might know where the diary was? Your whole life—everything you'd built, everything you were—would be over. You'd be the daughter of a notorious murderer, not the daughter of a war hero. And maybe people would start to look into what happened with Greg a little more carefully. No. None of that could happen. You'd already let five of your friends die. Now one more had to go to keep your secret."

Susan Marks turned and fixed Patty with a devastating gaze.

"What was the one thing you could count on with Allison? Her schedule. She ran every morning and she stopped on Arrowhead Point. That was perfect. Easiest thing in the world to fall off a place like that, and that there would likely be people nearby who would see the entire thing go down and be able to swear—absolutely swear—that no one else was up there. Honestly? I'm kind of worried that *I* gave you the idea. When we came into your shop on the first morning we were here and we were looking at your cakes, Janelle asked how you decorated them. You said that your trick was working from the outside in. I said, 'Like a crime scene.' No one ever listens to me when I say stuff like that, but I think you did. If Allison fell, the area would be roped off and investigated from the outside in. That means *time*. Time for something to vanish. And what vanishes on a hot rock in the sun?"

There was a pause as the assembled worked out whether or not this was a rhetorical question. Finally someone broke the silence with a tentative "Ice?"

"Ice," Stevie said, forcing her inner confidence out into her voice. "There was no time for anything elaborate—no molds or anything like that. What you could do was make some sheets of ice. Put them on the point so that when Allison stepped on them, she slid right off. The evidence either melted away as the sun came up or some of it fell off with her. When the police examined the rock, there was nothing there. You had everything you needed—large sheet pans, a professional-sized freezer, large capacity containers like the kind used to transport elaborate food items—and one more thing, the only thing that left a trace."

Stevie dug into her bag one more time and pulled out the remains of the Camp Sunny Pines shirt.

"I went up to Arrowhead Point when it reopened," she said. "I poured out some water from my bottle to see how steep the surface was, then I got on the ground. I didn't know it then, but I rehydrated something that was dried on the rock, and it won't come off. That's because it's dye—food dye. You made some large, flat pieces of ice, tinted with dye to darken them. No one would notice it, and in time, it would all wash away with the rain. It was good I was there when I was, before the storm. Because this"—she held the shirt higher for emphasis—"this can be examined. It can be identified, right down to brand and type."

Patty opened her mouth and closed it several times, like a fish gasping on the shore.

"This is absurd. . . ."

"Here's the thing," Stevie said. "Sabrina is a witness now. She's speaking from the dead. And everyone here"—she motioned, indicating everyone in the room—"they heard it. And everyone who hears this podcast—"

"Oh, it's a television show now," Carson cut in. "For sure."

". . . or watches this show . . . they're going to study you as you are right now, in this moment. This is your chance to tell your side. Because if you don't, other people will tell it for you. Everyone will judge you. You won't be able to escape it. You have a chance, right now, to say whatever you want to say. . . ."

"A piece of advice," David said, folding his arms casually across his chest. "I'd tell her what she wants to know. The last person in your position tried to deny it too, and it didn't work out well for them."

"My father was a *good man*," Patty said. "He did *everything* for me. He *lived* for me."

There was a tremor in her voice, one that reflected the seismic activity that must have been going on inside of her— the rush and tumble of decades of psychological weight coming down—all the blocks and boulders she'd stacked to keep the truth as separate as possible.

"Your dad was a Nazi," David corrected her. "And he murdered five of your friends."

Patty stiffened and fell silent.

"Something you're probably asking yourself right now," Stevie went on. "How do I have this diary? You chased us. You saw us jump into the lake. You heard me scream that it was gone. I bet you checked. Were you there all night? I bet you checked the path, to make sure I hadn't dropped it by accident. I bet you looked everywhere, to be really, *really* sure. Did you come back at dawn to check the lake to see if it was floating on the surface? Did you get in the water to look for it?"

The flicker of anger that passed over Patty's face told Stevie the answer was yes, she had absolutely done that.

"So," Stevie said, "you're wondering how I got the diary out of the lake undamaged."

"*I'm* wondering," Nate muttered, his voice tinged with awe.

The expectant silence in the room was delicious.

"What happened is that the diary never went into the lake," Stevie said.

"Wait," Nate said. "What? I was there. You said . . ."

"I said it went into the lake, yes." She tried—unsuccessfully—not to smile. "I made sure you heard me scream. I don't remember doing much else, because . . . I'd just fallen off a cliff into a lake. But I made sure to do that. I wanted you to think it was gone."

Patty shifted in her seat angrily.

"Are you saying you hid it?" Nate asked. "When? We were running the whole time."

"I have to thank Carson for this one," Stevie said.

"What?" Carson said. "Me?"

"I didn't have a lot of time, but I did have this . . ."

Stevie pulled out the wood-patterned Bag Bag, the one made of the same material that was used on her cabin wall.

". . . stupid bag that looks like wood. It's a really good pattern, right? Photorealistic. It fooled me too. I don't blame you for not seeing it. It took me awhile to find it this morning, and I knew what I was looking for. Just before we jumped, I stuck the diary in there and I chucked it. Even if we didn't make it, I thought . . . someone might find it. I had to keep it safe."

Then something odd happened. Patty began to laugh.

Paul Penhale stood up.

"Patty . . . ," he said in a husky whisper. "Patty . . . what did you *do*? Look at me, Patty. What did you *do*?"

She wheeled around at him, her eyes bloodshot from tears of laughter. Her face was contorted in a grimace of rage, relief, or some emotion that Stevie did not know. Something was breaking free inside of Patty Horne.

"You should say thank you," she said. "You should say *thank you*. Todd Cooper? You know what he did to your brother. Everyone knew. The whole town let him get away with it. He *told* us what he did. He *told* us he hit Michael.

Diane covered for him. Eric definitely had his suspicions, but he never stopped hanging out with him. Same with Greg. Same with me. We were all complicit. And what do you think they'd be doing if they were alive? Todd was a monster. Eric was a dealer. Diane was a stoner loser. Greg was a dirtbag. My father tried to tell me, but I wouldn't listen. In fact, if we're all being honest, the only person anyone really mourned was Sabrina. Perfect Sabrina. But who was hanging out with Todd Cooper that night? Perfect Sabrina. Who was making out with my boyfriend at my house when I wasn't home? Perfect Sabrina. Spare me your sanctimony. And whatever this was . . ." She waved at the screen, Stevie, the Bounce House, the crowd. "None of this is . . . real. This is some murder-obsessed kid making things up."

Sergeant Graves chose this moment to get up and walk over to Patty Horne.

"I'd like to speak to you outside, please," she said.

"I'm not going outside with you."

"If you like," the detective said calmly, "I'm happy to speak to you in here as well. Outside was for your privacy. Ms. Bell came and spoke to me earlier and told me what she knew. I was able to get a warrant this afternoon. You own a firearm."

It was not a question.

"I have a warrant for that, and for your DNA to do a familial match against the sample recovered from Eric Wilde's shirt. I have a swab with me. It will only take a minute of your time."

She nodded toward the back of the room.

"I have two officers with me to assist," she said. "If you could just go over and join them, we'll continue this conversation somewhere private. I'll be by once I speak to Ms. Bell for a moment."

Sergeant Graves waved Stevie over to a door leading to a small back patio.

"You didn't mention that you recovered the diary," she said to Stevie.

"Surprise?"

Sergeant Graves pulled a glove from her pocket, slipped it on, and took the diary from Stevie.

"And the shirt," she added.

Stevie handed over the remains of the shirt.

"We're also going to talk about the shooting that you failed to mention. So you and your friends are going to stay in this building so we can get some statements and sort this out."

They stepped back inside and Sergeant Graves dismissed most of the assembled. Stevie noted that many people had already recorded some of the events and were clearly posting them online. Carson was pinging around the room, trying to prevent this, but that bird had flown. He came over to Stevie and let out a long sigh.

"I'm going to sell so many of those bags," Carson said, not nearly as quietly as he should have.

30

THE MOON WAS HIGH OVER THE LAKE. THERE WERE BUGS, OF COURSE, thousands of them, but the four people sitting side by side on the dock didn't care. They swatted and slapped at them occasionally, but it made no real impact. The natural bug spray that Janelle had brought along only seemed to amuse them.

"I don't know about you," David said after the silence had grown too long, "but I'm bored now."

He reached for the bottle and gave himself another spritz of the sticky, citronella-sweet bug spray.

It had been an hour since Stevie and her friends had been dismissed by Sergeant Graves. There would be days ahead of this, of statements, of forms and conversations. But for tonight, they were done, and they had offered themselves up to the bugs as food.

"Okay," Nate finally said. "Why?"

"Why what?" Stevie said.

"Didn't you tell us you had the diary?"

"I'm sorry," Stevie said, sighing. "I had to do it that way. See, all the stuff with Allison—aside from the food dye—that's

379

all guesswork. The thing that tied Allison's death to Patty was the diary. If Patty thought I didn't have the diary, she had to be really, really curious about this big gathering that was happening. I had to be sure she would go, and I had to be sure she was going to be genuinely shocked. I needed to startle her so badly that she might freak out and start talking on camera in front of people. I had to make sure she really thought she was safe up until the last second before I got out the diary."

"What do you think will happen to her?" Janelle said.

"A lot of it will be hard to prove," Stevie said, "but there are some things out there. There are traffic cameras in town at the stoplights, so they'll be able to see if she left the bakery early that morning. They can look for the shell casings in the woods and see if they match her gun. That may be the thing that really gets her—shooting at us."

"The documentary won't help," Nate said. "She's going to be the ugly kind of famous once they see her reaction to what you said."

"Sometimes bad people get away with it," David added. "But I feel like this one won't. This town is mad."

Something whooshed just over their heads. Stevie flinched.

"Bat," Janelle said. "They're here to feast on all these insects."

"I'll take that as a sign," Nate said, standing and stretching. "I'm going to go write."

The other three turned to look at him.

"What?" he said.

"You know *what*," Stevie replied.

"I had some ideas, that's all. Since that kid has been following me around, telling me I don't know my own book.
Anyway. Do your thing."

He walked off back toward the camp.

"That kid was right," Stevie said. "The kid told me he was
going to make Nate get back to work on the book, and he did
it. He . . . annoyed him into it."

"And I . . ." Janelle also stood. ". . . am going to go talk to
Vi. I'll see you back at the cabin."

This left David and Stevie.

"So," David said after a long moment.

"So," she replied, looking down at her legs.

It was time to talk, which she was bad at. This kind of
talking, anyway. The feeling, apologizing, heartfelt kind of
talking. Breaking-down-murder talking was one thing—this
kind was actually scary.

"I'm sorry," she said. She spat it out—flung the sentence
away from her.

"I knew what I signed up for with you. We aren't like the
other children."

Stevie scratched at the exposed skin at the top of the cast,
near her elbow.

"Yeah, well . . ." Words had not failed her when she was
talking about crime. Crime was easy—this was the hard stuff.

"What are you going to do? About this England thing."

"Well, you'll be at Ellingham," he said. "Busy. Too busy for me."

"Stop it."

"No," he said. "I mean it. You just got famous again. You solved the Box in the Woods murders."

"Yeah, but . . ."

"I'm just saying. You'll be at school anyway. And I'm not going to lie, the idea of someone my dad can't stand sending me to college is pretty tempting. It would *feel* good . . ."

A *but* hung somewhere between the moon and the lake.

". . . for a day or two. But that's the part of me that's like him. The part that thinks everything is a competition, everything is about winning, and having enemies. And in the end all I'd be doing is taking money from another person who wanted to buy me. The guy isn't asking for anything—he's nice—but he's *also* sticking it to his enemy. I don't want my life to be about that anymore. So . . . I'm not taking his offer or his money."

Stevie's head shot up and she looked at him eagerly.

"I have a little in savings," he said, "and I can get a loan. I don't have enough for a year, but I can do a semester. There's a program I've already applied to. Not super long. Maybe you can come to England for the break. They have crimes there. Lots of them. Everybody's getting murdered all the time. Jack the Ripper—did they solve that one?"

"No," Stevie said. "There are a few suspects, but part of

the problem is that Jack the Ripper is more of a media creation than a . . ."

He moved closer, leaning his body into hers, careful not to put pressure on her broken arm.

"This is why I love you," he said, "you murder-obsessed freak."

Love?

"Yeah," he said in response to the unvoiced question. "I just confessed, and I'm ready to do the time."

The lake was still but for the buzzing of the bugs and the gentle swoosh of the bats. Behind them, there was the sound of laughter from the campers and distant singing of campfire songs. But Stevie did not hear them. She was so engrossed in the kissing that everything else was blocked out, including the water snake that slid behind them and slipped into the silent waters of the lake.

Sometimes, it's better not to know.

Author's Note

Frances Glessner Lee is a real person, and everything I said about her Nutshell Studies in this book is true. The studies are still used to train investigators to this day. The Smithsonian has digitized them and put them online; they have even enabled virtual reality so you can go inside the tiny rooms and examine the details. I used this source, as well as *The Nutshell Studies of Unexplained Death* by Corinne May Botz, which has close-up photographs of the studies and explanations of some of the scenes. They are not solutions, really; the point of the studies is to learn to observe. As the quote at the opening of this book states, the investigator's job is to clear the innocent as much as it is to identify the guilty. The studies are about finding truth, which can be complex.

If you are interested in true crime and investigation, they are well worth the time. Be aware that the studies are detailed depictions of death, and despite the fact that they are incredible works of miniature, they are also graphic in nature.

Acknowledgments

Much of this book was written during the pandemic of 2020, while New York City was hammered by the disease. It would quite literally not be possible without the lifesaving efforts of all the people on the front lines who treated, fed, drove, rung up, and ran the city. I wrote it while listening to the wail of sirens and the nightly claps for the medical personnel going to the hospitals. My first thank-you must go to everyone who kept us all going—and there are so many of you. Wherever you are, thank you.

Thanks always to my agent, my friend, my general partner in crime, Kate Schafer Testerman of KT Literary. Where would I be without you, buddy?

Many, many people at HarperCollins have made Stevie's detective work possible. I must thank them all. Thank you to my incredible, passionate editor, Katherine Tegen, and the amazing editorial team: Sara Schonfeld, Alexandra Rakaczki, and Christine Corcoran Cox. On the production and art side—the people who make things beautiful and the book physically possible to hold and read—thank you to: Vanessa Nuttry, David DeWitt, Joel Tippie, Katie Fitch, Leo Nickolls, and Charlotte Tegen. And the book would never make it into the world without the efforts of the marketing and publicity teams, so more and more thanks to: Michael D'Angelo, Audrey Diestelkamp, Jacquelynn Burke, and Anna Bernard.

We left our apartment just once during the summer. My friend Cassandra Clare has a writing barn, and she offered it to us as a refuge from the city. It was the first time we had spent time outdoors that year. Because of her, I was able to remember the feeling of being out in the woods, jumping into a lake, letting the sun settle on my skin. I counted dragonflies. I drank my morning coffee outside, under the trees, with my dog, Dexy. And with our friends Holly Black and Kelly Link, I got through some of the blocks I had on the book. That week of fresh air carried me the rest of the year. To them—to all my friends—thank you.

And last, but never least, thank you to my husband, here known only as Oscar. He knows what he's done. Oh, he knows.